One-Eighty

Marie James

Copyright

Acknowledgments

Huge shout out this time around to the #1 man in my life! My dear, sweet husband, you are amazing! Thank you for making my dreams come true and supporting me relentlessly from day one. This wouldn't be possible it is wasn't for your support!

My amazing BETAs, you ladies are the absolute best! Laura, MaRanda, Brenda, Jamie, Michelle, and Jo thank you so much for the help on this book! Mary, you amaze me each and every time we work together! Thank you for your help and all of your support through this process!

Laura Watson! Thank you! You keep my head on right. I couldn't do this without you!

Wildfire, you are an amazing group of ladies, and I'm so blessed with the opportunity to work with you gals!

Another shout out to RRR Promotions and Natasha for helping get this book out into the world. As always you nailed it!

Readers, I can't even begin to tell you what you mean to me. Without you, I'd have no reason to write these books. Thanks for your continued support!

Until next time!
~Marie James

Synopsis

He loves what he can't remember —she can't forget the truth...

PIPER

Arrogant, controlling, and an absolute jerk.

He's everything I loathe, and everything I want to forget.

But he doesn't remember a bit of it.

One accident, one misstep, changed everything.

Changed him.

Now, he's different and unbelievably sexy.

But I refuse to fall for a bully.

DALTON

Sexy, smart, feisty, and perfect.

She's everything I want, and nothing that I remember.

What she says I am, I refuse to believe.

For her, I will be anything.

I will *do* anything.

Even destroy the bully from before.

Epitaph

"Tell me every terrible thing you did, and let me love you anyway." ~Sade Andria Zabala

Prologue

Dalton

They tell me I used to love the color black.

There are many things from my past that I hate.

Myself and the dark color surrounding me are the two things leading the pack right now.

People whimper and cry beside me, and I'm just numb, so broken that my pieces can't combine enough to form wetness in my own eyes.

I deserve this.

I deserve watching the love of my life with her ashen face and hands crossed on her stomach in constant repose as the preacher talks about her devotion to life and helping others.

I deserve the looks from her mother and father that speak of the million ungodly things they wish would happen to me.

I deserve the blame my own parents planted at my feet for my involvement in the steps that led up to today.

I deserve it all.

The torture.

The accident.

The getting my heart ripped from my chest because of an undiagnosed brain bleed that snuffed out the life of the most beautiful girl in the world.

She was fine when I left the hospital that day. Even her mother assured me she would be okay.

She didn't deserve this.

She didn't deserve the monster that tormented her daily.

She didn't deserve to suffer at the hands of an idiotic boy and the army of bastards willing to hurt her at his command.

She deserved the world, and yet she gets a wooden box and six feet of dirt, all the while I'm left on earth without her.

I can't do that.

That can't happen.

Our story doesn't end this way.

It should be me in that casket. Me leaving this world behind so she can shine in the bright light of the sun and live her life to all its glory.

It should be me.

It should be me.

It should be me.

My hand trembles as I reach into the inside pocket of my sports coat.

I'm not scared or afraid of what comes next.

It's the anticipation, the thrill of joining her that makes my blood sing, the unused energy making my fingers twitch.

July sun glints off the barrel as I hold my salvation to my head and pull the trigger.

Chapter 1

Dalton

"Why don't you explain the text you just sent?" I do my best to keep a rational tone, but the topic of discussion always leads to a heightened sense of awareness, one I usually manage to keep others from seeing.

"I figured it was self-explanatory," Kyle argues on the other end of the line.

He'd just sent a text that reads: **You won't believe what one of the guys has planned for Mary tonight.**

Remaining silent, I wait him out. I have nothing but time; hence, the reason I'm standing in my driveway washing an already clean car. Well, spraying the wheels specifically. I've already taken the T-tops off my '71 Stingray Corvette in preparation for the wild night I plan to have in celebration of the school year ending yesterday. I'm finally a senior, and ruling Westover Prep has always been my legacy, but now it's official.

"Vaughn has been toying with Mary for weeks."

"The sophomore?"

"He's a junior now," Kyle corrects. "He's convinced her to come to the party tonight at my place. She's certain he's all but in love with her. When she arrives, he's going to text her to come upstairs, only to find him messing around with someone else."

His chuckle makes me cringe, which is a confusing reaction to what he's just told me. The junior varsity baseball players all have to do something outlandish for initiation in order to become part of the varsity team, but I can't remember when taunting Mary became a group endeavor.

It was always *my* thing, until it wasn't. These days, I don't have to do a thing to make her life miserable. I have a half dozen or more friends vying for my attention that torment her for me. I mean, it doesn't stop me from having a little fun at her expense, but I could take a few days off, and she wouldn't start to think I was suddenly a nice guy.

"I bet she cries just like that time we knocked over the corn display at the grocery store and blamed her. I swear her face was as red as a tomato. Elijah's dad was pissed at her. Remember her blubbering trying to explain what happened?"

Grinning at the memory of that day, I continue to spray the already-shining chrome of my wheels. Tormenting the girl next door has been a regular part of my day since the very first day of kindergarten. I was willing to be her friend back then. She was the prettiest girl in pigtails after all, but after choosing to play with another kid over me, it was game on. I'm not second best. Never have been, never will be. That was the day I decided to make her life a living hell. I was a heathen at five, and now I'm unstoppable. I've reminded her of that every single day since.

Sounds petty, doesn't it? Well, petty and repetitive is what you get in small-town Westover, Colorado. We literally have nothing better to do and even repeated pranks are funny when you're bored.

Hearing footfalls, I turn just in time to see Piper "aka Bloody Mary" Schofield walking up my driveway. The nickname "Bloody Mary" came from an unfortunate incident in sixth grade. The fact that her first menstrual cycle started at school when she was completely unprepared has given our class more than enough ammunition. I wouldn't be surprised if several kids in class don't even know her real first name. More than once, I've even overheard teachers mistakenly call her Mary before correcting themselves. Those are the best days. The ones where she's reminded just how much power I have in our small town.

The Mary walking up my drive right now looks nothing like the timid and standoffish Mary that was at school yesterday, or any other day since I met her, for that matter. Gone are the frizzy layers normally crowding her face. In their place are smooth, luxurious curls, either highlighted by the nearly setting sun or professionally colored. The soft, golden curls bounce almost hypnotically as she moves, and irritatingly, my fingers itch to touch them.

She's always been pretty, even though I'd never admit that out loud to anyone, but this evening she's a knockout. Her smoky eyes barely even look my way as she walks past me as if I don't exist.

My jaw drops as she saunters by me with more arrogance and assuredness than she's ever displayed before. She'd never act so haughtily in the presence of others, but her brazen demeanor right now irritates me even though there is no one here but me to witness it.

Normally, she'd cower away, make plans to come over when she knows without a doubt that I'm gone. We live right next door to each other, easily able to see the other's driveway from our living room windows, so it's not like she can be surprised I'm standing here. She wants to be seen. The realization strikes a chord with me.

"Speak of the devil," I mutter.

"What's that?" Kyle asks in my ear, and I frown at the fact that she's somehow managed to make me forget I was on the phone.

"Nothing. See you tonight." I hang up as I watch her ascend the front steps of my house.

Although her hair and makeup are done, she's dressed as she usually is at school in khaki shorts and a loose t-shirt, her clothes hiding her tiny frame. I'm surprised she came over, knowing she would have to walk past me to go see my younger sister, Peyton. They aren't friends exactly. Mary isn't really friends with anyone but one other girl in our class, something I've made sure of over the years, but I overheard my mom talking to my sister last week that her failed state math test will keep her from going to high school in the fall, and she needed Mary to help her study for the retake in a little over a month.

One problem with tormenting the girl next door is struggling not to get caught. Not only do we live in a small town, but our parents are good friends. The balancing act has been part of the fun these last couple of years and knowing that Mary can never get away from me completely is just another method of torture I like to remind her of.

As I'd guessed, my sister comes out on the porch after Mary knocks on the door.

Graduation is tonight, and Kyle's house has been volunteered to host the after-party. He lives just outside of town, so there's a decreased chance of the police crashing. His place is always the best place to get loud at. Besides, his parents are always gone, so the lack of supervision makes for the optimal party place.

Without a care, I watch my nemesis show my sister something on her phone. Both girls smile, and the radiant sparkle in Mary's eyes rubs me the wrong way. She's not supposed to be happy. She's not supposed to be brave enough to walk past me without flinching or worrying about what I'll do to her. She's supposed to cringe in fear at just the mention of my name and skulk into the shadows terrified of my next insult.

I'm agitated even further with the way my cock seems interested in the way her hair swishes back and forth across her back as she shakes her head in response to something my sister has said.

I'm not supposed to want her.

I'm supposed to ruin her.

Instinctively, my lips lift in a sneer as she turns back in my direction, but I falter for a split second as she glances my way. Her bright blue eyes still carry the sparkle that shown when she was speaking with Peyton until they lock with mine. Darkness clouds the vibrant blue, and it's enough to snap me out of whatever trance she'd placed me in.

Without another thought, I turn the hose from the wheels of my car and direct the flow straight at Mary. Her once lush curls drown and flatten in the water flow. Shock fills every feature of her face as the dark makeup around her eyes begins to melt down her face. Disappointment washes over me when a dark tank top is made visible under her now soaked t-shirt, rather than a bra or her bare tits.

Her eyes slow-blink as she stares at me in surprise, as if there's no way I've just done this. Her hands are open at her sides as if they too can't believe what just happened.

"You seemed a little dressed up for youth reading at the library," I say with as much seriousness as I can manage. "I guess your plans for the night have changed."

Shrugging, I turn the hose back toward my car. I don't know how long she stands there staring at my back, but I can't let her go to the party as the sexiest girl in our senior class. If I notice how hot she is, that means others will too, and I need Mary to stay in the gutter right where I put her years ago. Teenage boys are controlled by their dicks, and no matter how much the guys don't like her on my account, that would change very quickly if they'd seen what I just did.

Chapter 2

Piper

"What a waste," I mumble as I aim the blow dryer at my ruined hair. "Two hundred dollars down the drain."

Fresh tears burn the back of my eyes, and although I'm trying my best not to cry, I know I'm going to fail. I always fail. Even after years of Dalton Payne meeting the expectation of being the biggest jerk ever born, he still has the ability to make me cry. I've gotten better at hiding it from him and his blockheaded friends, but all bets are off when I get home.

I made it in the house and upstairs unnoticed, a feat I don't always manage, after he, unprovoked, sprayed me with the water hose. I'd let my guard down. After getting a very expensive balayage, nutrient wash, and had my hair curled to perfection, I had my makeup professionally done at the mall in Colorado Springs. It took less than ten seconds for him to destroy it. Stupid me imagined that he'd see how the smoky eye makeup made my blue eyes pop, and he'd finally see me. I would no longer be Bloody Mary, but a pretty girl who deserved to be treated better than he's ever managed in his entire life.

As predicted, I lose my battle against my tears, but I watch in the mirror as they roll down my red cheeks. I don't want to ever forget how he's treated me. One more year of torture is all I have to suffer before I can leave this godforsaken town and be rid of all of this. My fingers itch to grab the only thing that has brought me comfort over the last two years, but my bedroom door opens before I can find my reprieve.

"Let me get dressed," I tell my friend Frankie before closing the bathroom door.

I tell her almost everything about myself, but some things I can never speak out loud. I trust her more than anyone else walking this earth, but trust is a funny thing, and I don't think I'll ever trust anyone completely.

My inner thighs tingle with need as I cover my dark secrets with a pair of blue jeans before pulling on a loose shirt. I don't bother to look in the direction of the dress I had picked out for this evening. My now frizzy hair and makeup-less face wouldn't work with the formfitting satin I'd previously planned on wearing.

Frustrated, I swing open my en-suite door and look at my best friend. She's staring out the window, and I already know exactly what she's seeing.

"I've changed my mind. I'm not going to the party tonight."

"You have to go. We've been planning to attend for weeks," Frankie argues as she turns her head slightly in my direction but not enough to lose sight of what's below.

"What are you doing?" I ask as if I don't already know the answer.

"I'm watching a half-naked Dalton fucking Payne wash his car."

"We hate Dalton, remember?"

"But we don't hate Dalton's body," she says with awe in her voice.

"I haven't noticed," I mutter, reaching for a hair tie.

Frankie's knowing chuckle rubs me the wrong way. Of course, my tormentor would be the best-looking guy at Westover Prep, the captain of the baseball team with more muscles than any teenager should ever be allowed to possess, and the brightest green eyes I've ever seen outside of a Hollywood movie ad. Even with all of that, he chooses to torture me daily, just because he can.

"The boy lives to make my life miserable," I remind her, even though there's no way she can forget. She's been on the receiving end of his hostility more than once, as well. "His attitude makes him ugly."

"Jesus," she mumbles, unable to hide the appreciation in her voice. "Why does he have to be a dick?"

I shake my head at her antics as she bites her lip, still watching him.

I clear my throat to get her attention. Reluctantly, she turns around in my direction.

"What?" Her eyes widen as she finally gets a full view of me. "I like the color, but I thought they were going to do more with your hair?"

"It didn't work out," I mutter. I don't know why I don't tell her about his latest assault. No one knows the extent of his behavior. I stopped telling my parents in fourth grade when they gave the 'boys will be boys' speech and urged me to just 'kill him with kindness.' Maybe I'm too embarrassed to lay all of my unwitnessed humiliation at her feet.

"I can braid it," she offers. "I imagine Vaughn will love it no matter how it's fixed."

"I already said I'm not going to the party."

I guess your plans for the night have changed.

Dalton's words from earlier begin to make more sense after the hose down. He must've found out I was planning to attend.

"I have a bad feeling. Nothing good can come out of me going there tonight."

Frankie is shaking her head, immediately rejecting my plans to back out. "Vaughn is going to be there. He likes you and won't let anyone mess with you."

"He's a baseball player," I remind her. She's smart enough to figure out the implication.

"He's JV. It's not the same thing as Dalton's varsity team."

"I can't-"

"Nope," she says, pressing two fingers against my mouth to shut me up. "We're going. The jeans aren't bad, but at least put on a tank or something. You look frumpy in that over-sized t-shirt."

I try for twenty more minutes to back out of the party, so long that we miss graduation and instead of following a ton of other people to the party, we're stuck arriving alone. I'd planned to meet up with Vaughn and sit with him at graduation, but he texts to let me know an out-of-town family member had stolen the seat he was saving for me. I inform him that I'm running late, and we decide to just meet each other there.

"This is what everyone comes to school and raves about?" Frankie scrunches her nose as she peers out the windshield of her car. "This is just like homeroom only with alcohol."

I take in the scenery and can't help but agree. The same people who gather in groups in class are doing so on Kyle Turner's front lawn. Each person has a solo cup or a bottle of beer in their hands.

"I don't want to do this." I've said it a dozen times since Frankie arrived at my house a couple of hours ago, but only now does it look like she's going to agree with me.

"Ugh." She cringes. "Bronwyn is here."

"Of course, she's here. She's Dalton's toy," I remind her.

Dalton can have his pick of any girl at Westover, and he uses his selection freely, at least from what I've seen at school and the comings and goings at his house.

If Dalton is the king of our school, that makes Bronwyn the queen, if only because she's declared herself as such, and no one has been brave enough to contest it.

"We need to do this," Frankie says with resolve she didn't possess mere moments ago.

"We can just go back to my place and watch Vampire Diaries reruns," I offer.

"What about Vaughn?" I shrug, unsure if even Vaughn is worth heading into the lion's den. "I'm leaving first thing in the morning."

The reminder makes my heart plummet. I've known for the last two months that Frankie is obligated to her grandmother's farm in Utah this summer.

"I want to leave knowing that you'll have someone who will force you to leave your house more than once a week for church."

"I'm going to be tutoring Peyton," I counter.

"At your house," she clarifies.

It's true. Going to the Paynes today was unplanned, and when I tutor her this summer, there's no chance I'll be doing that at Dalton's house. I never would've agreed to help if that was the case.

"How does this party have any bearing on my summer?" I look away from the front of the house when I see Vaughn walking up the front lawn. I don't want Frankie to see that he's here, or she'll never let me leave. Just seeing him clap hands with several of the guys from the varsity baseball team makes my palms sweat.

"Vaughn," she angles her head to the front of the house, having noticed him, "he will make you leave the house on all the dates he's going to take you on."

Frankie has been the one driving the bus with this entire Vaughn situation. I've been leery from the start, but she keeps telling me that we're going to be seniors, and everyone in our class is growing up. She assures me that no one will mess with me this coming year. She only believes this because I've stopped telling her about the instances of bullying she hasn't witnessed.

I should know better. I shouldn't have even let things get this far, but I can't seem to convince my lonely teenage heart that, at some point, the scales have to tip in my favor. Today may just be that day, the day where I stop being Bloody Mary and become just Piper. I've wanted nothing more for as long as I can remember.

"Okay," I agree quietly.

"Okay? Really?" Frankie shoves open her car door before I can change my mind. Frozen, I sit in the front seat and watch as she rounds the front of the car to open my door. "Come on."

Hesitantly, I get out of the car and immediately reach for my phone, firing off a text to Vaughn to let him know I'm here. When he doesn't respond right away, I tuck the thing in my back pocket and look up at my friend.

"You're sure about this?"

"Not one bit," she says with a false smile, tucking her arm under mine and walking toward the front door of the house.

Most of the people that were standing around have now made their way inside, so it's only the two of us in the cool night.

"This is going to be epic," Frankie assures me with a soft pat of my hand. She opens the front door without even knocking and drags me along to walk in like we own the place. That's always been Frankie's style, and if it weren't for her, I wouldn't have experienced half of the things I have in life. She has a way of encouraging me to step out of my comfort zone. Tonight, however, I'm not comfortable at all.

The world doesn't end when we breach the threshold of Kyle Turner's house. The music blasting through the hidden surround sound doesn't screech to a halt when Frankie closes the door behind us, effectively trapping us inside with the monsters.

A quick glance around the room doesn't reveal Vaughn, and I avoid the corner where Dalton and his closest cult followers lurk. Instinctively, I reach for my phone once again. The sooner I make contact with Vaughn, the sooner I can get out of this place.

Chapter 3
Dalton

I flinch when Bronwyn shifts her weight on my lap. Her bony ass digs into the top of my thighs, but my grunt must make her think she's turning me on because she does it twice more before I can clamp my free hand on her hip.

"Be still," I hiss.

She giggles like a little girl, and the noise grates on my nerves.

"Am I turning you on?" she coos, her beer breath a little too close to my nose.

"Just be still," I repeat.

Tonight is the first party of the summer, but you wouldn't be able to tell just by walking in. It's the exact same as last week's party and every weekly party before that. I'm certain I'd have more fun sitting at home playing video games, but the expectation is that I'm here and having a good time. The only good thing I have going on right now is one hell of a good buzz.

Kyle always has the best alcohol selection since his parents own and operate several liquor stores in the state. It's also one of the reasons his house is always hosting the parties. His parents work late on the weekends when sales are optimal.

The front door opens, and although I'm not one to usually watch who arrives, my eyes have been laser-focused on the thing tonight. Just as I had hoped wouldn't happen, Mary and her only friend Frankie just showed up.

Bronwyn yelps when my fingers dig into her hip at the sight of the two girls who have no damn right to be here. I've kept Mary from every single party to date. Who the hell does she think she is showing up tonight?

Surely, she wouldn't believe for a minute that Vaughn was seriously interested in her. She's well aware that every guy in Westover has been warned away from her. I know from her ridiculously high GPA and number one ranking in our class that the girl is smart enough to figure out when someone is going to prank her. She's managed to thwart several pranks of my own due to diligence and her guard always being up.

"What is it, baby?" Bronwyn asks, and it takes everything in me not to cringe at her bad breath and jerk my head back. "Wanna go upstairs and have a little fun?"

"No."

My short answer doesn't seem to bother her. Whatever you want to call this situation between Bronwyn and me is past its expiration date. It has been for a while, but at the same time, pickings are slim to begin with in Westover, and I had a really wild time sophomore year. Cocky as it may seem, I can take my pick of the girls in school and many from the nearby college, but I'm not really one to revisit.

"Did you see who's here?" Kyle asks as he leans in closer when Bronwyn climbs off my lap and mutters something about getting another beer.

Hopefully, she'll get several more and won't be interested in coming back over here.

"Who?" I ask even though I know he's spotted the same petite girl I just did moments ago.

"Bloody Mary is here."

I allow my eyes to drift to her when he nods his head in her direction. She doesn't look our way, but I'd be a fool to think she didn't locate us the second she stepped inside. She knows she's safest when she can locate her predators and keep away from them.

"So?" Pretending to be uninterested, I turn my head, so it looks like I'm paying attention to the people dancing in the center of the room.

She's back to her old self in jeans and a t-shirt that's two sizes too big for her, but even seeing her like she is now doesn't make the memories of what she looked like earlier fade from my mind. Her hair is not as frizzy as it normally is, but the curls are gone as well as the sultry makeup she was able to hypnotize me with earlier.

Her friend, Frankie, points toward the kitchen, miming getting a drink, and I watch as Mary shakes her head when Frankie holds up two fingers, clearly asking her if she wants one as well. Smart girl not planning to drink tonight.

Mary stands alone only halfway through the foyer, looking lost and out of her element. Her lips turn down in a frown when she looks down at her phone.

"This is going to be so much fun," Kyle says, rubbing his hands together mischievously as he stands from the couch. "Catch ya later."

I don't bother speaking as he crosses the room, giving Mary a wide berth before shooting up the stairs. Someone else takes Kyle's spot on the sofa, but I don't acknowledge them. Thankfully, they don't try to engage me in conversation either.

For what seems like forever, I stare at Mary as she stares down at her phone. She types something on it several times like she's texting, but they must not be responding because she's growing increasingly agitated. The irritation doesn't fade when Frankie shows up at her side and offers her a red solo cup. Her head shakes back and forth as her thumb hitches over her shoulder, indicating that she's going to leave.

"Here, man." One of the incoming JV baseball players offers me a shot glass, and I turn it up, slamming it in one go just to get him out of my hair. Like he's never tasted alcohol before, the boy refills my shot glass before I can pass it off.

That shot goes down easy, too, but most of my drinks have for the last two hours. I feel heavy and somehow detached from what's going on around me. In the soft light from the overhead chandelier hanging in the entryway, Mary actually looks ethereal. I know if we weren't in Westover, if I'd seen her walk into a party, never having met her before, I would try to talk to her. I'd do my best to persuade her to follow me upstairs so we could talk where it wasn't so noisy.

But we are in Westover, and as petty as holding a grudge over not getting picked to play with in recess so many years ago is, I've dedicated my free time and reputation on tormenting her. There's no way I can change any of that now.

When I blink, I realize Mary is no longer standing in the middle of the room, frowning at her phone. My body moves before my mind can tell it where to go, but the house isn't so big that I lose track of her for long. By the time I make it across the room, I see her tucking her phone into her back pocket as she climbs the staircase.

Needing to watch her humiliation, I follow behind her, my drunken thoughts needing the reminder of who this girl is to get back on track.

Softly, she taps her knuckles against the first door on the right. Kyle's little brother isn't home tonight, but that doesn't stop someone on the other side of the door verbally granting her entrance, but as soon as she opens the door, her feet freeze before she can step a single foot inside.

"Oh, God!" she shrieks, reaching for the doorknob. "I'm so sorry."

A round of laughs follows her as she slams the door closed. I have an idea of what she just walked in on, and I can feel my cheeks raise in a drunken smile. Undeterred, she walks deeper down the hall, knocking once again on the next door. This room is Kyle's, and I know it's going to be empty because he keeps it locked during his parties. He doesn't care if people fuck in his brother's room, his parents' room, or the two guest bedrooms up here, but his room has always been off-limits.

Except, the knob turns when she grips it. Cautiously, she pushes open the door. This time she doesn't yell or apologize. She's frozen in the doorway as her face runs the gamut of emotions. At first, she's surprised, but then her brows furl before her chin starts to quiver.

"Wh-what's going on?" Mary asks, her voice quavering.

"Isn't it obvious?" a guy says.

Kyle is going to shit a brick if he comes up here and finds people fucking in his room.

"Did you actually think I'd want you, Bloody Mary?" That has to be Vaughn speaking.

Not wanting to miss the show, I step closer so I can see what's going on in the room. I anticipate seeing Vaughn wrapped up with some girl. At least that's sort of what Kyle hinted at. Nothing says *I don't really like you and never did* than getting a girl to a party so she can catch you with someone else.

Vaughn is definitely in the room, and he's with someone else, but instead of some no-name freshman, it's Bronwyn on her hands and knees with his dick in her mouth. I blink twice, certain that I'm not seeing what my brain is trying to convince me is right before my eyes.

But when I reach over Mary's shoulder and shove the door open further, things go from bad to worse. Not only is my girlfriend sucking off a dick that isn't mine, my best friend is plowing into her from behind.

"What the fuck is going on?" I snap.

All three participants, slow from hours of drinking, turn their heads in my direction at a snail's pace.

Vaughn and Bronwyn's eyes fall on Mary, and my girlfriend has the damn gall to smile around Vaughn's less than spectacular cock at the sight of her standing there in shock. Kyle doesn't even bother to stop thrusting as his eyes find mine.

His eyes are glazed, cheeks red from both the alcohol he's been pouring down his throat all night and the exertion he's putting forth to fuck my girl.

My ex-girl, I should say. There's no going back from this.

I'm livid, beyond pissed. I'm not angry because I love her or anything. Bronwyn is actually a vile human being and always has been. I'm enraged because what she's doing reflects on me. What kind of man am I if I can't keep my girlfriend from fucking around on me, at a party I'm also in attendance at no less? I'm nobody's fucking chump, yet here I stand watching my best friend drive his cock into her over and over. I'll be the butt of every damn joke from here on out.

How do I reign at Westover Prep when I can't keep one damn girl in line?

Mary chokes out a sob before she turns and hightails it away from the door. Only now does Bronwyn refocus and see me standing in the doorway.

"Dalton?" she squeaks, too slow in her thinking to both acknowledge me and shove the guys away at the same time.

The shove comes seconds later when her brain finally catches up to the situation.

"It's not—" she begins before licking at her swollen, spit-covered lips. "They forced me!"

Fucking typical Bronwyn, blaming anyone and everyone she can to take the culpability off herself.

Like she's done a million times before, Bronwyn turns on the waterworks, but the emotions on her face don't even begin to match her words.

"He was going to find out sooner or later," Kyle grunts, increasing his hold on her hips as he continues to slam inside of her. "Hold still. I'm close."

Vaughn hasn't said a fucking word, and when I look in his direction, I find out why. Limp dick hanging to the side, he's laid back on the mattress passed the fuck out.

"I'm not even surprised," I mutter.

I don't bother to close the door when I turn to leave.

Somehow, I manage to make it down the stairs without toppling ass over end, and as if they can feel the shift in the atmosphere around me, people get out of my way before I get the chance to shove through them. It's disappointing, really. I was looking forward to taking some of my anger out on them.

My keys are out of my pocket before my feet hit the grass on the front lawn. I'm spitting nails, contemplating going back inside and beating the shit out of my best friend by the time I make it to my car.

Just as I pull the door open, it slams back closed. The tips of my fingers burn from the abrupt release.

"The fuck?" I yell when I turn to see who's fucking with me.

Now would not be the best time for Kyle to come out and try to talk some sense into me. He couldn't even be bothered to pull his cock out of Bronwyn long enough to fake some stupid ass excuses like she did.

He was going to find out sooner or later.

His words echo in my head. Does that mean this isn't the first time they messed around? Tonight wasn't some drunken mistake, which seemed like a good idea while filled with alcohol, that they'd both regret if they could even remember the details in the morning.

But it isn't Kyle or Bronwyn now standing against my closed car door.

"Get the fuck out of my way, Mary," I growl.

One thing I've never done while torturing her all these years is put my hands on her, but right now, it doesn't seem like a bad idea. She must not recognize the pure hatred in my eyes because the girl doesn't even flinch when I growl at her.

"Not going to happen, Dalton. Give me the fucking keys." She holds her tiny hand out like I'd ever let her drive my car.

No one drives it—not even my parents.

"Move," I snap. "Or I'll move you myself."

Her arms cross over her chest, but when I reach for the door handle again, she has the damn nerve to slap the keys out of my fucking hand.

"You're pushing your fucking luck," I warn, but before I can bend to collect the keys from the grass at our feet, she already has them clutched in her hand.

"You're not driving," she snaps, finally taking a few steps away from the car to put some distance between the two of us.

"I'm leaving."

"You can walk, or you can ride, but you're not driving home drunk."

Glaring at her doesn't seem to have the effect it normally does, and if going by the tension in her slender jaw, I don't imagine she's going to change her mind anytime soon. I don't make a habit of drinking and driving, but my go-to plan, crashing here until I sober up, isn't going to happen tonight. I never want to step foot on this property again. If I do, I may end up charged with murder, and I'm too good-looking for prison. Plus, neither Bronwyn nor Kyle is worth the damn trouble.

"Get in the passenger seat or walk," she hisses.

Chapter 4

Piper

Although I haven't had anything to drink besides water tonight, that doesn't stop my foot from trembling out of control each time I press the gas pedal. I know how Dalton feels about this car. I don't think there's anything more valuable to him in this world, and that's saying a lot because he's the most materialistic person I've met.

Why I insisted he let me drive, I don't know. Actually, I do know. He's drunk, and my parents would never forgive me if I saw him leave and didn't try to stop him. I couldn't go back inside and try to track down Frankie, and she didn't answer my text when I sent her one once I got outside. Dalton is my fastest way home.

"Put on your damn seat belt," I tell him for the tenth time as I pull away from Kyle's house and head in the direction of our neighborhood. He doesn't. It's like he's refusing to even acknowledge I spoke in the first place.

"This is all your fucking fault," he spits from the passenger seat. He doesn't even respect me enough to look in my direction while he insults me.

Dalton is mean when he's sober, but it seems he's even more noxious when he's been drinking.

"You would blame me for not being able to control your girl," I mutter.

When I opened that door, finding Vaughn, Bronwyn, and Kyle in their compromising positions, I was pissed. Not because Vaughn was with someone else, but because I was stupid enough not to listen to my gut in the first place. Then, like the soft-hearted pushover I was, I felt bad for Dalton. Not only was his girlfriend cheating on him, but she was doing so with his best friend. Frankie would never do something like that to me, and she knows dang well I'd never do anything like that to her.

What I walked in on was soap opera worthy. Things like that aren't supposed to happen with high school kids. Girls our age are supposed to get upset when their boyfriends look at other girls too long, and guys should be getting upset when girls don't wear their letterman jackets or smile too brightly at other boys. They aren't supposed to get caught having threesomes with people they aren't in relationships with. Or maybe that's what these stupid parties are always like. If so, count me out. I want nothing to do with copious amounts of alcohol and demoralized teens. How half of our class hasn't ended up pregnant or with STDs, I'll never know.

"You shouldn't have even been there," Dalton says as if speaking to himself.

Leave it to him to blame me for what was going on in that room. Like I had any control over his friends. My only mistake was thinking for a second that a boy at Westover Prep would be interested in me. I'll never make the same mistake again, that's for dang sure.

"You belong at the library, not at some house party," he continues.

Even with the wind whipping around in the car from the T-tops being gone, his words still manage to stay inside the car and stick to me like poison.

I don't argue with him because he's right. I'll never be able to get the sight of Vaughn's penis out of my head. Thankfully, Kyle was situated so that even though I could tell what was going on behind Bronwyn, I couldn't actually *see* the details. In no way, shape, or form did I think seeing my first in-person penis would happen like it did tonight.

"You fucking ruin everything!" Dalton roars as his fists come down hard on the dash.

The movement startles me, but even though the wheel jerks in my hands, I manage to keep the stupid car on the road.

"You can't take a hint? You must like the fucking teasing because you just keep showing up for more and more. Why can't you just get out of my fucking life for good?" He's still not looking at me, but with each ragged breath he takes, the angrier he gets. "You spend all of your time thinking you're better than everyone else. Piper Schofield can't be bothered to care what others think of her."

His tone is mocking, and I'd like to say I ignore him, that I concentrate on driving since I've never been behind the wheel in this part of town before, but that's not the case. The tremble in my feet and hands from worrying about Dalton's car transitions to heated anger and hatred for the boy in the seat beside me.

"You don't have a fucking clue what it's like to be me!" I roar, turning my head to look in his direction.

His face is marked with tears, and the sight of the wetness on his cheeks disorients me for a second. Inwardly, I wonder if these tears are like mine, and he's crying because he's so angry. There's no way he's actually heartbroken over Bronwyn. They were frenemies at best. Then his lips turn up in a demonic sneer.

"You're fucking pitiful." His words are calm. There's no sign of the rage and hostility that echoed through the car just moments ago. "You're just the girl everyone loves to pick on. Everyone hates you. There isn't one person at Westover Prep that likes you."

As far as insults go, these aren't so bad. Lord knows I've heard worse. I've been through years of misery from him and others, but tonight they strike a harder chord.

I shake my head, turning my attention back to the rows of trees that provide a false sense of security on the side of the road. Between the trees and the asphalt, I know for a fact that there's at least a ten-foot-wide ravine. For a single second, I wonder what it would be like to drive us both over the edge of the cliff, but as quick as the urge is there, it's gone. Imagining death isn't new to me, but I'd never do that to my parents. Permanent pain isn't something I'm into.

"Even that girl you showed up with tonight was in on the joke," he interrupts, continuing like I didn't just counter his claim.

"That isn't true. Frankie is my best friend. She..." I squeeze the steering wheel until my hands ache from the effort. My eyes snap back to his. "No."

His head bobs. "Yes, she was."

My mouth runs dry, and tears burn the backs of my eyes. It's not possible. Frankie has been my best friend for years. She hates Dalton and his shitty friends just as much as I do. Then a thought hits me. She was adamant about going to the party, wouldn't take no for an answer when I tried to back out. She didn't even bother to hide the ogling of Dalton from my bedroom window earlier when she arrived at my house. She wouldn't be dumb enough to fall for his playboy ways, would she?

"And Bronwyn and I broke up. We planned the entire thing."

Now I know he's lying. He was just as shocked as I was when he shoved that damn door open, but my brain hasn't had time to sift through the bullshit he's spewing to get to the bottom of his words and find the truth.

The car begins to shake, and when my eyes snap to the front, I realize that my front tire has slipped off the road and is kicking up the rocks on the shoulder.

"What the fuck are you doing?" Dalton roars.

My eyes begin to roll as I move the steering wheel to the left to get us back between the lines, but I must not be doing it fast enough for Dalton because he grabs the wheel and pushes hard to the left. Things might have been okay if we weren't coming up too fast on a blind curve. Both of my feet press the brake as I pray that there's isn't anyone on the other side of the curve, but my prayers aren't heard.

Lights blind me as I struggle against Dalton's hold on the steering wheel.

By some miracle, we avoid the other car, but the fishtailing is too much to compensate for. When the front passenger wheel hits the gravel again, the car has had enough. Even knowing that we're going to wreck, I somehow manage to wonder why the trip down a ravine is so bumpy. Having driven in Colorado since I got my permit, I always pictured it more like a flying experience. Thinking the car would leave the roadway and soar until I met death at the bottom with a *Thelma and Louise* type crash and explosion.

Instead, I'm jolted back and forth as the car tumbles. I'm weightless, then jarred to the side, over and over. Dalton is going to be pissed about his car, but when I look over to the passenger seat, it's empty. Nothing but leather and the flash of lights fills the seat that once held the angry boy as the car topples.

The sounds of scraping metal and snapping of tree branches fade away until nothing can be heard but an eerie hissing and the sporadic tumble of smaller rocks as they slide past the wreckage.

"Da-Dalton," I manage, but his name comes out as a whisper.

Wetness fills my eyes, but my shoulder screams in pain when I try to wipe it away. It feels like glass is clogging my throat when I try to yell out for Dalton again.

"H-help!" My scream is more like a soft plea, and as much as I want to stay here until help arrives, it hits me that help may never show.

If the car we swerved past kept going, we wouldn't be missed until tomorrow.

With all the strength I have and favoring the injured left side of my body, I manage to get my seatbelt off. My phone is still in my back pocket, but when I pull it free and hit the home button, I realize I have no service. I don't know how far down the ravine we are, but I know I won't have a chance of getting help if I can't get back to the road.

"Dalton," I call again as I climb from the very top of the car.

Sliding safely from the T-tops makes my stomach turn. Just knowing that Dalton exited the car the same way while the car was rolling down the hill is enough to make me vomit. I'm undiscerning of where I get sick, having only enough energy to turn my head to the side to lose the contents of my stomach.

Tears sting my eyes, joining the wetness already there as I try to get a better footing on the rocks. I'm able to climb to safety from the T-tops, but that, combined with Dalton refusing to put on his seat belt may be what kills him.

I repeat his name as I slip and slide up the rocks. The only way I know I'm heading toward the road in the pitch black is the pull of gravity at my feet. The sharp incline is hell on my calves and nearly impossible with only one working arm. I don't spot Dalton on the way up. My phone flashlight is bright but still only manages to give me about five or six feet of visibility.

I pause when I hear what I think is a whimper, but even after staying still for long moments, I don't hear it again.

"Dalton, can you hear me? Make a noise," I yell when I finally manage to get to the top.

Shivers hit me with the force of a train when I point my phone down the ravine and realize that the car is so far down, I can't even see it from my vantage point.

"Are you okay?"

I spin around at the masculine voice, but it isn't Dalton standing behind me but an older man with a look of abject fear in his eyes.

"Thank God, you're okay," he says as he walks closer.

"M-my fr-friend." I point down the ravine as my teeth begin to chatter.

"Come on," the man says with his hands out. "I have a first aid kit in my car. I called an ambulance as soon as I saw you go over."

"We have to help Dalton," I tell him as I dig my feet into the gravel on the side of the road, preventing him from pulling me toward his car.

"There's nothing that we can do for him until help shows up." That doesn't make any sense. The man in front of me is an adult. They're supposed to know how to handle situations like this. "Let's get something on that forehead cut of yours."

Before I can object, the sounds of sirens fill the air. Only then do I notice a road flare burning in the middle of the road about forty yards away. I don't know which direction I'm facing. I don't know which side of the road we went off of or how close we are to town. Everything is happening so fast and yet slowing down at the same time.

It seems like hours before the ambulance and rescue personnel show up after hearing the sirens for the first time, but then it's like there are a hundred people swarming the scene. I refuse to go in the back of the ambulance, insisting that Dalton will need it when they find him.

The EMT frowns when he looks at me, and I can see in his eyes that he doesn't think Dalton will need an ambulance. Thankfully, he stops short of telling me that a body bag will be more likely for the boy that's tormented me for years.

People are hollering; guys are tied to ropes and rigs as they're lowered down toward the car, while I sit in the open door of a police car and watch it all in the flash of red and blue lights.

There's a commotion, but my brain isn't really registering any of it. It's almost like an out-of-body experience when the bottom of a bright orange rescue basket peeks over the ledge. Inch by inch, Dalton is revealed as the pulley system brings him to safety.

He's rushed past, carried by two men on either side of the rescue basket, but when I stand to tell him I'm sorry, it's clear that he'll never hear another word I say.

My head swims, guilt and fear filling it until I can see nothing but blackness and death.

Chapter 5

Piper

Through the steady beeps of a distant machine and whispered voices, I do my best to assess my surroundings without opening my eyes. I've done this very thing several times already, before falling back into the torment of my nightmares.

I know when I open my eyes and acknowledge the people in my hospital room, I'm going to have to answer for what I've done. I'm putting that off as long as I can. Guilt burns a hole in the lining of my stomach.

I don't think most people would bat an eyelash at the opportunity to rid the world of their tormentor. I imagine, just like me, they lie in bed late at night and dream of a slew of demises fitting for the ones who've made their lives a living hell. After years and years of abuse, I, myself, have thought about numerous possibilities to relieve the earth of Dalton Payne.

I pictured my hands around his throat, cutting off his oxygen and ceasing the vile words from his mouth. I've imagined watching him getting attacked by bears and doing nothing to try to stop it. I've even wondered what it would be like to hold his head under water until he stopped moving.

I didn't think it would ever happen. Getting rid of someone requires guts, stamina, and most importantly, the ability to get away with it.

I don't have any of those things.

He's made sure of it. Dalton and his clan of groupies have chipped away at my self-esteem and self-worth until I've been left with nothing.

Tonight, however, I'm single-handedly responsible for killing the tyrant.

I hate Dalton Payne.

Hated Dalton Payne.

I haven't had a change of heart but despising someone who is no longer alive doesn't seem fair.

His life is over.

My life will also be over once I open my eyes, but the bravery I need to face my actions is nowhere to be found. My body trembles, shaking uncontrollably.

This isn't like the time I broke the back window at my grandmother's house, or the time I forgot the bathroom sink was running and the water overflowed for hours onto the floor. This isn't a mistake that a couple of hundred dollars and a trip to *Home Depot* can fix.

I've ended a life, and there are serious repercussions for doing something like that.

Maybe the police will believe me when I tell them that Dalton grabbed the wheel. He caused the wreck, not me. But it's my luck that they'll still handcuff me and take me to jail. It's honestly where I belong. If I hadn't let him make me angry, if I had paid more attention to the road instead of the horrific things he was saying, we'd both be home right now. I wouldn't be in a hospital bed, and he wouldn't be in the morgue.

"Piper?" I don't recognize the voice calling out to me, but my eyes flutter again.

When they open fully, the overhead light blinds me, and I'm forced to squeeze them shut again.

"Can you dim the lights?" the unfamiliar voice says. "She's going to be sensitive to light for several days."

"Piper?" That's Mom's voice, and just the sound makes tears form in the corners of my eyes. "Can you hear me?"

I nod my head, just a quick up and down because my body is screaming from pain. Every movement is like getting pelted with rocks.

"Wh-where am I?" I manage.

"You're in the hospital," the person other than my mom answers. "I'm Dr. Columbus. You were in a motor vehicle accident. You sustained a pretty serious concussion. You also have a severe sprain to your left wrist and several fractured ribs. You're pretty banged up all over, but you'll make a full recovery."

It's not fair. I shouldn't be whole. I shouldn't be good as new after a few weeks of healing. Not while the other person in the car with me is…

I try not to let myself think of him again, but the memory of wondering what it would be like to drive us over the ravine hits me hard. A choked sob escapes my lips, and warm fingers wrap around my right hand.

"Shh, baby. It's going to be okay." Emotion clogs my mother's throat, and I wonder how she can make promises right now.

She should be well aware of what I'm facing. I can only hope that they will let me heal before they cuff me and cart me off to prison.

"What's your pain level?" Dr. Columbus asks. "On a scale of one to ten?"

"Thirty-five," I mutter because it's true. I think even my hair follicles hurt right now.

"I'll get the nurse in here with some meds to ease that," he assures me.

What seems like hours later, a soft voice tells me that she's administering pain meds into my IV, but I don't have enough time to thank her before I slip back into my nightmare.

The wreck is on constant replay in my head. The guilt hits me when I'm awake, and the sight of Dalton being carried past me by the rescuers invades my dreams. Even in my mind, I correct that they're not performing a rescue at that point but a recovery. A lump lodges in my throat at visualizing his gray, ashen face covered in blood. His sandy-blond hair is so saturated with blood that his matted locks look black. He's motionless, his once hostile mouth slack and not showing any sign of the trauma he's suffered.

In my dream, I sob. I cry for the man he'll never become. I grieve for his family and the pain they must be feeling with his loss. And as much as I hate to admit it, I weep at the knowledge that the boy that had made it his life's mission to ruin me still has the ability to do so from the grave.

Each time the accident and the aftermath replays in my head, the regret and anguish only multiply. It doesn't diminish or dilute as I relive it over and over. If anything, it gets worse. It doesn't change, even when I want to reach out for him as they carry his body away. Even as I have the foresight of what's going to happen while still driving the car. I still get angry at his hateful words. I still pay more attention to him than the road in front of him. We still go over the edge, and he still dies.

I suffer through this over and over and over, and by the time I wake up again, my body hurts more than it did the very first time I woke up to face my new reality.

When I whimper, the hand I didn't realize was holding mine clenches tighter. Rather than open my eyes and beg for more meds, I focus all my attention on that single contact. From the size and the warmth, I'm certain my mother is the one holding on to me. She's tethering me to the here and now.

"We just don't know yet," a defeated woman says from the other side of the room. "The doctors said all we can do is wait. The swelling hasn't shown any sign of diminishing. How is Piper doing?"

My already dry throat turns into a desert when my brain allows me to recognize the woman talking. How is Dalton's mom so calm, asking about the girl who killed her son?

"She's in and out," Mom whispers.

"Will she be okay?" Mrs. Payne asks.

My mother's fingers tighten on mine, and I wonder if it's guilt that makes her pause for a long moment before answering. She waits so long, I begin to think the doctor was lying to me about my recovery prospects.

"She's going to be fine," Mom finally says.

"Oh, thank God," Mrs. Payne answers. "I don't know what I'd do if things were any worse."

Tears burn my eyes once again. What grace it must take for this woman to be relieved that I'm not going to die. If I didn't know her as well as I do, I'd think she was happy that I'll live just so she can see me suffer for what happened to Dalton, but Cynthia Payne is never one to say something she doesn't mean. The woman is the epitome of no filter and opinionated. More than once over forced family dinners, she's openly asked Dalton and me why we haven't started dating yet, so sure that our once-in-a-lifetime love was already written in the stars and destined for forever.

Dalton, of course, just grunted his response, and I know it took everything in his power not to get sick at just the suggestion of willingly touching me or having any feelings for me other than the hatred that would swim in his eyes when our parents weren't looking.

"Have they spoken to you about what to expect?" Mom asks Mrs. Payne.

"The induced coma will help the rate of swelling, and with any hope and a million prayers, they won't have to do surgery. His left arm is broken, but we won't know the full extent of his injuries until he wakes up."

What?

"Well," my mom says with a sigh, "Dalton is one of the most determined, strong-willed young men I've ever met. I'm certain he's going to be fine, but we're constantly praying. Let us know if you need anything."

What?

The machine beeping near my head changes tempo, the annoying cadence nearly tripling in rhythm.

He isn't dead? I didn't kill Dalton Payne?

He isn't dead *yet*. My brain chooses now to lean toward pessimism. Which means I only have a slight reprieve until Mrs. Payne changes her tune. There's only so much decorum a woman can maintain in the face of her worst nightmare coming true.

"D-Dalton," I mutter.

"Shh, sweetheart," Mom coos near my ear. "You're fine. Everything's fine."

Even her assurance, something that's always calmed me when I'm upset, doesn't help right now. Nothing can help me right now.

But if Dalton is alive, even if he's in an induced coma, I need to see him. I need to tell him I'm sorry for what I've done that landed us both here. I need to let him know that I forgive him for all the hateful things he's said to me, for all the tricks he's played, and all the times he's made me cry.

I don't care about any of it anymore. The only thing that concerns me right now is coming clean. I can live with the stain of hurting him on my conscience, but the agony of him slipping away before he knows how apologetic I am is enough to burn a hole through my soul. I'm already facing hell on earth. The last thing I want is an eternity of the very same.

"D-Dalton," I repeat. "I n-need to see him."

"Shh," my mom says again. "Get some rest. You can see him when you're strong enough."

I struggle against her hands as they clamp on my shoulders. She doesn't understand, and there's no way for me to explain. My confession isn't for her to hear. It's only meant for one person, and she's in my way of making that happen. But my body is weak, too unsteady even to manage to keep my eyes open while she holds me down.

I don't know how long I fight to get out of the hospital bed, but it couldn't have been long. By the time I collapse against the thin mattress, I'm breathing hard and crying uncontrollably.

As if he can hear me from here, I repeat *I'm sorry, I'm sorry, I'm sorry,* over and over until blackness claims me once again.

Chapter 6

Piper

My time spent in the darkness transforms after hearing that Dalton is still clinging to life in a coma. Although still ashen gray when the rescuers carry him past me at the scene of the accident, he no longer has his eyes closed. Sometimes he merely watches me until the angle of the rescue basket prevents him from making eye contact. During more vivid dreams, Dalton accuses me of ruining his life. He threatens me with more pain than he's ever administered before, and during the worst times, he glares at me with confusion, asking me with his eyes why I had to do something like this to him.

It's these moments that bring me the most heartache. Even with the years of torment, I wouldn't wish any of this on my worst enemy, and that person just happens to be Dalton Payne, by his choosing not my own.

I have more episodes of wakefulness, but I'm still unable to understand how much time has passed since the accident. Mr. and Mrs. Payne stop by to visit regularly, each time asking how I'm doing, and every time they arrive, I close my eyes, so I don't have to interact. It's the coward's way out, but I have no other recourse. At least not one I can think of during the minimal times when my head isn't throbbing.

Today, however, I'm unable to close my eyes fast enough.

"How are you feeling, Piper?" Mrs. Payne asks as she steps inside my hospital room.

My dad has returned to work, but as a local pediatrician, his office isn't far from the hospital. My mom stepped out, claiming to need to make a few calls, but I don't doubt that she's growing restless just watching me lie in bed for days on end. I, too, want to escape this place, but the doctors treating me haven't mentioned a discharge yet.

"I'm okay," I croak.

"Your mom tells me that you may get out of here in a couple of days."

I merely nod. What else can I say right now? I want to tell her I'm sorry. I have this gut-turning need to explain what happened. Even as crappy as it would be to place blame on Dalton for grabbing the steering wheel, he's at least partially responsible for what happened. Had I wrecked just from the vitriol he'd spit in my direction on our way home, he'd still be partially culpable for the end result, honestly.

But her son is clasping on to life, and that doesn't seem fair.

No doubt Dalton would point fingers and blame in my direction all day long, even if he was one hundred percent responsible, but I just don't have it in me.

"Do you hurt?" Mrs. Payne asks when my face screws up when I try to re-situate my lower half on the bed.

"I'm okay," I tell her.

As much as I'd like the physical pain to go away, it's the torment in my dreams that have prevented me from asking for pain meds today. Plus, the sooner I can get up and move around, the sooner I can go home. I'm tired of the hospital, disgusted by the sterile smells surrounding me. It's going to take weeks to get the scent of this place off my skin.

"I wanted to apologize for what Dalton did."

Despite the debilitating pain in my body, my head snaps in her direction. My eyes go fuzzy from the sudden movement, but when my eyes refocus, I find her at my bedside with her head hung low.

"I'm sorry?" It's a question, not an apology on my part.

Confusion forces my brows together when her shoulders begin to shake with tremors.

"He shouldn't have been drinking. He shouldn't have been driving." Her head lifts, eyes rimmed red and overflowing with tears. "Why did you get in the car with him?"

My head shakes, the back-and-forth motion making it feel like I'm swimming in a murky pond. My confusion before has nothing on how I'm feeling right now.

"I don't understand," I manage when it's clear she still wants answers.

"He's so strong-willed," she says, her chin quivering in a way that makes me wish I could reach out and hold her.

Her pain is clear in the forward slump of her shoulders and the wary look in her emotion-filled eyes.

"I know he wouldn't let anyone drive that stupid car, but I wish you'd have gotten a ride with someone else at the party. At least you could've avoided all of this pain and suffering." She sobs again as she lowers her face into her trembling hands. "I don't know what I would've done if you had..."

She doesn't complete her sentence, but the intent is clear. Does she think Dalton was driving? I guess it makes sense. Even I was shocked when Dalton climbed into the passenger seat after I insisted he wasn't going to drive home intoxicated. Someone else driving his car is unheard of, but she doesn't have a true account of what happened.

I swallow, needing to tell her the truth, but instead of the words leaving my lips, I keep them clenched tight.

I blame my own weakness, my fear of dying in prison if Dalton doesn't make it, but I know that the guilt that settles in my stomach will eat a hole in it the size of the seventeen-year-old boy that's hidden somewhere else inside the hospital.

The truth will come out eventually, and I'm a coward for not confessing now, but I have no idea how everyone will react. I don't want to face this alone without my mom and dad here, even though their own disappointment is something I've been avoiding the last couple of days as well.

"How is Dalton?" I ask, rather than answering her questions.

"He's..." She sobs again, and I wait for her to tell me that his condition is deteriorating. "They've weaned him off the drugs that put him in a coma since the majority of the swelling has diminished. He's woken up a couple of times, but he's disoriented. He didn't remember us when he woke the last time. Dr. Columbus is confident that he'll get his memory back soon, but there are no guarantees."

As she begins to explain that a specialist has been called in and should arrive sometime tomorrow, I let my mind wander.

He doesn't remember?

That could work in my favor but holding on to the truth with the hope that he never gets his memory back is like pulling the pin on a grenade and praying it doesn't blow your hand off when you get distracted. There's no way this could work.

The repercussions of letting everyone believe Dalton was driving will only multiply and be exponentially worse when they find out the truth.

But I don't open my mouth. I don't confess. I don't take the opportunity to tell Mrs. Payne that I was driving. I don't tell her that I'm sorry for my own actions. I let her walk out of my room fifteen minutes later with tears still streaming down her face believing that her son wronged me, not the other way around.

I don't even open my mouth to clear up the confusion when my mom returns, or when my dad gets off work and comes to sit by my bedside. I keep my lips sealed and my wishes in my head. I don't reach for God. I don't pray that Dalton never remembers. I feel like that's an even faster way to end up in Hell. Surely sinning, then praying that the sins stay hidden would be frowned upon by not only God but anyone who's privileged to hear the wishes.

The next day, I do my best to ignore the conversation Mr. Payne and my dad have on the other side of the room, but it's impossible to distract myself with anything else. Due to my severe concussion, I'm not allowed to do much of anything. My phone has been taken away. The remote to the tiny TV mounted on the wall has disappeared. I'm not allowed to read. Dr. Columbus told me to rest and to avoid thinking at all, if possible. He's reiterated more than once that my symptoms are acerbated by anything that really requires brain function. I snorted with derision when he told me that last part. He doesn't have any idea what I'd give to never think of the things that have been plaguing me over the last couple of days, but without anything else to do but lay here, all I think about is the accident and how I could've done a million things differently to have prevented it.

"I don't even know how this is possible," Mr. Payne tells my dad. He has the same slump to his shoulders that his wife had yesterday. They're both defeated and frustrated. "He doesn't have a clue who he is or who any of us are. How do you forget your entire family?"

"I thought you said he remembers you, but he doesn't have any recollection of the last decade or so," my dad responds.

"All he remembers are flashes of early childhood," Mr. Payne clarifies. "He doesn't know who Preston is, and he freaked out to the point he had to be sedated again when Peyton showed up. His last memory of her was when she was a baby."

"The brain is a complex thing, Devin. Things will get better with time. Many patients with amnesia get some, if not all, of their memories back. Dalton is young and strong, and if I had to bet on his recovery, I'd put my money on his memory loss being temporary. The swelling in his head isn't completely gone, but things will change drastically when it is. You just have to have faith."

"How is Piper doing?" Mr. Payne asks. I don't know if he's genuinely concerned or if he needs a change of subject.

Thankfully, I have my eyes closed. The sun went down several hours ago, but time doesn't seem to matter anymore. Sitting in a hospital bed with nothing to do makes everything run together.

I feel both sets of eyes on me, so I do my best to keep my breathing rhythmic.

"She's doing loads better. Dr. Columbus said he'll discharge her tomorrow if her scans look good. She'll still be in the soft cast for a few more weeks, but they expect a full recovery."

"Thank God," Mr. Payne mutters.

They exchange a few more minutes of conversation, but eventually, Mr. Payne says goodbye and leaves.

Exhausted, my dad settles in the chair beside my bed. I still don't open my lying mouth to spit the truth about what happened, and as time goes by, I wonder if I'll ever build the courage to utter those incriminating words.

Chapter 7

Dalton

It's been twenty-three days since the accident.

Eight days since I woke up from a medically induced coma to parents who seem to have aged overnight. I lost all my memories since I was a young child, and I gained a brother.

Preston is ten, and I've never seen the kid before in my life.

Peyton is no longer a chubby-faced, curly-headed baby sucking on her thumb in a crib and learning how to stand. She's almost fourteen and heading to high school.

My bedroom, where I've spent most of the last five days since being discharged from the hospital, is familiar in that the window and closet and bathroom doors are in the same place.

Gone are the matchbox cars and Legos. In their place are sports trophies and textbooks.

I don't have the mind of a five-year-old. I don't even feel that young, but all the experiences I've had since I was that age seem to be gone. My speech and vocabulary seem to have been maintained, but I don't have a single recollection of elementary school or junior high.

Although the strangers who call themselves my parents told me it's the summer before my senior year, I don't recall my first three years of high school. Other than clues in my room, I don't have any idea who I am—or *was*.

I'm athletic according to the accolades overflowing the shelves on the far wall, but at the same time, I must be intelligent due to the textbooks on the desk in the far corner. I feel smart like I know things, but it's impossible to just pull facts from thin air when there are a million other things to worry about right now.

I was ashamed but still a little thrilled when I accessed the search history on my phone. I discovered a slew of things about myself. I like fast cars, facts about outer space, and apparently, I have a thing for nerdy girls who do porn. My cheeks were on fire by the time I cleared my history and deleted saved screenshots of all of the half—and sometimes completely—naked women in plaid skirts and glasses.

One thing I do know from that discovery is that I *still* like nerdy girls who do porn, but my head was throbbing after looking at my phone for so long, so I just put it away.

I'm lying on my bed just staring at the wall, mentally willing all of my memories to come back when there's a gentle tap on my door. I'm sure the old me would know just by the sound which person in the household is there, but the Dalton I am now doesn't have a clue.

Mostly, my parents and siblings leave me alone, and I don't know how to tell them that I'm lonely and want company. Our interactions so far are stilted and filled with awkward silences, but at least I'm not isolated in my room with strict instructions to rest. Each time I see my mom or dad, I can feel the pain they're suffering from at my lack of recognition.

"Come in," I say loud enough for the person on the other side of the door to hear.

"Were you sleeping?"

"No," I answer. "Come on in... Mom."

She smiles at the moniker, but it doesn't meet her eyes. She's an intelligent woman, an attorney I'm told, just like my dad. She's well aware that I'm calling her that just to ease some of the tension between us. I'm not certain it helps. Hell, it may be making things weirder, but I can't bring myself to call her by her first name.

She stands stiff just over the threshold in my room, and it makes me wonder, not for the first time, what kind of relationship I had with my family members before the accident. They all seem happy that I didn't die, so I guess that's a good thing.

"What's that?" I ask, pointing at the thick leather-bound book she's clutching to her chest when it doesn't seem like she remembers what she came in here for.

"This," she says with a quick smile as she begins to move toward me, "is the family photo album. I'll be honest. I haven't been the best at keeping up with the day-to-day memories, but I figured this would be a good start for you. Most everything we have from the last seven or so years are all in digital form, but your father is getting those printed so you can look at them."

I smile, knowing exactly what she's doing. Dr. Columbus and the specialist, who visited the hospital after I woke up, both suggested that I immerse myself back into my life. They recommended looking at pictures and watching the shows I loved when my headaches subsided. They encouraged me to associate with the same people I did before, but neither Mom nor Dad seems too keen on that idea, even though they wouldn't explain exactly why that was.

All of this is with the hope that something will trigger memories. They assured me that these memories could trickle in over time, come at me full force all at once, or could be gone forever. They also said that some memories could come back while others didn't. Neither doctor would placate me or even speculate which of these they think would happen with me. They reminded me that I was lucky to have survived being ejected from my car during the accident, and although they were reluctant, they even admitted that my intoxicated state and lack of reaction time might have been what saved my life.

"I'll…" I pinch the bridge of my nose between my fingers, "I'll take a look at these things later. My head hurts pretty bad right now."

"Okay." She takes a step back after placing the photo album beside me on the bed, and her disappointment is clear.

They haven't pushed me much. They haven't even mentioned anything about punishment for drinking and driving, which resulted in wrecking my car and nearly killing the neighbor girl. I recall being in a timeout for an eternity when I used my jumbo crayons to color a mural I thought was worthy of being showcased at *The Louvre* on my closet wall when I was three, but I guess it's hard to discipline someone who doesn't even remember what in the world happened that night.

"You can keep that as long as you need to."

Before I can thank her for the effort, she's out the door and down the hall. When her bedroom door closes with a soft click, I know what's happening. If I followed her and pressed my ear to her door, I'd hear her sobbing. It's happened more than once since I got home, but I don't know if it's because I've ruined their lives and put them in debt with hospital bills. I don't know if she cries because she's grateful I'm still alive, or if she's upset that I can't remember much about her. I don't have it in me to ask.

Tired of the claustrophobia that comes hand in hand with staying in the same room for days, I climb off my bed and walk down the hallway. I don't turn toward my parents' room but toward the stairs. Maybe sitting on the back patio will help. There's a huge in-ground pool here, and even though everyone assures me that I'm a great swimmer, all I can remember is the one time I slipped and thought I was going to drown in the bathtub when I was two.

As I walk past my brother's room, I lift my fingers to the tiny scar right above my left eye that I got the day I slipped in the tub. I cling to that memory because I don't seem to have many these days.

Preston's door is halfway open, and when I peek in, I find him sitting on a black beanbag in the middle of his room while he races cars around a track on his TV.

"Mind if I play?"

My little brother jolts when I talk, and the surprise is still on his face when I cross the room in his direction.

"Play?"

"Yeah." I shrug. "I won't be able to play for long because my head will start hurting, but I'm bored."

I don't bother admitting that my head is already throbbing as he scrambles to pass over the other controller. I can deal with a little pain if it means I don't have to be alone right now.

Preston starts another game, one that allows two players, and somehow the buttons on the controller are familiar. Even the track my silver sports car is navigating is familiar. My car races in the lead, and I don't even have to look down at my hands to figure it out. It's almost like an out-of-body experience. I have not a single recollection of playing this game before, but my hands seem to have played it a million times over.

"Wow," Preston praises when I lap him on the screen. "Impressive."

I'm smiling, having a good time for the first time since leaving the hospital, but then out of nowhere, a black car sideswipes my car. The silver car on the screen spins out of control before stopping in the middle of the track with a small puff of smoke coming from under the hood. It's not a huge accident. There isn't blood pouring from the doors or anything, but it hits me in the chest like a cannonball. I drop the controller as Preston's little red car rushes past me to the finish line.

"Wanna play aga—" My brother's jaw snaps shut when he looks over at me. "Is it your head?"

"Yeah," I lie before standing from the floor to leave his room.

"Hey, Dalton." I turn in my brother's direction. "Thanks for playing with me."

I nod my head, a little weirded out that he seems so grateful that I spent ten minutes playing a video game. If anything, I should apologize for having to cut it short.

"You never took the time before," Peyton says when she sees the look on my face after I step out into the hallway.

"So, I was just busy all the time or something?" That would explain all the trophies in my room and his surprise at me asking to play.

"No," she answers, her voice flat. "You were just that big of an asshole."

Chapter 8

Piper

Surreal. That's the only way to describe how my night is going.

What started out with me helping my mom make dinner has turned into an impromptu gathering with the Paynes. All of them, including Dalton.

My archnemesis is sitting in the recliner in the den while my mom, Mrs. Payne, and I put the finishing touches on dinner.

This entire scenario isn't odd. My parents have been friends with the Paynes for as long as I can remember. It's the addition of Dalton, that is unusual. Normally, he's too busy with friends or sports practice to come over. His parents normally just take him a plate to eat when he gets home late.

His eyes found mine the second I answered the door and his parents stepped out of the way. He didn't say a word to me as he walked into the house, but the look in his green eyes was nothing like the millions of times he's glared at me in disgust. I directed the guys to the living room, and thankfully, that's where they have stayed.

"How are you feeling, Piper?" Mrs. Payne asks as she transitions the mashed potatoes from the pot on the stove to a serving dish on the counter.

"Pretty good. My arm only hurts late in the evening. I'm off the prescription pain meds and only taking over-the-counter stuff when it bothers me."

Her face scrunches up, and I recognize the same look of guilt that was on her face when she told me she was sorry Dalton wrecked his car with me in it.

"That's good." Her voice is small and still tinted with shame.

It makes me feel ten times worse, but Dalton has been home for over a week now, and from overhearing conversations between my parents, he still hasn't remembered anything from that night.

"I'll be as good as new before long," I assure her.

My physical ailments may heal, but the torment from my lies will haunt me until the truth comes out, and even if he never gets his memories back, I imagine I'll feel the weight of my sins for the rest of my life.

"I hate to even ask this of you," Mrs. Payne begins as she places the potato pot in the sink, running water in it to soak, "but would you consider still tutoring Peyton?"

She's hopeful when she turns around to face me, but I can tell by the look in her eyes that she's already anticipating my rejection. According to her, her son almost killed me. Why would I volunteer to help her family when she believes they caused me pain and suffering?

"Of course," I answer before I give myself time to talk myself out of it.

"Really?" Shock fills her voice. "That's very kind of you."

I just nod, busying myself with getting silverware from the drawer.

"Can I ask another favor?"

"Sure." I'm filled with trepidation when I look at her again.

"Preston usually visits my parents in the summer, but with everything that's happened, we didn't feel like it was a good time for him to be separated from the family."

Translation—Dalton doesn't remember him, and it won't happen if he's gone.

"I was hoping you'd be able to keep an eye on him during the day while you're tutoring Peyton." She takes a deep breath and continues before I can respond, "He's pretty self-sufficient. Mostly stays in his room playing video games, so you won't have to keep a constant eye on him."

I almost tell her no, but the guilt won't let me. "Sure. No problem."

"I'll pay you double what we agreed to for helping Peyton."

I merely nod before walking out of the room to set the dining room table. If I turned down the money, it would look suspicious, so while I put the silverware by the place settings, I think of places I can donate it to for charity. I can't keep it. It's effectively blood money, and I've done enough bad things to last a lifetime.

The unspoken part of watching Preston seems to be that I'll now be doing my tutoring at the Paynes instead of going over junior high math equations in the comfort of my own bedroom like I had planned. I chalk it up to penance before heading to the den to let the guys know dinner is ready.

My hands are trembling by the time I take my seat. Somehow, Dalton ended up sitting right beside me. Every other time he bothered to show up for one of these meals, we take seats as far away from each other as possible. It decreases the possibility of any of our parents discovering the hostility between the two of us.

My mom smiles at me when I pull my chair further under me, and I hope she didn't notice that I also moved it a few inches closer to Peyton. Even the distance I've managed to put between Dalton and myself doesn't ease the tension. I know exactly what tonight is. It's a show of reunification, a way to test the waters and see if the relationships between the families will survive the tragic accident that nearly took the lives of a child from both families.

Both Mr. and Mrs. Payne seem subdued, a contrast to their normally boisterous demeanors, and telling from the look on my dad's face, he isn't impressed with the new seating arrangement.

Throughout the meal, I chat with Peyton about schedules and what we need to study tomorrow. I avoid conversation with Dalton, and it seems he's avoiding interacting with everyone. I'm succeeding at pretending he isn't even in the room until I hear his fork clank on his plate for the millionth time.

"Crap," he mutters when his utensil strikes the china once again.

When I chance a glance in his direction, I notice him struggling to cut the pork chop on his plate. He does it for another minute longer before I swear if I hear his fork fall one more time, I'm going to pick it up and stab him with it.

"Here," I snap, yanking the fork from his good hand and reaching for his knife, "let me help you."

My words come out on a hiss between clenched teeth, and when I lean over to begin cutting, the back of my arm brushes his chest. We both tense but at least he doesn't spew some hateful stuff in front of my parents.

"Thank you," he whispers when I finish, placing his knife to the side. I leave his fork on his plate, knowing dang well I don't want to chance touching him again to hand it over. "I can't wait to get this cast off. I feel useless with it on."

I straighten in my chair, pushing my glasses up my nose and manage a side glance to see if his face betrays his statement. He's not sneering at me or giving me a heated glare that says he remembers what happened and is only lying in wait to explode my life. He would be the type of guy to pull some stuff like that.

"You're welcome," I respond when I don't see any of the past hatred in his eyes.

After the weirdest dinner on the face of the earth, I offer to do the dishes while everyone else retreats to the living room. I'm avoiding everyone, and I have been since I was released from the hospital. I've only spoken with Frankie a handful of times because I can't get Dalton's words out of my head. Deep down, I don't believe Frankie had anything to do with Vaughn's little prank, but I can't talk to her without wanting to tell her the truth about what happened that night.

Not one single person saw me climb behind the wheel of his car, so that means everyone in town is under the impression that Dalton was driving. My lie of omission has spiraled out of control, and I haven't been able to think of a way to confess and survive the fallout.

Once the dishes are done, I take the back exit out of the kitchen, so I don't have to face the people in the den, but once again, my plans are foiled. Dalton is leaning against the wall in the hallway, and at first, I wonder if he's trying to avoid everyone as well.

"Hey," I say as I try to walk past him.

"Piper," he whispers, and the single word from his mouth makes my legs turn to stone.

I haven't heard him use my real name in years. I've been *Mary* to him and every other person in my school for as long as I can remember.

Before I can convince my legs to start working again, Dalton is standing in front of me. When I take a step back to avoid contact, I hit the wall, and he just keeps coming. Two steps are all it takes before his body is pressed against mine. I turn my head to the side, tears already burning my eyes. I thought I had a little longer before we were going to hash out what happened that night.

Air rushes past his nose as he inhales. His breath is warm on my shoulder when he releases the breath. His casted arm hangs at his side, but his elbow is bent enough that I feel his fingertip brush my hip.

"Fuck," he mumbles when he breathes me in for a second time. "Please tell me you're mine."

My entire body is shaking. This has to be another one of his sick games. This is Dalton Payne, and there are no boundaries for his cruelty.

The heat of his body and the gravel in his voice are unfamiliar. My pulse skyrockets with his proximity, but I can't find the words I need to speak right now. Terrified like a mistreated dog, I just stand there and shake, praying with each second that passes that I'll eventually make it to my room unscathed.

He presses against me harder, the erection straining in his jeans an unspoken threat against my stomach.

"Piper," he whispers again.

"P-please," I beg, the tremble in my voice as clear as his cruel intentions.

Before he can threaten me, a door closes somewhere, and it's enough of a warning to make him step away from me.

"See you tomorrow, Piper." His tone doesn't hold the warning it normally does, but his history of depravity speaks for itself.

When he's far enough away, I shove past him and race up the stairs.

I lock my bedroom door for the very first time in my life.

Chapter 9

Dalton

The growl of my stomach is the only thing that pulls me from my bedroom. I didn't race downstairs when the doorbell rang, and I didn't bother plastering my ear to my bedroom door when the sound of Piper's voice managed to make it up the stairs.

She hates me. That much was clear last night when I met her in the hallway. Actually, it was clear long before that. It was in the look on her face when she opened the door, and in the attitude she barely managed to cover when she helped me at the dinner table.

I may have lost my memory, but my ability to read social cues seems to be fully intact. The thing I don't know is if she hated me before the accident or hates me because of it.

I wanted to talk to Peyton about it when we got home last night, but she doesn't seem to be my biggest fan either. I'm a popular guy which I discovered after accessing my social media platforms a couple of days ago. I'm tagged constantly in posts, and even though I didn't seem to post much myself, all of the things I did share showed me surrounded by smiling faces. I'm the captain of the varsity baseball team. I was nominated to homecoming court last year even though I don't seem to be a football player.

Yet, even with all of the social proof that I'm popular and a fun guy to be around, not one person has stopped by. The messages in my inbox are either from people wishing me well that I've never messaged before or are stagnant leftovers from before the accident. There wasn't one single message thread between Piper and me. I knew that when I went to dinner last night, but it didn't keep me from hoping that we were closer than the need for messages. I'd looked her up online before going over there, hoping that the sight of her would bring back memories from our accident. I wanted a little more understanding of the girl I nearly killed. Apologizing for something I can't remember strikes me as insincere for some reason, but the dated pictures on her mostly unused profile didn't force any memories.

Peyton and Piper are both leaning over some worksheets spread out on the kitchen table when I make it into the room. Neither looks up at me as I walk by even though I make sure to make enough noise to be noticed.

I grab an apple and sit on the opposite side of the table. Being avoided by family members is one thing but being ignored by Piper strikes a different chord with me. I actually hate it. Her indifference settles in my stomach like acid, and I'm pretty sure I'd do just about anything to have this gorgeous girl look up at me without contempt in her blue eyes.

They discuss a few more problems, and even when Piper sets a timer on her phone and Peyton works against the clock, the girl doesn't look up. She busies herself by flipping through a math workbook and tearing out pages they'll work on next.

The timer goes off just as Peyton's phone rings. When my sister stands to take her call, Piper leaves the table as well. I watch her as she moves around the kitchen, pulling bread, butter, and slices of cheese from various places and placing them all together on the counter. She still doesn't look at me when the first sandwich hits the skillet she's heated on the stove.

I've had enough. Enough of being ignored. Enough of having no memories. Enough of not knowing where I stand with her and why.

She doesn't respond to me when I stand from the table, but the same tension that was in her body last night tenses up her shoulders when I step closer to her. I don't press against her or touch her with the fingers of my casted hand like I did last night, but I'm close enough that I know she can feel the heat from my body.

She doesn't ask me to step back, but she doesn't close the distance between the two of us either. Her breaths are ragged and quick, the only form of acknowledgment.

"I thought about your lips all night," I whisper, and it's the damn truth. Even when I tried to close my eyes to think of something else, it was the top curve of her cupid's bow that infiltrated my mind. It must be one of the downfalls of not having anything else inside of my head to pull from. "And the scent of your hair."

My nose brushes the curly strands of her hair hanging down her back as I inhale. I'm straining in my jeans, and even though I have no memory of ever touching a girl, I also somehow know that making it to seventeen without doing so is highly unlikely. My cock jerks like it's well aware of what it's missing.

"Unless you're going to help, leave me alone," she hisses.

"Kiss me, and I'll leave you be," I bargain.

I also have no memory of pressing my lips to anyone before, but deep in my gut, I feel like it's something I'm probably good at, and there's only one way to find out.

Instead of turning to face me, Piper scoops the grilled cheese from the pan, slaps it on a plate, and walks away.

I'm staring at her retreating back when Peyton walks into the kitchen.

"What the hell have you done now?" my younger sister spits.

"Nothing," I lie. Well, as far as I see it, I'm lying. I didn't do anything to her, but maybe Piper really does hate me. "I was trying to talk to her, and she just walked off."

"I highly doubt that," Peyton mutters before taking her seat back at the table.

"What's her problem, anyway?"

"You," my sister says without pulling her eyes from the worksheet in front of her.

Her response floors me.

"When I said you were an asshole?" She looks up at me. "You were worse with Piper."

"So, I ignored her like I did Preston?" Like I don't have enough guilt for being an absentee brother.

She huffs, but there's no humor in the sound. "You tortured her. Like going out of your way to be mean to her. Pranks, tricks, and insults were some of your favorite things."

"I thought we were dating," I mumble, still looking in the direction Piper disappeared to.

"Hardly. That girl is way too smart for that."

"We were in my car together," I remind her.

"She was probably there against her will. I can't imagine any other reason for her to want to spend time alone with you."

"That stings."

"It's the truth." Peyton taps her pencil on the paperwork. "Now get lost so I can study. I'm already behind."

I don't answer, just nod my head and turn to walk away.

"If you want to know what your life was like before the accident, maybe ask your best friend. Spend a few hours with Kyle, and then you'll easily see how things really are."

Her suggestion is ominous, but I'm desperate for answers, so I shoot Kyle Turner a message as I leave the room.

Instead of hanging out downstairs, I head back to my bedroom to hide. When I see Piper coming out of Preston's room, I merely nod my head and move to the far side of the hall so she can walk past. I can't confront her or say another thing to her until I have answers.

It takes him twenty minutes to respond, but we agree to meet in a few hours so he can answer some questions. There's no way I hate her. It doesn't make sense, but it also doesn't stop the dread from settling in as I wait to meet Kyle. I don't think Peyton has any reason to lie to me. She seems to be the least worried person that I lost my memories. I don't think she'd have an ulterior motive for telling me what she did downstairs.

All I know is no matter what has happened in the past, I plan to make Piper see that I'm the best decision she could ever make.

Chapter 10

Piper

"I need you to run to *Corner Street Diner* and pick up dinner," Mom says as soon as I step inside of the house. "We're running late. Still playing catch up at the office."

Of course, she guilts me first. My mom is a nurse at my dad's office, and since they both missed tons of work while I was in the hospital, I can only imagine what chaos they went back to once I was released from the hospital.

"Cash is on the counter," she adds as she walks past me to head to her bedroom.

I don't even have time to argue before she disappears down the hall. *Corner Street Diner* is over five miles away, but Mom walks back into the room several minutes later after changing her clothes to find me standing in the entryway, figuring out how I'm going to walk the whole way there and make it home before the food gets cold.

"We discussed this," Mom says with a sharp sigh.

"I can't. Why don't we go there together?"

Even riding in the car from the hospital was enough to make me want to ask for Prozac for my nerves. She's asking me to get behind the wheel and actually drive myself there.

"I have a ton of charting I have to do," she counters. "You'll have to get comfortable in a car one day. That day might as well be today. Go on. I'm sure the food's ready."

She shoves the two twenties from the kitchen counter into my hand and ushers me out the front door.

This has to be some form of child abuse. She could've easily ordered something to be delivered to the house.

My hands are trembling, much like they did the night of the party, when I climb behind the wheel and crank the car. I'm taking a few deep breaths, convincing myself that I'll be fine when my phone rings. The sound is so abrupt in the silent vehicle that I screech.

"H-hello?" I say when I finally manage to press the connect button on the dash.

"Piper?" Frankie sounds far away, but it may just be the pounding pulse in my ears that makes it difficult to hear her.

"Hey."

"Do you have me on speakerphone?"

"I'm in the car," I answer.

"I'll let you go."

"Don't," I snap.

Not including the last time I drove, I have an otherwise spotless driving record, and hands-free phone calls have always been a part of my experience when I'm behind the wheel.

"Talk to me while I drive," I beg.

I don't speak my fears out loud, but I know Frankie will understand.

"I can do that. I was calling to see how the first day of tutoring went."

"That's not why you called." I chuckle as I put the car in reverse and back down the driveway.

"It is," she insists.

"You wanted to know what it was like at the Paynes. Don't be afraid to ask."

"You got me. So how was it?"

"It was fine." I smile when she huffs.

"And how is Dalton?" Going straight for that is exactly what I expected when her name flashed on the dash, but when it happens, it makes a chill settle in my bones.

"The night that we wrecked, Dalton told me that you helped plan the trick with Vaughn."

"Piper, I would never do that." Her voice is filled with conviction, and I feel bad for even considering the possibility. "He's spiteful. He's gorgeous, but he's evil incarnate. I'd never do anything to hurt you, but more so, I'd never do anything to help that piece of shit."

I frown when my best friend cusses. Vulgar language seems to be ever-present with most teens our age, but we were never fond of it. My grandmother once told us that people who use foul language do so because they aren't intelligent enough to use different words. She told us more than once that classy women don't speak like that. We wanted to be classy when she told us that over ten years ago, and it sort of just stuck with us.

"He's still gorgeous," I mutter.

"What was that?"

"Even with the bruises on his face," I clarify. "He's still very good-looking."

"That's—complimentary." Wariness fills her tone, and I bite the inside of my cheek as I pull up to a red light halfway to the diner. "Did something happen that's making you not so anti-Dalton?"

Please tell me you're mine.

His words from last night echo in my head but confessing that to Frankie will never happen.

When I don't answer, she uses a different tactic. That's the thing about best friends, even over the phone she can tell there's something going on.

"Has he gotten any of his memories back?"

Last night, I was certain that he remembered everything and was just waiting until the right time to spring the truth on everyone. For Dalton, he'd wait until the truth would have the biggest impact on my life. This morning, when he watched me from the other side of the table, all I could feel coming from him was hunger and not the kind that accompanies predator and prey.

He had every opportunity to confront me in the hallway after I took Preston his lunch, but he just walked right past me without a word.

"He doesn't remember anything," I finally answer. "Not even his little brother or any of his friends. I don't think he remembers how he treated me."

I've been mulling over that possibility since last night as well, but this is the first time I've said as much out loud.

"What does that even mean? Is he treating you differently?"

"He's—nicer. He hasn't insulted me once. Not last night, and not earlier today at his house."

"Don't fall for that crap, Piper," Frankie warns. "The guy has amnesia. He didn't have a personality transplant. He's been vicious since the day he was born. A bump on the head didn't change that. He's the same person he's always been."

I don't argue with her. I don't try to describe how even his eyes seem different now. They don't quite sparkle, but they also don't seem to be filled with malice and ill will any longer either.

"Give me a second, Frankie. I have to switch you over to my headphones."

As I pull my headphones from the glovebox, I cringe, noticing Kyle's truck parked down the block. It would only be wishful thinking to hope that he wasn't at the diner, but since this is the only establishment on the block, I know he's inside.

Maybe the accident will somehow garner goodwill from the second biggest jerk in our class?

"You still there?" I ask after pushing the buds in my ears.

"Still here."

"I think Kyle is here," I mutter.

"Kick him between the legs if he says anything to you, or better yet, smack him upside the head with your cast."

"It's a soft cast," I remind her as I open the driver's side door and step out. "It would probably just hurt me more."

"Then go for the nuts."

I chuckle, tucking my phone into my back pocket before heading to the entrance.

"Oh fuck," I mutter when I first step inside.

"What is it?" Frankie doesn't chastise me for the slipped cuss word. She sounds nervous for me.

"He's here," I hiss.

"Kyle?"

"Dalton," I correct, and it kills a little part of my soul to see the boy I had let myself imagine had changed just a little sitting across the diner with the same group of jerks he's always been around. Vaughn is even at a table adjacent to his with a wide smile on his face as he watches Kyle act out some stupid story.

"Looks like things are back to normal," I mutter as I turn toward the counter.

We frequent the diner so often; the owner has my food waiting for me once I reach the pay counter. The transaction goes smoothly, and I'm certain the guys in the back corner haven't noticed me as I leave, but my luck never works out like that.

"You looking for me?" Dalton asks just as I step outside on the concrete.

"Hold on, Frankie. Let me get rid of this jerk."

"Frankie?" Dalton asks, his brows drawing together in confusion.

"Is that your boyfriend?"

"Tell him to suck a bag of dicks," Frankie urges in my ear. "Or kick him in the sac!"

"Yes," I answer, but I don't honestly know if I'm answering Dalton or agreeing with Frankie that I should do either of her raunchy suggestions.

"You have a boyfriend?"

"He really has lost his memories, hasn't he?" Frankie whispers like if she speaks at a regular tone, he'd be able to hear her.

"Isn't that what I just said?"

The news should make him back up, but it doesn't. If anything, he inches closer.

"How about you stay out of my way, and I'll stay out of yours?" I suggest.

"That's the last thing I want," Dalton says as he manages to step even closer.

His voice is doing that same husky thing it did last night and earlier in his kitchen. I don't like it, but I can admit in my own head that I don't *hate* it either. After years of him yelling and insulting me, it's actually a nice change.

"What is he doing?"

"Don't," I tell him when he leans in closer, his mouth parted like he's going to kiss me.

His eyes are laser-focused on my mouth, and the attention makes them tingle.

"I don't know where your lips have been," I add.

"Is he trying to kiss you?" Frankie screeches in my ear. The hysteria is almost loud enough to make me rip the buds from my ears. "I bet he's an amazing kisser."

Jesus, whose side is she on? And how in the heck does she go from hating him to opinions about his kissing skills?

"I've never kissed anyone before."

Frankie snorts in my ear before I can manage the sound myself.

"Well, I don't remember kissing anyone before." His green eyes dart from my lips back up to my own eyes twice. "You'd be my first."

"Dang," Frankie moans. "Even from five hundred miles away, he's turning *me* on."

"Now isn't the time," I snap at Frankie.

"Some other time then?" Dalton asks, that same damn casted hand gripping my hip.

"More like never," I answer before turning around and getting the hell out of there.

Chapter 11

Dalton

"Never?" I mumble as Piper drives away. I huff a humorless laugh. "That's never going to happen."

"What was that?"

I look over to find Kyle standing right beside me. He was so engrossed in his telling of a party he went to last week that I was hoping he'd stay in the damn diner. I guess I'm not that lucky.

"Nothing," I mutter, taking a step away from the curb.

I need distance, distance from thoughts of her and distance from the guy who claims to be my best friend. Since he picked me up from my house, he's been kind of an asshole. All he wants to talk about are the parties we attended together and the girls he's slept with. There's no real substance to him, and I'm honestly shocked that we're friends. He's nothing like I picture myself being.

I wonder for the third time if losing my memories are more a godsend than an actual tragedy. The first time I got a glimpse at who I used to be was when Peyton intercepted me at home outside of Preston's room.

The second time came the following day when she told me how awful I'd been to Piper.

"Dude?" Kyle knocks my shoulder with his. "Why did you lean in like you were going to kiss Mary?"

"Mary?"

He points down the street in the direction Piper went, but the different name isn't my main focus. Is he blind? There were several girls that have come and gone from the diner since we've been here, and yeah, I can see their beauty, but no one compares to Piper, absolutely no one.

"She's gorgeous," I tell him. "Why wouldn't I want to kiss her?"

Kyle snorts. "I realize you don't remember anything about people in Westover, but Mary isn't an option for you."

I want to argue with him. I'll do everything in my power to make that girl see how good we could be together. Holding on to the hope that she eventually comes around has been my primary focus since walking into her house last night.

"I mean," he scrapes his hand over the top of his unruly hair, "I guess you can hit that, but fuck her in the dark and keep it to yourself. You do not want people finding out. You may not have believed me when I told you the first time, but you rule Westover, and there's no faster way to get knocked off your throne than people finding out you're messing with her."

Frowning, I stare at him. If staying on this so-called throne means I have to forget Piper, then I'll give it up myself.

"Can you take me home?" I ask, rather than argue with him about Piper.

Kyle's clearly an idiot and standing here while he gives me instructions on how to lead my own damn life isn't something I'm fond of doing.

"Sure," he claps me on the back, "come on."

"You said Piper was gorgeous," Kyle starts once we're back in his truck. "You don't even know gorgeous. Let's get some of the crew together at your house. We'll invite all of our friends and the hottest girls from school. You'll see how easy it is to score then."

"I'm not trying to score," I mumble, not loud enough for him to hear over the pounding music coming from the radio.

He bops his head back and forth like he's auditioning for a music video. As much as I like the beat blaring through the speakers, I sit idle in my seat. I don't want to be anything like this guy, and I kind of already hate the old me if he's an example of who I was.

"Why my house?" I ask. If he hates Piper, then that means my other friends do too. Piper will be there tutoring Peyton, and I don't want them to get anywhere near her.

"Really?" He arches an eyebrow but doesn't take his eyes from the road. "You have a pool."

"I can't be the only one with a pool."

"You have the *best* pool," he clarifies. "Plus, your sister is hot."

"No," I snap. "Stay the fuck away from my sister."

I don't know my sister very well, but she doesn't seem the type to go for a jerk like Kyle, but I have to get the warning in, regardless.

He smiles wide, but he doesn't agree—such a damn slimeball.

I don't know why I finally agree to host a pool party at my house on Friday. Maybe it's because I'm bored. Maybe it's because I'm a glutton for punishment. But deep down, I think I'm going to take it as an opportunity to set all these people straight. Maybe Piper will come around if I defend her in front of everyone.

The bad thing about making split-second decisions is that, most often, you regret them, and I want to cancel the plans I made with Kyle before I even make it back inside my house.

When I make it to the top of the stairs, I turn right instead of heading to my room on the left. Peyton's bedroom door is open, but when I stick my head inside the room, it's clear she isn't here. Her windows face to the east, and lucky for me, that means that she has a clear view of Piper's house.

My eyes focus on the window that has coral-colored curtains. I don't know if that's Piper's room, but it's highly likely since I know from the dinner visit to her house that her parents' room is on the main floor.

Leaning forward, I realize that since this is a corner room, exactly like Peyton's, she has one window on the side and one in the front, so she's able to see the road and our front yard. I make a mental note of that, already thinking of ways to be seen by her.

"What are you doing?"

I spin around at my sister's voice. She's wearing a frown, arms crossed over her chest as if she caught me in here rifling through her things rather than just standing at the window and peering out.

"Wanna switch rooms?" I ask, instead of explaining my presence in her space.

She chuckles as she steps further into the room. She comes to stand beside me, her eyes also glued to the side of Piper's house. "You've asked me that same question a million times."

"I have?" It seems I'm not entirely different. Some things have remained the same even after the accident.

"Yep," she answers. "Especially since Piper's boobs showed up."

My cheeks heat, and I don't know if I'm embarrassed for being so transparent or if it's because my younger sister realizes my perversion.

"It has the best light," I argue like an idiot. I have no damn clue about light angles or sunshine infiltrations and telling from the incredulous snort that erupts from my sister, she's well aware that I don't either.

"She's never going to like you," Peyton says as she steps away and sits on the corner of her bed.

"I don't even remember being a jerk to her," I remind her.

"And she'll never be able to forget. You were cruel to her, and your friends are just as bad."

My brows scrunch together. I hate hearing about the past, especially since there isn't a damn thing I can do to change it.

"I'm not like that anymore," I argue. "She can't hate me forever."

"If you think that, you don't have a clue about a girl's ability to hold a grudge. Give up on Piper, Dalton. It's never going to happen."

"Tell me about her," I say rather than agreeing to back off.

My sister's frown deepens, but she doesn't seem annoyed, just resigned that I'm not planning to give up any time soon.

"She's a straight-A student, ranked number one in your class. She's probably going to get a full-ride scholarship to her college of choice. I don't think she wants to be a doctor like her dad, but it wouldn't surprise me if she goes to medical school anyway."

"Why would she become a doctor if that's not what she wants?"

The concept doesn't make sense to me.

"She's a people pleaser." She sighs. "For example, she doesn't want to be stuck coming over here every day seeing you, but she didn't turn Mom down when she asked. She does shit she doesn't want to do to make those around her happy."

"That's fucked up," I mumble.

"Yeah," she agrees. "She spends a lot of time at the library. I think she tutors there or leads the children's storytime or something like that, teaching kids to read."

This is all great information to have, but I really need to know what I did to her to make her life miserable, call it penance, or even a way to possibly correct some of my misdeeds.

"How did I treat her?"

"Like shit," she answers without pause.

"Can you be more specific?"

She rolls her eyes. "I don't know everything. I'm just now heading into high school, and we weren't exactly close before the accident."

"But you know some things, right?"

"I know that you and your friends made fun of her the day she started her period in junior high. You've called her Bloody Mary since that day."

So that's where Kyle's name for her came from.

My nose crinkles. "Really?"

"That's not even the worst thing."

I get the feeling I'm not going to like the rest of the information my sister is about to lay at my feet, but instead of telling her I've heard enough, I insist she goes on.

"What else?"

"You filled her car with trash from the park. Your friends throw food at her in the cafeteria. You even sprayed her with a water hose the same day you two got in the wreck. She showed up here to iron out our tutoring details, looking amazing, and when she walked past you in the driveway, you turned the water hose on her. You were a real bastard."

Peyton is right. I was a complete asshole. But how do I convince Piper that I'm no longer that guy?

"I'm pretty sure you or one of your friends posted videos online of her doing embarrassing things, and I know for a fact that you've messed with her assignments so she'd get horrible grades."

"Jesus," I mutter.

"And that's only the things I know about," she says with a heaved sigh. "Like I said, you were a complete asshole."

"I'm not that person anymore," I argue once again. How many times do I need to say it before people actually start to believe it?

"Good luck convincing her of that."

Chapter 12

Piper

"Can we talk?"

I don't even acknowledge him as I walk past.

I've been here all day, and somehow, he's managed to stay in his room and away from Peyton and me while I tutored her.

I continue to ignore him as I head to the kitchen to pack up my things for the day.

"Piper?" he pleads. "Can we please talk?"

There's sincerity in his tone, but I'm no fool. I won't fall for whatever game he's playing. I did that once in fourth grade, and it came back to bite me on the rear.

"I told you to leave me alone," I mutter as I cram my pens and a couple of spirals into my backpack.

"I left you alone all day."

"Try forever next time," I snap as I zip my backpack.

I refuse to acknowledge that I watched the bottom of the staircase all day, waiting for him to saunter into the room. I even kept my ears peeled, wondering when he was going to show his handsome face. I don't know if I'm disappointed or grateful that he didn't.

"Why are you so hateful?" When my eyes snap up to his, I see his face transform.

It's easy to tell he regrets asking the question in the first place, but even if he can't remember what he's done to me, his true colors are already starting to reappear.

"That's rich coming from you."

"Can't you forgive me?"

"No." And it's the truth. There's no level of forgiveness I can offer him. The pain from what he's done is too great. He could become a model citizen, helping the homeless and dedicating his life to those less fortunate, and it still wouldn't change my opinion about him. A zebra doesn't change its stripes and all that.

"I don't remember being a jerk to you. It's not fair for you to hold that against me."

I sling my backpack over my shoulder with so much force I wonder if it's going to leave a bruise on my back from the impact. Hurting myself because of him only serves to piss me off even more, but it's not like it's the first time.

"Just because you can't remember doesn't mean I should forget the years of torment and torture I suffered at your hands and those of your crappy friends."

"I'm not asking you to forget," he clarifies, "but a little forgiveness would be nice."

"You don't deserve my forgiveness."

"And I'm sure that's true, but that doesn't mean you can't. It's obvious that you're a better person than me. You volunteer at the library and help teach little kids how to read. I know that girl could forgive."

I take a step back from him. "How do you know that?"

Is he remembering? How long do I have before he realizes that I was driving his car the night that we wrecked?

"Peyton told me."

My jaw tenses and I'm already formulating the words I need to have with his sister. We're not best friends or anything, but it seems like some break in girl code for her to give information to the one guy she knows I hate more than anyone else in this world.

"Peyton should keep her mouth shut," I snap as I take a step around him.

Instead of staying in his kitchen, Dalton follows me to the door, and then he stays on my heels as I walk across his lawn to my own. He's still at my back when I unlock my front door.

Mrs. Payne texted not long ago to let me know that she was on her way home, and Preston would be fine until she got there if I wanted to leave. I couldn't get out of there fast enough, yet, I'm still being followed by her obstinate son.

"What will it take?" he asks, walking into my house behind me and shutting the door behind him.

"There's no chance," I tell him, but my pulse quickens when the closing of the front door echoes around my empty house.

My parents won't be home for another hour or so, and just the thought of being alone with Dalton where no one can hear me scream if he tries to hurt me makes me hyper-aware of my surroundings.

The curtains are pulled tight, the only light infiltrating the foyer streams in from the arched window above the front door. The silence is deafening, filled only with the ragged sound of my breathing.

"Y-you need to leave." I hate the tremor in my voice. It speaks of weakness, and that's always something I try to avoid around him.

Dalton has never physically put his hands on me before, and the only time I thought he would, was when I refused to give his keys back outside of Kyle's house after he caught him and his girlfriend together, but this new Dalton may think it's a good idea. I have no way of knowing if the crash did more to his brain than wiping his memories. Did I read somewhere that head trauma patients are known to have regular bouts of aggression and hostility?

"We're just talking," he says, and as if to get his point across, he takes a few steps away from me.

He doesn't make a move to leave, but the several feet between us calms me some. It gives me a greater chance of getting away if he lunges for me.

A long breath rushes past my lips when I realize he's not going to leave until I give in. And since that's never going to happen, I need to figure out a way to make this boy understand that forgiving him isn't something I'll ever be capable of.

"Where are you going?" he asks when I turn away from him and head toward the stairs.

I don't answer him, and as I predicted, he follows me up the stairs. I've never had a boy in my room before, and that isn't lost on me when Dalton follows me into my private space.

Like a fool, he smiles as he looks at my coral curtains. His eyes glisten like there's some inside joke I'm not privy to. It only serves to frustrate me more.

"My dad will kill you if he catches you in my room," I mutter as I fling my backpack onto my unmade bed.

He doesn't say a word as his eyes skate over everything in my room. I almost hate that I'm not a tidier person. I shuffle around, scooping up dirty clothes and straightening the things on my desk.

"It smells nice in here." His nose tips up as he takes a deep breath. "What is that? Lavender? Lilac?"

"Really?" His head drops back down, and the heat in his stare forces a wave of goosebumps down my arms. I ignore them, just like I ignore the way his tongue traces his lips. Why does he have to be so good-looking? "You know notes of my body lotion, but you can't remember your family?"

His brows furrow. "I know my family. I mean, I know who Mom and Dad are. My memories of Peyton are a little off since she's no longer a baby."

"You don't remember Preston at all?"

Sadness fills his eyes, and the flash of pain on his face makes the walls around my heart lose a little fortitude. It also makes the guilt ramp up to its highest yet. He can't remember a primary person in his nuclear family because of what I did. His memory loss is more than just forgetting what a jerk he was. It's wiped out entire people. That wouldn't be so bad if the only ones on that list were Kyle, Bronwyn, and the rest of the evil minions, but knowing he can't remember his brother makes my heart ache.

"What's that look for, Piper?"

I swallow thickly, breaking eye contact with him.

"Wh-what look?"

"I don't want you to feel sorry for me."

"I don't." It's a partial lie, but that's the thing about accidents—you can't pick and choose what the suffering will be.

"Forgive me." It's not a question or really a demand, but the repetition of his insistence reminds me why I came up here to begin with.

Instead of refusing him once again, I turn toward my closet. The box I need is all the way on the top shelf, and just like every other time I've needed it down, I head back into the room to get the step stool in the corner of my room.

"Let me," Dalton offers, cutting in front of me to stand in the middle of my oversized closet. "Which one?"

I point to the second box to the left, thankful that he reaches for it and hands it directly over. His efficiency keeps me from staring at the sliver of golden skin that's revealed when he reaches up.

My hands shake as I take it from him, but I don't know if it's because I'm fixing to attempt to trust him with my secrets or if it's because of the scent of his cologne and the warmth of his body with our proximity invade my senses.

I exit the closet as fast as I can and go to stand on the far side of my bed.

"What's in there?" Dalton asks as he closes my closet door. "It's not a weapon of some kind, is it?"

I huff. "Do you know how hard it would be to get blood out of my carpet? I'd never be able to hide it from my parents."

I cringe with the words, remembering all the blood covering his ashen face as he was carried past me and put in the ambulance.

"You sound like you've spent some time planning my death." He chuckles, but his statement hits a little too close to home.

"You're not worth the prison time," I mutter.

"Notebooks?" he asks, not bothering to hide the disappointment in his voice when I pull open the top of the box.

I chose the box that has my journals in it from the end of sixth grade through the summer before high school. This box doesn't contain the most horrific things that have happened to me, but it will give him some idea of why I can't do what he's asking. I can't forgive him for the things that will leave lasting scars on my soul.

"I want you to read these," I tell him as I pull a stack of journals from the box and offer them to him.

"Read?" He shakes his head. "Why don't you just tell me what's in them."

The manipulative smirk on his face as he barters is all too familiar.

"Never mind," I hiss and shove them back in the box.

"What?"

"You want to ask things of me that I can't give you, but you don't even want to take the time to understand why. It seems like the same old Dalton to me."

"Wait." He places his hand on top of mine, preventing me from folding the box flaps down. "I only asked you to explain them because my head kills me from the accident. Reading is one of the main triggers."

I know he's telling the truth because it was the same for me the first couple of weeks. I can only imagine how bad his head hurts considering how extensive his injuries were.

"No big deal." I shrug my shoulder as I jerk my hand out from under his. The contact is too much. His fingers are too warm, not cold and calculating like I always imagined they would be.

Tell me you're mine.

I step away as the memory from the other night in my hallway hits me full force. I don't need to think of his masculine scent or how perfect he felt against me in the hallway. Those things will only lead to more trouble. Trusting him or even believing that he has changed will only make things ten times worse when he reverts right back to the old Dalton.

"I'll read them. It may take me a century to get through them, though."

Against my better judgment, I pull a stack of journals from the box and hand them over.

"Now, please leave."

Instead of arguing, Dalton turns around and walks out of my room. I don't breathe easily until the sound of the front door closing echoes through my house.

Chapter 13

Dalton

"This is great," I lie as I shovel another bite of dried chicken into my mouth.

Mom smiles at the compliment, but Peyton snorts. I cut my eyes to hers, but all of her attention is focused on moving her food around on her plate. She hasn't eaten much, and I can tell by Preston's lack of enthusiasm from being pulled away from his video games that family dinner time isn't part of the norm for us.

Do my parents think that changing things up will make me remember faster? I want to open my mouth and remind them that the doctors told me to get back to my normal life, but I don't want to hurt anyone's feelings.

"Is it okay if I have a few friends over to swim in the pool on Friday?"

My dad nearly chokes, and I don't know if it's because he doesn't like the idea or if the dry chicken got lodged. Peyton raises her eyes to glare at me, but I keep my eyes on the head of the table. When Dad takes a sip of wine, attempting to get rid of the stuck food, his eyes dart to my mom.

"Friends?" Mom asks cautiously. "Do you remember the kids from school?"

Sadness fills her eyes and I know she thinks that I remember them when I haven't shown any signs of remembering my family.

"No," I answer honestly, "but Kyle suggested it when I saw him earlier this week. I'm hoping it will trigger something."

"I don't like that boy," Dad mutters.

"He mentioned a party Saturday night, but I figured staying close to home would be a better idea, considering what happened the last time I went to a party."

It's a low blow, and I'm well aware of the manipulation, but I'm a teenager after all, and using everything I have in my arsenal to get my way is just second nature.

"You're no longer allowed to go to parties," Mom says, but her tone suggests that she's gearing up to argue over laying down this rule.

I feel Peyton's eyes burning a hole in the side of my head, and even Preston seems tense like he's waiting for me to lose my shit. I don't. The thought doesn't even cross my mind. The last thing I want to do is go to a party. Not counting the fact that I'm certain I don't even like the people who call themselves my friends, I don't relish the idea of being away from home. Here, Piper is next door, and I know I'm safe.

"It's just a couple of friends. I'll make sure to clean up after," I barter.

"Just a couple of friends," Dad agrees. "But no alcohol."

"Of course not," I agree.

Dinner is even more tense after my parents agree to let me host a few friends, but they don't take back the offer. To make things easier to accept, I help Mom with the dishes and carry on a conversation with my dad about the car. I haven't seen the wreckage, but he seems to think that the body will be salvageable. I don't bother to tell him that I have no interest in the car.

After finishing up in the kitchen, I stop by Preston's room with the hopes that we can play a few video games, but when I poke my head in his room, he's enthralled with his own game and chatting with someone on his headset. I leave him to it and go to my own room.

I pull the stashed journals from under my pillow and resign myself to reading about all the terrible things I did to Piper Schofield. I know that the only reason she gave these to me was that she wants to cement her reasoning for being unable to forgive me, but I see it as an opportunity to get to know her better and for a way to see how bad I was, so I know to never do those things again.

The inside cover of the first journal I pick up lets me know that it's from the summer before she began sixth grade. There are hearts and sketched flowers adorning the front page and the name Dillon written over and over.

I don't know if I'm friends with this Dillon guy, but I already hate him. The first entry describes in nauseating detail her trip to the park with this jerk. Although mostly benign to my teenage standards, it's clear that she really likes this guy. He pushed her on the swing and held her hand while they walked up the block to get ice cream. She had about a million hearts on the page when she wrote about him kissing her on the cheek when he walked her home.

My head is throbbing by the time I make it through the first journal, nauseated by the number of times she mentioned this boy. Not once was my name mentioned, and I can't help but feel like I wasted the last hour reading about her young love.

"What are those?" Accusation fills Peyton's tone when she steps inside my room, finding me with a scowl on my face and Piper's journal clutched in my hands.

"Piper's journals," I answer before tossing the one I was reading onto the pile with the others.

"You stole her journals?"

"I didn't steal them. She gave them to me to read."

"Fat chance. Why would you take her things? How did you even get them?" She continues to glare at me. "Did you break into her house? You were an asshole before, but I'm sure you were never a criminal!"

"She gave them to me to read," I repeat. "I wouldn't steal her things."

Even as the words leave my mouth, I wonder if they're completely true. I don't think they are. If there was something I could take of hers that would give me some insight on how to make her hate me less, I think I'd take that chance.

"Seriously," I tell her when she continues to glare at me.

"Why would she do that?"

"Probably to get her point across about how awful I've been to her." I look down at the journals. "Will you read them to me?"

"No way," she answers immediately. "I already know how big of a jerk you were."

"Please?" I pinch the bridge of my nose. "My head is killing me."

She watches me for a long moment before sighing and holding her hand out for one of the journals. When she takes it and sits across the room, I stand and close the bedroom door.

"I don't want Mom and Dad hearing this shit," I mutter when she gives me a quizzical look.

"Believe me, they know you're an asshole."

"Was," I remind her. "They know I was horrible to Piper?"

Wow, that only makes what I've done worse. How do they sit at the dinner table with the Scofield's with smiles on their faces knowing that I tortured Piper on a daily basis?

"I don't think they know you were mean to her. I don't think Piper has said anything to her parents either."

"That's a relief," I mutter.

"Yeah, isn't it awesome that the girl has been suffering in silence?"

Derision fills my sister's voice, but I guess I deserve it.

"Can you just read?"

She sighs before flipping open the cover. "Wow. These are really old."

"Sixth grade," I tell her.

"The first day of school was worse than I could've imagined," she begins. "Even though I was wearing the same style clothes as the other girls—"

"Maybe just summarize?" I tell her. It'll take forever if she reads these damn things word for word. I need to get to the bottom of my assholery quicker than this.

"Fine," Peyton huffs as her eyes start scanning the page.

"Bronwyn is the meanest girl she's ever met. They made fun of her in the bathroom. Kyle tripped her in the cafeteria."

Peyton flips through the journal quickly.

"Does it mention a guy named Dillon?"

Her eyes meet mine for a brief moment before she refocuses on the journal.

"It looks like his dad got a new job, and they moved to Oregon in November of that year. Her parents wouldn't let her go trick or treating that Halloween." She continues to flip the pages. "Her and Dillon dressed up as Raggedy Anne and Andy and stayed at her house and watched movies. Oh, shit!"

"What?" I lean closer on my bed.

"Her house got egged that night. It says," she flips the page, and then another, "she didn't know it was you and the other guys in class until she went back to school on Monday, and everyone was talking about it. Smug is the term she used to describe you when you confessed to it."

"That doesn't seem so bad. Just a stupid prank kids play."

"Wait—" She holds up her finger to silence me. "This is worse than I thought it was. Remember, I told you about making fun of her when she started her period?"

I nod, but she doesn't see me because her nose is still in the journal.

"Apparently, it happened during a field trip. No," she gasps as her eyes snap up to mine. "You didn't. Please tell me, you didn't?"

"I wouldn't remember if I did," I remind her. "What does it say?"

"You stuck pads to her back. She didn't notice them until the teacher pulled her aside when your class got back to school."

I scrunch my nose. "That's disgusting."

"I don't think they were used, but that's still a complete asshole thing to do."

"How did she know it was me? If she didn't notice them until the teacher pointed it out, it could've easily been anyone else."

"Don't you get it, Dalton? Everything everyone did to her was because you either told them to or because you treated her so poorly; they did it to impress you."

"What else does it say?"

"I almost don't want to keep reading. It's awful. I'd be suicidal if even half this shit happened to me."

Her words hit me like a knife in the gut. The man I am now would be devastated if something happened to Piper because of me. The guilt of her getting hurt in the crash already weighs me down, but I wonder how the old Dalton would feel if he had pushed her to the point of hurting herself.

From what I've been told and what Peyton is reading in the journals, I'm not so sure he'd even care.

Chapter 14

Piper

I don't know if Dalton read the journals and realized that what he's asked of me is impossible or what, but he didn't show his face once on Thursday. It didn't keep me from expecting him to pop up out of nowhere and insist, once again, on my forgiveness.

Today is going to be different, however.

Peyton dropped the bomb that Dalton was having a few friends over. The information came as more of a warning, letting me know that Kyle was in charge of the invites, and that meant that the worst of the group would be in attendance.

Dalton must not remember a damn thing because I can't see him remembering what happened between Kyle, Vaughn, and Bronwyn and being okay with letting them come over to his house.

"I could kill him," Peyton mutters as her pencil eraser flies over the problem she was working on. "I can't concentrate on a damn thing with all of that noise."

I cross the room to the far window and glance down at the source of her irritation. The first couple of hours this morning, it was peaceful. Now that the pool is full of teenagers splashing around, they're reaching epic levels of irritation.

From the looks of it, there are more than just a couple of people down there. Every guy from Dalton's group of friends is in attendance. Even Vaughn is splashing water in the face of a sophomore girl. The sight of him makes me want to spit nails, but he's not the only person that makes my blood boil.

Bronwyn is sitting so close to Dalton that she's practically on his lap. Even without his memories, he's gravitating right back to the same situations he'd be in if the accident never happened.

There's more skin on display than I've ever seen, all of the beauties from my class wearing the tiniest bikinis. The guys are all shirtless, muscles for days shining golden in the sun. They're all beautiful, goldens gods, and every one of them has the blackest hearts.

"It's like a party at Hugh Hefner's grotto," I mumble as I turn away from the window.

"Who?"

I shake my head instead of answering her. She may be almost fourteen, but I'm not explaining porno magazines to this girl.

"Wanna go down?" Peyton asks as I plop down on the bed beside her. "It's not like I can concentrate with all the racket."

"Not a chance in hell," I answer honestly.

"It's almost lunchtime," she reminds me.

"Can't Preston make his own lunch for a change," I argue, but then feel bad. Even though I'm not keeping the extra money for keeping an eye on him, his parents are still paying me to do just that.

"If we left him alone, he wouldn't eat. I don't know how his eyes aren't crossed at the end of the day after playing that damn game for sixteen hours straight."

"His fingers are going to curl up with arthritis," I add.

She laughs, but instead of staying to work out a few more problems, she closes her book and heads to her bedroom door.

"Come on, maybe we can make lunch without being interrupted by the idiots in the pool."

I follow her out of the room, stopping by Preston's room to ask what he wants for lunch.

"You make the best grilled cheese," he tells me with a smile.

"Flattery will get you everywhere. Keep it up, kid." I wink at him before heading down the stairs.

Peyton is already in the kitchen, standing in the open door of the fridge.

"What did he decide on?" she asks as she pulls a container of yogurt from the shelf.

"Grilled cheese."

She busies herself, getting out what I need for sandwiches while I grab the skillet from the cabinet.

"I think he only likes it because he can eat them one-handed," Peyton says with a grin as she grabs a butter knife.

"False. He said I make the best grilled cheese sandwiches he's ever tasted."

She snorts. "And he told Mom yesterday that no one makes chocolate milk better than her. He insisted that her milk to chocolate syrup ratio was out of this world."

"So, he's manipulative?"

"Yep. Dad was getting on to him about playing so much on his video games, but Preston interrupted him to ask if he'd been working out, telling him that his arms seem more muscular than usual."

"And how did Raymond respond to that?" I ask with a wide smile on my face.

"Dad forgot that he grounded him from the video games."

We both laugh loudly at the kid's antics.

"He's going far in this world," I tell her just as I place the first piece of buttered bread in the skillet.

"Let's just hope he doesn't end up like Dalton," Peyton mutters as she peels a slice of cheese from the stack and hands it to me.

"Do you think he's different? Does he seem different to you?"

She takes a long moment to respond, and I keep my head down watching the bread heat. I shouldn't have asked. I shouldn't be doubting how much I hate him. It doesn't change anything. There are some things that are too terrible to come back from.

"He is," she finally says. "He hasn't insulted me once. He's been taking time to play games with Preston. He even complimented Mom's shitty dinner the other night. Before the accident, he wouldn't have even been around to eat with us."

"But?" I ask because it feels like she's leaving something out.

"But look outside. He doesn't remember, yet all those jerks are still here. I can only hope that the way he was before wasn't actually who he *is*. You know? I have my fingers crossed that the jerk that used to live here stays gone forever. I kind of like who he is now."

I kind of do, too.

I don't speak that out loud, however.

"Well, if it isn't Bloody Mary."

I freeze at the sound of Vaughn's voice, and Peyton grows tense beside me as well.

The playful atmosphere that welcomed us when we were talking about Preston's ability to redirect people is sucked out of the room in an instant.

"Oh, Vaughn," Bronwyn coos, "I'm so happy you think I'm pretty."

The hairs on the back of my neck stand on end as she repeats verbatim one of the messages I sent to Vaughn earlier this year. I know it was all a joke, a way to get me to that party so they could humiliate me, but the sting had worn off a little. Getting into a major accident and thinking I killed someone had a way of making the other things that happened that night a little less important.

I should've gone home the second Peyton told me Dalton had friends over. I'm a fool for still being here.

"Oh, Piper, you're the prettiest girl in school, and every guy knows it," Vaughn adds.

What he doesn't know is that was one of the lines I had on replay in my head. It was the first time I let myself consider that he was full of it, but my teenage heart wanted so badly to be liked by someone that I ignored that feeling in my gut warning me away from him.

"What are we discussing?"

As if things couldn't get any worse, Kyle chooses now to join us in the kitchen.

"Oh, hey, Bloody Mary. Are you making us lunch? I like wheat bread."

If I didn't know any better, the tone in his voice could easily be misconstrued as friendly. Kyle Turner has never been friendly to me a day in his life.

"You people are supposed to be outside. My mom and dad don't want anyone in the house," Peyton tells them.

"Grown-ups are talking, little Dalton," Bronwyn snaps. "Best keep your nose out of our business unless you want a four-year dose of what Mary has gotten."

I understand the threat immediately. They will easily treat Peyton the same way they've treated me, and I don't wish that on anyone.

"It's fine," I tell Peyton.

My back is still to the jerks as I finish Preston's sandwich. When I turn off the stove, I let myself imagine slapping Bronwyn in the face with the hot skillet, but violence doesn't seem like the answer. She'd only be viler if I hurt her.

"Why are you even here?" Vaughn asks, and I can tell he's moved closer to me. "Are you trying to weasel your way into Dalton's life? He may have forgotten who you are, but none of us have."

Bronwyn and Kyle both express their agreements with a series of grunts.

"Are you so desperate for his attention that you come over and make him lunch?" Bronwyn adds.

"Say something," Peyton urges from my side. "They only do it because you don't stand up for yourself."

I want to tell her how wrong she is, but she doesn't know about the time I shoved Bronwyn into the lockers in second grade when she pulled my hair while in line waiting for the bathroom. Even seven-year-old Bronwyn was a spiteful little girl. She retaliated that time by cutting off my ponytail at a sleepover we both attended later that month. I was in tears when my mom showed up to get me, but even then, I didn't tell her what had really happened. I've spent my entire life hiding the truth and my pain from my parents.

"That's it," Bronwyn snaps. "You just put yourself on the list, little Dalton. I hope you're happy right now because once school starts, you'll wish you never defended her."

I see red. They've been picking on me for years, but threatening Peyton is going too far. None of them seem surprised when I spin around to face them. Angry tears are already rushing down my cheeks, and I hate that I cry when I get mad. I'm usually able to save the tears for home, but today it's just all too much.

"You'll leave her alone," I hiss.

"You won't have any friends," Bronwyn continues as if I'm not standing here with steam erupting from my ears. "Even the girls you hang out with now will turn on you for a chance to be in our crowd. You won't have any more true friends."

"True friends?" I snap. "Is that what you consider you assholes?"

I point at each of the three tormentors standing in front of me. I focus on Kyle.

"Were you Dalton's true friend when you slept with his girlfriend at that party?" Kyle sneers in my direction, the ugly snarl only worsening the evil look in his eyes. I ignore it. "And you, Bronwyn. Does being a true friend mean that it's okay to spend your time performing oral on one guy while the other has sex with you?"

Peyton gasps.

"Oral?" Bronwyn says with a chuckle. "Sex with me?"

"It's like she's eleven or something," Vaughn says. "Good thing you told me not to try to sext with her. She would've known something was up then."

"First off," Bronwyn hitches her thumb to indicate Vaughn, "I was sucking his dick while this one fucked me—hard."

Bile fills my throat at her words, the memories of that night coming back in full color, but what irritates me most of all is her talking about this stuff in front of Peyton. Not only is she young, but Dalton is her brother. Some things just shouldn't be shared with a sibling, but I guess I'm the one who brought it up, so this is just another mistake I can own.

"Why don't you fill me in on what happened at the party?"

Bronwyn, Vaughn, and Kyle spin around so fast to face Dalton, I'm surprised that they don't fall over.

Standing in the doorway of the kitchen with his arms crossed over his shirtless chest, he doesn't look very impressed with what he just walked in on.

Chapter 15

Dalton

"What. About. The. Party?" I repeat when my so-called friends turn around to look at me.

Shock fills their faces at the sight of me, and I can tell that all of them are worried about what I might've overheard before I made my presence known. I heard enough that I'm annoyed that I didn't cancel this damn pool party like I wanted to a million times this week.

"Oh, that's right," Piper says, and even when she's being mean to me, I've never heard her sound as spiteful and vindictive as she does right now. It's possible she hates these three people more than she hates me, and that's saying a lot because the girl can barely stand the sight of me. "You don't remember. Let me tell you exactly what happened at the party."

"Don't," Bronwyn hisses, and I can tell she isn't the nice girl that's spent most of the day trying to convince me that she's my girlfriend.

Bronwyn was shy when she first showed up today. She kept her distance with a couple of other girls she arrived with, but as the day passed, she got braver. I found it odd that she hasn't called or stopped by if she was my girlfriend, and it was even stranger that she didn't speak to me when she first got here. There's a reason she's kept her distance, and I'm certain it has everything to do with what I just overheard.

"Vaughn here," she says, pointing to the boy I've barely tolerated since meeting him at the diner, "thought it would be funny to convince me that he liked me. He wanted me to show up at the party at Kyle's that night to humiliate me."

My blood boils at the thought of Piper liking this piece of shit, but I'm also angry with myself for setting all of this in motion so many years ago.

"When I showed up, he texted me to meet him upstairs." My fists clench at my sides. "When I got up there, your girlfriend was in the middle of a three-way. Vaughn was enjoying her mouth while your best friend…"

She pauses, darting her eyes in Peyton's direction.

"Apparently, Kyle was fucking her," my sister says before Piper can think of a polite way to explain what happened.

"Is that so?" I look at Kyle for confirmation.

"You know how it is," he begins. "All the JV guys have to pull a prank to get on the varsity team."

"Hmm," I muse. "So, you and Bronwyn were just helping him out?"

"Exactly," Kyle says with a smile on his twisted lips.

"And you thought I would be okay with that?"

His eyes dart to Bronwyn, but it's clear that they were both hoping I wouldn't ever find out about that night.

"Okay with it?" Bronwyn says with a throaty laugh. "You were in on it."

Peyton snorts in disbelief.

"So, I helped you guys plan to set Piper up?"

"Doing that to *Mary* was *your* idea," Bronwyn answers.

Piper stiffens across the room, but I can't focus on her right now.

"So, I wanted to do something so vile to *Piper*," I emphasize her real name since Bronwyn insists on using the insulting one, "that I thought it was a good idea for you to suck Vaughn off while getting plowed by Kyle?"

The three of them share a look before nodding at the same time. They're full of it and must think I'm an idiot if they imagined I'd fall for this mess.

"I should've told you sooner," Piper says.

"You need to leave," I snap.

Piper's eyes widen as she looks at me, but she just nods and turns to walk around the group.

"Not you, Piper," I clarify before looking at the people standing in my kitchen. "Get out of my house and take all of those idiots in the pool with you."

Kyle opens his mouth like he's going to say something, but he sees the look on my face, and his jaw snaps closed.

"Now," I spit.

Piper walks away before Kyle, Vaughn, and Bronwyn move a muscle, and as much as I want to go after her, I want to make sure they don't damage my parents' property on their way out. I don't know much about them, but they seem like the malicious type. Peyton follows her out of the room, and I'm glad that my sister will be there to comfort her until I can get to her.

Bronwyn scuttles out of the kitchen first, followed closely by Vaughn.

Three-ways and betrayal in Westover? What is this, an episode of Game of Thrones? I started the series yesterday when I was avoiding Piper, and even while I was watching it, I thought it was just a little too much drama for me. That show has nothing on this bunch of spoiled brats.

Kyle stops beside me, and it takes all I have not to punch him in the face for what he's done to Piper.

"Is this part of your plan?" He smiles at me like we're sharing some sort of inside joke. "Are you trying to get on her good side so you can score?"

My jaw tenses.

"I'm all for it, dude, but I think alienating your friends to get a piece of ass is taking things a little too far."

"Get. Out," I spit again, seconds away from grabbing him by the hair and physically removing him from my house.

"I'm your best friend, Dalton. Don't let a little sex with Bronwyn ruin all of that."

Is this guy for real?

I don't know how I know what they said were lies, but somehow, I do. Surely, I wasn't so bad that I would've been okay with my girlfriend sleeping with other guys, and if I was that guy, I'm just glad he's gone.

The thought of anyone touching Piper makes my skin crawl, and flashes of murder infiltrate my brain. Even if I didn't really like Bronwyn all that much while we were together, I know deep down I wouldn't have been okay with sharing her, if only for proprietary sake.

"You need to leave before I hurt you." He merely stands there and glares at me like I'm speaking a language he doesn't understand. "Get the fuck out of my house. I don't need people like you and them in my life."

"Us?" He doesn't bother to hide the confusion in his tone. "*You* started all of this years ago. *You* called her Bloody Mary first when she got caught with blood on the back of her jeans in sixth grade. *You* put the spiders in her locker because you found out she was terrified of them. *You* convinced her to eat Reese's in fourth grade, knowing she was deathly allergic to nuts. *You* were the reason she ended up hospitalized that day. All of that was *you*. We were just following *your* lead."

"I don't remember any of that," I seethe.

"Doesn't mean it didn't happen. Listen, man. I know you're pissed right now, but eventually, you'll get all of your memories back, and you're going to regret alienating all of your friends."

"Why are you still here?"

"Don't say I didn't warn you," he huffs, but thankfully, he walks away.

I stay in the kitchen for a few minutes before heading back out to the pool. The last couple of people are drying off, preparing to leave.

"I think it's great that you put them in their place," a girl I hadn't been introduced to says as she walks past me. "There may be hope for you yet. Westover will change if you make them."

I don't respond to them, but her insinuation that people will still follow me no matter which direction I take things grates on my nerves. I don't want to be their leader. I don't want to be the one that influences what people think or how they react. I just want to be left alone, and everyone else needs to be their own person.

Bronwyn doesn't make eye contact with me when she grabs her bag and turns to leave. Vaughn also refuses to make eye contact, but at least he has the wherewithal to look ashamed of his role in what happened. I watch all the teens load up into a half-dozen different vehicles, and it doesn't even bother me when Kyle wraps his arm around Bronwyn's shoulder as he leads her to his car. They can have each other for all I care. The only person that matters to me right now is inside my house.

I lock the front door, but before I head upstairs, I grab the plate with Preston's sandwich on it. Piper has been cooking for him all week, and I don't want her hard work going to waste. I reheat the sandwich in the microwave and carry it up the stairs to my brother.

"Thanks," he says when I hand him the plate. "All of your friends gone?"

"Those people are idiots," I mutter.

"I'm only ten, and I could've told you that."

Chapter 16

Piper

"I hate that I cried in front of them," I confess through my sobs.

Peyton wraps her arms tighter around me. I'm grateful that she's here, grateful that she witnessed what happened in the kitchen and not Frankie. My best friend would've clawed their eyes out, and then she would've turned on me for not letting her know just how bad things had gotten with the kids at school.

"I'm normally stronger than this."

"You're the strongest girl I know," Peyton whispers.

I cry quietly for a few more minutes.

"Let me get you some tissue." She's off the bed, disappearing into her bathroom before coming back with a length of toilet paper.

"He's actually making them leave," she says when she crosses the room and looks out her bedroom window.

I watch her as she continues to look down at the people that have made my life miserable. Her brow is creased, and she looks like she wants to say something, but I'm sure my sobbing for the last couple of minutes is keeping her lips clamped shut.

"Just say whatever it is that you're thinking," I urge.

It's been hard with Frankie gone, but Peyton has made it easier to deal with the bouts of loneliness.

"What if he is different?" She turns to face me. "What if the guy who was mean to you for so long is gone?"

I open my mouth to tell her it doesn't matter but then close it so I can actually think about how that really makes me feel.

"It doesn't change anything."

"It'll change the future," she counters. "That's something, right?"

"I'm not saying I'm going to hate him for the rest of his life—"

"But you won't forgive him," she interrupts.

"I don't think I can."

"I think you should. I think he's genuinely sorry for how he's treated you."

"I don't think someone can authentically regret doing something that they don't remember doing," I argue.

"But you think it's right to continue to dislike him when he isn't that guy anymore?"

"I should've known you'd be on his side," I mutter.

"I don't know if you remember this, but Dalton hasn't always been nice to me either."

"He didn't torture you as he did me."

"Because I wouldn't just roll over and let him do it." Her jaw snaps shut.

"Tell me how you really feel about me," I snap. "I'm weak, a punching bag for every kid at Westover Prep. I deserve everything that has happened to me because I don't stand up for myself."

"That's not..." She sighs as she crosses the room to join me on the bed. "You're not weak. You stood up for me in the kitchen, but when they were picking on you, you just stood there and took it. Why do you defend others and not yourself?"

"Because it wouldn't matter. I only have one more year of this crap, and then I'm leaving Westover for good. There's no sense in stirring stuff up."

"You should—"

A knock on her bedroom door prevents the dispensing of what could only be immense levels of knowledge from the thirteen-year-old girl.

"Go away," she snaps so loud I cover my ears. "Sorry."

I laugh at her apology, but the chuckle fades away when her bedroom door opens, and Dalton pokes his head inside.

"What are you doing, creeper? We could be naked in here."

Dalton rolls his eyes at his sister, but when he looks in my direction, his eyes roam over my body, and I can tell from the look on his face that he doesn't hate the idea of seeing me naked. I swallow thickly before running the wad of toilet paper under my eyes. The action draws his attention to my face, and I hate that he's seeing me so upset.

My nose is running, and I know my eyes are puffy and red. He's not the one who made me cry this time, but the situation is way too familiar to all the times he was the reason I sat on a bed with tears in my eyes.

"Can you give us a minute?" Dalton asks his sister.

"No," she answers immediately. "This is my room, jerk."

I don't know if she's putting on a united front with me because she just wants to punish him or if it's because she feels bad for taking up for him earlier.

"Please?" he asks.

"It's okay, Peyton. Maybe just a few minutes."

She huffs as she stands from the bed. "Just holler if he acts like an asshole. I'll replace the cream filling in his Oreos with toothpaste."

I cringe at the thought as she walks out of the room.

"Leave the door open," she tells her brother. "She doesn't want to be alone with you."

"You told her that?" he asks after she's gone.

"I didn't say it out loud, but she seems pretty good at picking up social cues."

He frowns as he draws closer, but he must see the look on my own face because he redirects himself from sitting on the bed beside me to plopping down on the floor.

"It's clear that I did some super shitty stuff to you in the past."

I huff. "That's an understatement."

"There's nothing I can do to change any of that," he continues, avoiding my addition to the conversation. "I don't know what I can do to make it right. What I do know is that you're the most beautiful girl I've ever seen, and I'm certain that I realized that long before the accident."

Cold chills sweep down my arms. Oh, how my life would've been different if he would've realized any of this before now.

"So, it got me thinking."

"That's dangerous," I joke, trying to lighten the mood.

He chuckles, but his fingers continue to twist together in his lap. When he looks up at me, his green eyes are filled with so many emotions. Somehow, he no longer looks like the guy who has haunted my nightmares for the last twelve years, but I think this realization makes him even more dangerous.

"There has to be a reason for the way I treated you."

"Other than the fact that you're hateful and mean?"

Is he looking for a way to point the blame of his actions on me? How narcissistic is this jerk?

"Can you remember the first time I was mean to you?" he asks, not paying attention to my flippant question.

"The first day of kindergarten, you pushed me down and got my dress dirty."

He smiles, and the sight of his cheeks pulling up startles me. He's always been handsome, but he's different right now.

"I probably liked you even back then."

My brows scrunch. "Don't give me that crap. My parents used to tell me boys will be boys when I was younger, and I complained about you being mean to me. I don't care if you were too young to use words like *be my friend,* or *I think you're pretty,* hitting me, shoving me, and being mean to me was never okay."

"I agree."

My lips clamp closed with his swift agreement.

"Are you really still mad about what happened over twelve years ago?"

My eyes narrow. "What about the dead snake in my backpack in first grade, or the time you tore up my library book in second grade? Maybe I'm still mad about the spiders in my locker in third grade or when you sent me to the hospital in fourt—"

"Okay, okay." He holds his hands up near his ears in mock surrender. "I get it. I've always been an asshole."

"Exactly." I cross my arms over my chest, no longer worried about my puffy face and eyes. Maybe crying in front of him should've happened a whole lot sooner, but even as I think it, I know Dalton would've only used it for ammunition at a later date. Before the accident, he didn't care at all how what he did to me made me feel.

"I'm no longer denying it. I was a total douche."

"King Douche of all douches," I specify.

"Let me prove that I'm different."

My mouth runs dry with the request.

"I can't."

"You didn't even think about it long enough before you rejected it."

"I don't need to think about it. I was serious when I said we should just stay out of each other's way."

"And I'm serious when I tell you that every one of my waking thoughts is about you, and I can't sleep at night knowing that you're next door hating me."

"Maybe it's about time you lost a little sleep over the vile things you've done." I have to look away from him when sadness tugs the corners of his mouth down. "And I think trying to make me feel bad about it only proves that you're still the same guy."

"That's harsh," he mutters.

"It's the truth."

"I just want to get to know you, and I think if you get to know who I am now, you'll see that I'm not that guy anymore."

"And then what happens when all of your memories come back. Do you honestly think I'd waste my time with you only to end up back under your feet once that happens?"

"Even if I get my memories back, it won't make you any less beautiful. It won't make me stop thinking about your lips, wondering how they'll feel against mine. If anything, my memories will only make me realize what I've been missing all this time."

"That's enough." Just the mention of him wanting to kiss me makes me tingle, and that pisses me off.

"Just being honest."

"Well, keep that kind of honesty to yourself."

"Will you please give me a shot?"

"I'm not going to date you just because you begged."

His lips twitch. "I'm not asking you to date me, yet. At this point, I'd be happy with you not running away every time I walk in a room."

I look in his eyes, searching them for any form of deception. I find none.

"I'm not making any promises, but I guess it won't hurt me to stop being so rude."

"It's a start." He grins again. "I'll take it."

He offers his hand to me, but I glare at it like he's holding a squirming snake.

"Too soon?"

"Yeah," I answer. "Way too soon."

"Okay, then." He stands from the floor. "The original pool party was a bust, but that doesn't mean our entire day has to be ruined. Why don't you go home and grab a swimsuit? I'll convince Preston to leave his room for a few hours, even though he may have to stay in the shade. I don't think the kid has seen sunlight in weeks."

"What?" He's rambling so fast, I wonder if he somehow tricked me into agreeing to hang out with him, and I missed it somehow. "I'm not getting in the pool."

"Then you can sit in one of the loungers and watch me swim."

"No, thanks."

"You said you weren't going to be rude."

"Turning down your demand to go swimming isn't rude," I counter.

"It'll be fun, promise." He walks across the room and opens the bedroom door. "Peyton!"

"What?" his sister says as she steps out of Preston's room. "Did she claw your eyes out? I don't see any marks."

"We're on good terms," Dalton assures her. "Convince this pretty girl to go swimming. I'm going to go make snacks for everyone."

Dalton disappears out of the room, and Peyton turns around to glare at me.

"What happened?"

I shrug. "I agreed not to be so rude."

"Damn." She grins wide. "I wonder how he'd act if you agree to go out on a date with him.

"That's never going to happen."

"Never say never, *pretty girl*. Let's take a break from math and go swimming."

"I don't want to."

"Then sit on the lounger and watch us swim."

"That's exactly what Dalton suggested."

She winks at me. "Great minds think alike. Now go get changed."

I yelp when she slaps my ass, but I grin all the way out of her house to go get my bathing suit.

Chapter 17

Dalton

"She's allergic to strawberries," Peyton mumbles when she walks into the kitchen.

"Seriously?" Giving up on cutting the strawberries, I scrape all of them in the trash.

"What are you playing at, Dalton?"

My sister props her hip against the counter, and I can tell by the way her arms are crossed over her chest that she isn't impressed with me at all.

"What do you mean? I was going to make strawberry lemonade, but we can just have regular since she's allergic."

"If you're doing this as some type of messed up joke, I'll never forgive you." She straightens. "Better yet, if I find out you're trying to manipulate her or convince her you're a nice guy only to turn around and be mean to her again, I'll kill you."

I smile, loving that she's in Piper's corner.

"Have you always been so violent?"

"I'm serious, Dalton. She deserves better."

"I know she does," I agree. "I was only making lemonade, promise."

"My threat may not mean a damn thing to you, but I swear I'll make it happen."

She doesn't give me time to answer her before she walks out of the room. It seems I may have more than one person to prove myself to.

Piper doesn't knock when she comes back over, and I love that she must feel welcome in my house enough to just walk right in. Of course, she's wearing an economical one-piece. Only in my fantasies would she show up in a revealing two-piece. She's the complete opposite of the girls that were over here earlier, and I love that about her, too.

"I made lemonade," I tell her with a smile as I reach into the cabinet for four glasses.

Preston assured me he'd be down in a few minutes after his game was over, and I'm certain he means it. His eyes lit up when I stopped by his room to see if he wanted to hang out with us. If only Piper and Peyton were as willing to see past the way I used to act.

"Is it poisoned?"

I chuckle, but when I look over at Piper, I can tell she's at least a little bit serious.

"Well," I begin, "I almost poisoned you, but Peyton told me you were allergic to strawberries. I put them in the trash. You're allergic to nuts, too. Any other deadly foods I should know about?"

"How did you know I was allergic to nuts?"

"Kyle mentioned it earlier."

"Did he mention fourth grade, or were you two plotting on another way to hurt me?"

I ignore the skepticism.

"He mentioned I tried to kill you with a Reese's when we were younger," I admit. "And it may mean nothing now, but I'm sorry about that. Anaphylactic shock isn't just some stupid prank. That could've been really bad."

"We were just kids," she mutters. "Just so long as you wouldn't do it now."

She grabs the pitcher of lemonade and follows me to the back patio.

"When was the last time you were over for a swim?" I ask before placing the glasses down on the patio table.

"Never."

I'm shocked by her answer, but if I really think about it, I know I shouldn't be. If I started being mean to her in kindergarten, then I guess she never would've had the chance to come over.

"Well, you're welcome to it any time," I offer.

"Thanks."

Her response is muttered, so I do the only thing I know to do. I change the subject.

"I brought towels out already. Are you going to swim in your shorts?"

"I'm not swimming."

I don't argue with her or try to pressure her into getting into the pool. Hounding her until she gives in seems like something the old Dalton would do, and since I'm no longer that jerk, I let it slide.

"Okay. Well, if you change your mind, I'm pretty sure you'll have a good time."

"Cannonball!" Preston yells as he runs across the patio in dinosaur printed swim trunks.

He tucks his knees, wrapping his arms around his legs and flies into the pool.

"He knows how to swim, right?" I ask Piper when he doesn't immediately pop back to the surface.

"I sure hope so."

A second later, Preston's head breaks the surface of the water, and his face is overrun with a huge smile.

"I'll be back," I tell her before heading back inside.

She's settling in a sun lounger on the edge of the pool when I make it back out with a tray of sandwiches.

"You're not allergic to turkey on wheat, are you?"

"Are you making fun of me?"

"No."

"You sure are laying it on thick. Lemonade and sandwiches? You don't have to turn into Betty Crocker in an attempt to prove to me you aren't a jerk."

"Peyton helped," I tell her. "Plus, I was hungry. It's just as easy to make six sandwiches as it is to make one."

"Well, that's very nice of you."

I hitch my thumb over my shoulder. "There are chips inside, if you want me to grab them."

"This is fine, thank you." She grabs half a sandwich off the tray but doesn't immediately lift it to her mouth. I grab the other part and bite it in half, a silent way of proving to her that I didn't do anything to tamper with the food.

"Where's your cast?" she asks as I lift the second half of the sandwich to my mouth.

"Cut it off." I shrug. "It got in the way."

"You'll regret that when your bones don't heal properly."

"Probably so," I agree. "Seems I regret a lot of things these days."

She nods with understanding but then breaks eye contact. We watch Preston splash around in the pool for a few minutes until the pull to get in myself gets the better of me.

"Sure you don't want to swim?" I ask as I stand and pull my t-shirt over my head.

"No, thanks."

Her eyes are glued to my chest, but I don't flex to show off the muscles that I've clearly worked hard to get. I've tried lifting weights since I got out of the hospital, if anything just to kill time, but the strain makes my head hurt, and even though the cast got in the way, my wrist is nowhere near healed enough for that yet.

"Offer stands if you change your mind."

I turn away from her, not wanting to go, but needing the space. The sight of her laid out, even in that one-piece, makes me want to do naughty things to her, but the girl can barely stand the sight of me. No doubt she'll maim me if I try to run my finger up her leg like I've been dying to do since she showed back up.

"Cannonball!" I yell as I run to the pool.

Preston claps and celebrates like only a ten-year-old boy can when I resurface. Peyton joins Piper on the patio, but I can't hear what they're saying. Before long, Peyton slowly wades into the pool, and Piper is left sitting alone on the side.

"Don't look at me like that," my sister complains. "I tried to convince her to get in. She doesn't want to."

"Yeah, she turned me down too."

"Of course, she turned you down," Peyton huffs as she slaps the water in my face. "She's not going to fall in love with you in a day."

"Love?" I huff, looking back in Piper's direction after wiping the water from my face. "I could only hope."

"Then go talk to her," my sister urges. "Don't hang out here and ignore her."

I figured she's had enough of me today, but Peyton knows more about girl shit than I do, so against my better judgment, I swim to the end of the pool that Piper is at.

"The water feels great," I tell her as I rest my chin on the edge of the pool. "You should get in."

She glances from me to the sparkling water several times before her eyes finally meet mine.

"It does look enticing."

"Plus, I'm in here." I give her a wide grin, but she just rolls her eyes. "Too douchey?"

"Just a touch." She holds her thumb and forefinger an inch apart for emphasis.

"Still. You should get in. I promise no more douchiness."

"And if I don't?" she challenges.

"I promise I still won't act like a douche. Maybe we can play Marco Polo."

"Yeah!" Preston yells. "Let's play Marco Polo!"

"Are you really going to disappoint my little brother?"

She raises an eyebrow. "You said you weren't going to be a douche."

"Last time, promise. Come on, Piper. Let's play."

I can see it in her eyes the second she decides to join us, and I'm ecstatic. Unfortunately, she keeps her shorts on as she slowly inches into the water from the stairs.

Being the oldest, I'm nominated to go first, but it doesn't take long before I manage to catch my little brother. He splashes too much when he swims, and it makes him an easy target. Preston tags Peyton in the second round, but I discover quickly that she let herself get caught because she's tagging me seconds into her turn.

"Damn, you're a quick swimmer," I mutter after coming up for air and sputtering since she dunked me when she caught me.

"I'm on the swim team, dummy," she says with a grin.

I look around the pool for everyone's position before standing in the middle and closing my eyes. I know who my target is, and I'm not letting her get away from me this time.

"Marco!" I yell, already positioning myself in Piper's direction.

"Polo!" Peyton and Preston answer.

"Oh, Piper. You're not playing fair," I tease when she remains silent.

Neither am I since I've got my left eye open a tiny slit.

"Marco!"

"Polo!"

Again, she doesn't play along, but before she can move, I'm right in front of her. I could easily grab her shoulders to tag her, but where's the fun in that? My hands clamp around her thin waist, and she gasps.

"Dalton." There's a warning in her tone, and I plan to put some distance between the two of us, but instead of quickly releasing her, I trail my fingers down her hips and the outside of her thighs.

Her gasp is audible, but it doesn't stop her from getting away from me.

We play in the pool for another hour, but she manages not to get caught by me again.

I was idiotic, and I know touching her without permission isn't the way to build her trust. I want to apologize to her when we get out, but she wraps a towel around herself and disappears inside before I get the chance.

Chapter 18

Piper

His hands on me—eye-opening is the only way I can describe it.

For a split second, I forgot who he was.

I forgot the last twelve years.

I forgot the way his lip would twitch with evil intent when he was preparing to do something mean to me.

I forgot all of the things that made me despise him.

And that's dangerous.

It's dangerous to my heart, my health, and, most importantly, my sanity.

"This should help," Peyton says as she hands me a cold bottle of water and two Tylenol. "I can't believe you didn't put sunblock on."

I pop the pills into my mouth and follow them with a long drink of the cold water.

"I didn't plan on getting out from under the awning," I tell her. "I should've just stayed out of the pool."

I should've never agreed to go out there in the first place, but I keep that piece to myself.

"We had fun," Peyton says with a lopsided smile. "And I was thinking the fun shouldn't end."

I quirk an eyebrow up at her. If she suggests anything that remotely has to do with spending more time with her older brother, I'm out of here.

Without a word, she disappears into her closet before returning with a huge cosmetic bag.

"Makeup?"

"More than makeup." She plops down beside me on the floor. "Facials, nails, the whole nine."

I consider the offer for a while. I haven't done that sort of thing since eighth grade when Frankie and I decided that if we had healthier skin, the kids at school would be our friends. I was still hopeful in those days, but Dalton made sure to cut me off at the knees when we arrived at school with glowing skin and our faces made up. Looking back, we probably had on more makeup than necessary, but what do thirteen-year-olds know about applying contours and blemish cream?

A lot, apparently, because Peyton is an expert with a makeup brush and eyeliner. Glancing at myself in the small mirror she's holding up, I turn my face back and forth. I look better than I did the night before the party, before Dalton turned the water hose on me in his driveway. It was my last-ditch effort to make people see me as more than a running joke, but that day in eighth grade was already in the back of my mind. It didn't work that time, so why would it work now?

Needless to say, it didn't. Even if Dalton hadn't ruined my look, the same people who ruined my life that night would've done the same regardless of how my makeup and hair looked. They don't have it in them to change.

"You look fabulous." She beams at me. "I wonder what the kids at school would say right now."

I sigh in frustration, but it isn't aimed at her, really. She has the same mindset I did when I was her age. My pessimism built for years, but it was firmly in place by the time I started high school. I don't want her heading down the same path, and even though I can't control what other people do, I can apply a little reality to Peyton.

"People at Westover Prep don't care if you change from an ugly duckling overnight."

"You were never an ugly duckling," Peyton counters with a frown.

"What I'm saying is it doesn't matter what you look like on the outside."

"Beauty is only skin deep? Really, Piper?"

"The people at school are mean because of what's inside of *them*. It has nothing to do with me."

"That's very—enlightened."

"It's the only way I've survived all this time, and I know when I leave Westover, things will be better."

"Because you can be anyone you want?" Her brows furrow.

"No, you're not getting it. There's nothing wrong with me. I don't have to change when I leave for college. I'll still be the same person I am now, and there are people out there who will appreciate that about me." I give her a weak smile, hating that my new beginning is still a year away. I long for it more than anything. "There are people who will value my opinion, who are mature enough not to belittle others just to get a thrill when they're bored."

"There are assholes everywhere," she mutters.

"There seems to be a much higher concentration in Westover."

"Will you stay the night?"

I grin. "That's a quick change of subject."

I'm stalling. The last thing I want is to be stuck in her house with Dalton just across the hall all night. I already can't get him out of my head when I'm at home. I know it'll be pure torture on my psyche to be mere yards away from him.

"I don't think that's a good idea," I tell her when she just watches me with hope-filled eyes.

"Please? We can make popcorn and watch scary movies," she offers.

"I hate scary movies."

"Then romantic comedies."

I cringe. "I hate those even more."

"We can watch whatever you want. Your pick."

I don't know much about Peyton, but I know I haven't seen any of her friends come over this week. I don't know if that's intentional because she's trying to focus on passing her math test so she doesn't have to repeat eighth grade, or if it's because she's in low supply of friends.

"Fine," I agree.

As much as I don't want to be near Dalton, I can admit that I've had fun tonight and I don't really want it to end.

"Yay!" Peyton claps her hands excitedly. "I'll grab you some pajamas."

While she rummages in her dresser for clothes, I put away the makeup and hair products.

"You can change out here. I'll change in the bathroom, then we can grab snacks and binge watch something."

I agree with a head nod, only stripping out of my still-damp swimsuit and shorts after her bathroom door clicks closed—only she's faster at getting dressed than me. I have the t-shirt over my head, but I'm just pulling up the pajama pants when she reenters the room.

I don't have panties to put on, but when her eyes focus at the center of my body, I know she isn't shocked that my lower half is naked.

What surprises her are the tiny lines slashed in my upper thighs. Some are white and silvery, while others are still angry and pink.

"Piper?" she looks up at me, and tears glisten in her eyes.

"It's nothing," I mutter as I finish getting dressed.

"It's not," she replies.

"Please don't tell anyone."

"You hurt yourself?"

"Not anymore," I lie. Well, it's sort of a lie. I haven't cut in a couple of weeks, but I'd be remiss if I thought I'd never do it again. I do have a year of torture at Westover Prep to get through.

"Don't tell anyone," I repeat.

"I w-won't."

I don't believe her, but there's nothing I can do about it right now. Maybe if I show her how happy I am, she'll believe that the self-harm is over.

"How about those snacks?" I'm gleeful to the point it's bordering on manic, but it doesn't work the way I hope.

She's quiet and reflective the entire time we're in the kitchen popping popcorn and loading up on sugary things. When we make it back upstairs, I give in and choose a comedy, praying it will take her mind off what she saw.

She laughs at the right parts, but the joy she expressed after I agreed to stay the night never returns.

She falls asleep before I do, and with the way my brain is running wild right now, I don't think I'll ever sleep again. If she tells my parents, I'll probably end up in a psych ward. My father, as a pediatrician, is well aware of the process of making that happen since he's involved often with teens who are on the very edge of a mental break.

I worry the edge of my lip until I taste blood, and that only serves as a reminder of the rusty taste in my mouth the night of the accident.

A noise in the hallway distracts me from my thoughts. The household went to sleep hours ago, so the noise is startling. Maybe I should sneak out and head home?

The noise happens again, and it's not like a thump but a soft patter. Making sure not to jostle Peyton, I climb out of bed and slowly make my way across the room. I hear the noise again when I press my ear to the door.

There's low mumbling, but I can't decipher the words. After minutes of listening, I determine that it's one person in the hallway having a conversation with themselves. Does Preston sleepwalk?

Afraid he's going to fall down the stairs, I slowly open Peyton's bedroom door. Only it isn't Preston pacing the length of the hallway, but Dalton.

His eyes snap up to mine when he notices me.

"What are you doing?" I whisper-hiss at him.

Is this part of the head trauma? Just what I need, more guilt to feel if he has insomnia because of the accident.

"I was contemplating knocking on the door."

I bite the inside of my cheek to keep from smiling.

"It takes ten minutes of roaming the hallway and arguing with yourself to decide?"

He nods. "I wanted to apologize for touching you in the pool. I should've asked permission."

"I would've told you no," I interrupt.

"I know." His lips twitch with a weak smile. "I think that's why I didn't ask, but it was still wrong."

"Apology accepted."

I turn and begin to go back into Peyton's room.

"Wait. I also wanted to show you something. Maybe to make up for my douche-baggery?"

I give him the side-eye, still not fully convinced he's a changed man. "Like what?"

"It's outside." He hitches his head in the direction of the stairs.

"I'm not falling for that."

"You need to trust me." He grabs my hand, urging me to follow him.

"That's probably never going to happen," I mutter, but I don't pull my hand from his.

We stay joined through the house as he grabs a blanket off the couch, and we head out the back door. I don't let go of his hand when he directs us around the side of his house. Thankfully, we're on the opposite side of his house that mine is on because my parents' bedroom is on that far wall.

"What are we doing?" I ask as he releases my hand to spread the blanket out on the grass.

"Just sit and wait."

There's a small rail fence on this side of his house because a privacy fence would block the view of the woods lining his property.

"We're going to get eaten by a bear," I mutter.

We're not touching, but I still draw my knees up to my chest to put more distance between us.

"We would hear a bear if he was coming for us."

"That's reassuring." I roll my eyes, but it's almost pitch-black out here, so I'm certain he doesn't see me do it.

"Just watch." There's a playful hint to his tone, and it takes a lot for me not to smile in his direction.

"Oh!" I gasp when a tiny light flashes a few feet away. Then it happens again and again.

"I know fireflies are rare in Colorado, but I noticed them the other night."

I watch in awe as the bugs twinkle and light up, communicating with each other. I watch so long I don't realize Dalton has moved closer until the warmth of his body on my left side makes me realize how cold my right side is. When I shiver, he wraps his arm around me so he can rub his warm hands down my arm.

"Real subtle," I mumble when he inches even closer. "I'm not buying this romantic bull."

Skepticism is one of my honed skills.

I turn my head in his direction. "What's next? You're going to try to kis—"

His lips are on mine before I can finish.

Electricity jolts through my body, and it's more than a spark between our lips created by the static in the air.

I have no explanation for what I do next. I'm supposed to open my mouth to tell him to take a hike, but that's not what happens. My mouth opens, alright, but only to give his slick tongue entrance.

Kissing him is wrong and magical.

It's forbidden and everything I didn't know I wanted.

It's cruel and perfect.

It's over before I want it to be.

When he leans in to kiss me again, I shove him in the chest.
"Don't ever do that again."
I'm on my feet and gone before he can say a word.

Chapter 19

Dalton

"Where's Piper?" I ask when I rush downstairs.

I hadn't meant to fall asleep. Before I closed my eyes, after hours of worrying I had only made things worse with Piper, the sun was already coming up. Now it's almost noon, and I seem to have missed her.

"She went home a couple of hours ago," Peyton answers over her chicken salad sandwich before turning to look at Mom and Dad.

They're both sitting at the kitchen table. My dad is reading something on his phone, and Mom is sifting through a thick folder. I know they've been prepping for a big trial, and they must always keep busy because of their dedication to work. I'm sure the wild teenager from before loved that they were always distracted, and it doesn't even bother me now, but I'm sure Preston would enjoy some of their attention every once in a while.

"What exactly do you wear to a viewing?" Peyton asks.

"Viewing? As in someone died?" I ask. "What did I miss?"

"Orville Clark passed away a few days ago. The viewing is today," Mom answers without looking up from her work.

This is news to me, but I can admit I haven't been paying attention to much going on around here unless it pertained to Piper who I've been singularly focused these days. "Did I know him?"

Peyton's brows draw together at my question.

"Everyone knew Mr. Clark." She frowns when she realizes what she said. "Sorry."

"He was a regular at the diner, either sitting inside when it's cold or out on the bench when the weather was nice," Mom explains. "He was kind of a town fixture."

The growl of an engine draws my attention to the front window, and when a beast of a muscle car pulls up in Piper's driveway, I do my best to act inconspicuous as I watch a guy with just as many muscles as his car emerge from the driver's seat. Although his arms are covered in muscles, he can't be much older than me.

Irritation runs through my blood when Piper's front door opens, and she runs to him. He catches her in his tattooed arms, spinning her around like the fools do in chick flicks after being separated for a long period of time. Her nose is buried in his neck, and his hands are dangerously close to her ass because her legs are wrapped all the way around his waist.

I don't even acknowledge my sister when she steps up beside me. If I open my mouth, I'd say something hateful, and it's not Peyton's fault that my girl is clinging to another man mere hours after having her lips on mine. I might've initiated that kiss, but she was a full participant. Until she wasn't.

We both stare out the window, watching Piper smile when the asshole finally puts her back down on her feet. She must've not gotten enough of him because they wrap each other in another hug, swaying back and forth for another long moment.

"Who is that asshole?" I spit.

"Oh," Peyton says as she's had some ah-ha moment. "That's who she was talking about in her journals. That's Dillon."

And things go from bad to worse. The sight of all of those stupid hearts in her journal are seared in my brain, and now they'll live right beside the ones of her tangling herself with him.

"He's here for the funeral. Mr. Clark was his granddad. Damn, he's smoking ho—"

"Stop," I hiss. "That's enough."

"He's a tasty little snack, isn't he?"

"Peyton," I warn.

"Yeah, that's wrong. He's not a snack. That boy is a five-course meal."

I turn to leave, and Peyton's laughter follows me all the way out of the room.

I spend the next half hour seething, walking a hole in the concrete on the back patio, but the tension in my body only seems to double by the minute. It's at catastrophic levels when I hear the jerk's car start up, and I'm damn near imploding when I peek through the fence and watch him open the passenger side door. He presses his palm to her lower back, guiding her inside. I don't miss the wide smile on his face or the devilish glint in his eyes as he rounds the front of his car and climbs into the driver's side. Then he backs out and takes off with my girl.

I pull out my phone to do some research, but *Dillon Clark* doesn't produce results for him. I can't access Piper's friend list because her accounts are on lockdown.

Frustrated, I head back inside and up the stairs. Peyton has to have more answers, and maybe she's done taunting me.

I find my bratty sister sitting in front of her makeup mirror in her room.

"I won't apologize for teasing you," she says as soon as I edge open her partially closed door. "Piper deserves someone like that hunk."

"What do you know about him?" I ask, instead of setting the record straight.

"Same as you." Her words come out distorted as she contorts her face to apply something to her eyelashes. "Only what was in the journals. He moved away years ago. She had a huge crush on him, and from telling by the way they acted a little bit ago, he feels the same way about her."

"Are you saying that shit just to get back at me?"

She turns to fully face me rather than looking at me in her mirror.

"You don't deserve her. You've already caused enough damage to Piper. Leave her alone."

"What did she tell you? I thought you were on my side."

She huffs, her focus back on the mirror as she applies lipstick.

"That was before I knew how bad things were."

"What changed?"

"Get out of my room, Dalton, and next time knock before you come in." Her eyes meet mine in the mirror. "Better yet, don't even bother to talk to me."

"What the hell, Peyton? I haven't done anything to you or her since I came home from the hospital. What gives?"

"She was right." My sister shrugs like it's no big deal to tell me to fuck off. "There's no way she can forgive you. The pain you caused changed who she could've been a long time ago."

"What's going on?" I prod, refusing to give up. I thought I'd made some leeway with Piper, and I know for a fact that Peyton was coming around. "What happened between playing in the pool yesterday, and now that's making you so hateful?"

"Let's just say my eyes are fully open."

"What does that even mea—"

"Can you go grab a pie from the diner?" Mom asks as she walks into Peyton's room. She's smiling, so she must not have overheard our conversation. "The diner is closed tomorrow, and we need it for the wake."

"Can't Peyton go?"

My sister huffs, and my mom stares at me like I've grown an extra head.

"She's not old enough to drive," Mom reminds me.

"You trust me to take your car?"

"Do you not want to drive?" she counters.

"I'm sure I remember how," I mutter. "I'm not afraid."

I don't remember shit from the accident, so reliving the trauma isn't a thing for me.

"I'll go," I agree.

"Money is downstairs by the front door. Get blueberry if they have it, apple if they don't."

I nod my head in agreement, trying to catch Peyton's eyes one last time before leaving the room, but she refuses to look at me.

Piper kissed me back last night. Yeah, she shoved me away before we could kiss a second time, but her lips were all about mine during the first one. I get the feeling that whatever my sister is upset about is something that Piper is less concerned over, but with the attitude she's flinging my way, I'll never get that information out of her.

Ignoring it seems like the manly thing to do, hoping that Peyton's irritation fades over time, but that'll be near impossible to do. Neither one of us go anywhere, so avoidance is difficult. Asking Piper about it would be the next best thing, but if my sister is more worried about it than Piper, bringing it back up may be the wrong way to go.

Why are women so damn confusing?

I growl in frustration as I climb into my mom's car. I have bigger things to worry about than my sister disliking me. I need to find out who the hell this Dillon guy is and what he is to Piper. My sister can stew in her anger until I have time to address it.

Chapter 20

Piper

"I'm sorry I couldn't make it back to town sooner," Dillon says after swallowing a bite of pecan pie.

"How was the tattoo convention in Vegas?"

"Amazing." His eyes light up at the mention. "There were so many people there. It was nuts but exhilarating as well."

"I bet. I can only imagine the number of scantily clad women walking around."

"You know it was the guys walking around shirtless that caught my eye," he waggles his eyebrows, "but there was more skin showing than I thought there would be. They had wet t-shirt contests daily and ink competitions."

"Did any of your work make it on the stage?"

His nose scrunches. "I haven't been doing tats long enough to enter anything, but maybe next year I'll have something to showcase."

"You've definitely spent the last six months since your birthday covering yourself up."

I appraise the bright colors on his arms. Dillon has always been an artist, but it wasn't until two years ago that he wanted to take his designs from paper to skin. I've seen some of his work in the pictures he texts, and he's already well on his way to being amazing.

"The guys at the shop love a blank canvas, so they did a lot of work on me. The pictures I sent you are mostly on them. Tattoo artists aren't afraid to get a little amateur ink."

"Didn't seem too amateurish from the pictures you sent me."

"I have a long way to go," he says before taking another huge bite of pie.

He's acting like everything is fine, but I know he's heartbroken about his grandfather. Mr. Clark was loved by everyone in the community, and his passing is hard on many of the people that knew him. But this is just how Dillon has always been. He hides his pain, just like he hid who he really was for a long time.

"Tell me about the Prince of Payne," he says after he swallows.

I nearly choke on my hot tea, sputtering it back into my cup. I forgot that's what we've called him for years, especially since his asshole tendencies fully matured.

"What are you talking about?"

"Don't pretend like you don't know what I'm talking about. I saw how your eyes darted toward his house before we left to come here."

"I'm tutoring Peyton," I explain with a shrug. "There's nothing going on with Dalton."

"You've always been a horrible liar. Now, spill."

"He's been… nice." I keep my focus on the table, knowing that if I look up at him, he'll know there's more to the story.

"Nice?" He chuckles. "Just how nice has he been to you, sweet Piper?"

"Don't call me that." I swat at his arm with the back of my hand.

He's sitting on my side of the booth, and I love that we've always sat like this. When we were younger, it killed me to sit beside him with the huge crush I had on him, but he came out to me before he left for Oregon. Since then, I have managed to tamp down my crush, and we've morphed into an amazing friendship. Although I never told Dillon I like him, he guessed when I tried to kiss him on Halloween many years ago. That's when he told me that he loved me, but he liked guys that way. He softened the blow by telling me I'd be his ideal girl if he weren't gay.

"How nice, Piper?" he prods.

"He hasn't said a horrible thing to me since the accident. He told his friends off when they were picking on me yesterday. He kissed me last night."

I wouldn't confess that last part to Frankie because she'd skin me alive, but I need to tell someone. Since Dillon will be heading back to Oregon in a few days, I figure he's my best bet. I can get advice, and he's less likely to blow his top as my other best friend would.

"Kissed, huh?" His lips turn up in a huge smile, and it kills me how handsome he is. "Was it a good kiss?"

"A great kiss."

"This is just like a romantic comedy."

"My life is more like *Carrie* than *Hope Floats*," I mutter, forking my pie across my plate.

His grin never falters.

"I was going to ask you what I should do, but you have those little hearts in your eyes, so I'm almost afraid to ask."

"Oh, my answer is simple. Make him fall in love with you and then break his heart into a million pieces."

My eyebrows hit my hairline. "Not what I was expecting you to say."

"Well," he taps his inked finger against his chin, "if a fine piece of ass like Dalton Payne fell in love with me, I'd marry his sweet little ass and never let him leave the house. He's the one who made me realize I was gay, remember?"

I do remember. Before Dillon left town, the crap Dalton and his friends pulled were child's play. Back then, there were several kids who got pranked, and their focus wasn't entirely on me. I think it had a lot to do with Dillon being around. He's a year older and looked out for me in school. He was also a typical boy and saw the hilarity of spiders in my locker and a dead snake in my backpack.

Things changed after he left, but that Halloween night, when I questioned how he knew he was gay, he confessed his utter attraction to Dalton. Even as much of a crush as I had on Dillon, I'd always caught myself watching my next-door neighbor. I couldn't deny that the boy was the cutest in my class. It was his spitefulness that has always kept me from admitting his good looks. It never stops Frankie of course, but I've never confessed my attraction out loud.

"I remember," I huff. "Yes, Dalton is attractive."

There I said it.

"Attractive?" Dillon laughs. "The man is sex on a stick covered in chocolate sauce. He's way beyond sexy. You should do exactly what I said, and if you fall in love with him, too, then that's a wonderful outcome as well."

"I don't think so," I object. "Even if he is nicer, there's no chance in hell I'll let myself have feelings for that boy."

"You mean more than you already have?"

"What?" I shake my head violently. "I don't care about him at all."

"And if he showed up here looking like my teenage wet dreams, you wouldn't bat an eyelash?"

"Not a dang chance."

A wide grin spreads his face, but then I notice movement across the diner, and I'll be damned if the man in question isn't walking in this direction.

"Put your arm around me," I snap.

"What?"

"Pretend to be my boyfriend," I hiss through clenched teeth.

Dillon sighs, but his arm slings around me like expected. He goes all out and nuzzles his nose up and down my neck. It's all for show, but that doesn't keep the cold chills from racing down my neck.

"Piper," Dalton says as soon as he steps up to our table. "Crazy, seeing you here."

"Best place in town for pie," I remind him with my shaky fingers pointing at my half-eaten slice.

Dillon chuckles into my neck before nipping at the skin.

I yelp, and it only serves to make Dalton clench his fists at his sides. If I'm not careful, he's going to end up attacking my oldest friend, and I can't help but worry about his unhealed wrist, especially since he took the cast off before he was supposed to.

And of course, worrying about my lifelong tormentor makes me angry at myself.

"Aren't you going to introduce me to your friend?"

Dillon chooses this time to pull his mouth from my throat. It takes everything I have not to wipe away the spit I feel drying there, and if I ever wondered if I still had those kinds of feelings for Dillon, those questions are now answered.

"Oh, hey, man. I'm Dillon." He offers his hand, and although it takes an endless span of time to accept, Dalton finally takes it in his.

They spend an eternity, eyes locked, hands clenching tighter and tighter in a show of machismo that Dalton doesn't realize is only one-sided.

Dillon is the first to let go, and I see victory flash in Dalton's eyes.

"Sorry to hear about your granddad," Dalton offers in a surprising show of sympathy. "How is your dad doing?"

"He was my mom's dad," Dillon corrects. "But she's doing okay. Papa was sick and didn't tell anyone. I think that hurts her more than anything."

Dillon's voice cracks, and it's the first sign of pain he's shown. I squeeze his thigh under the table in a show of support. His lip ticks up in the corner, letting me know that he understands the action. I hate that he's hurting, but Dillon always deals with pain and grief in his own way. He only shuts me out when he's sad. He doesn't exactly distance me from his person, but it's understood that if he doesn't want to talk about something, there's no way for me to change that. It's just who he is.

"So, you're friends with Piper?" Dalton asks as he settles on the other side of the booth.

"What are you doing?" I hiss before Dillon can answer him.

"I'm just getting to know Dillon a little better," Dalton says with a sly grin.

"And I'm trying to spend time with my boyfriend."

The grin disappears in a flash.

Chapter 21

Dalton

Boyfriend? No fucking way.

My knuckles crack when I fist them against my thighs, and hopefully, the conversations going on around us are loud enough to block out the sound.

What I can't seem to control is the clenching of my jaw with her declaration.

"Boyfriend?" I manage in a nearly civilized tone. "I didn't know you had a boyfriend."

"Have," she counters. "As in *have* one presently, not past tense."

"You haven't mentioned him all week." I challenge her with my eyes, but my glare doesn't make her look nervous at all.

"We've been dating for years," the asshole sitting across from me adds. "Since we were kids. We're soulmates."

"Nice." I never take my eyes off hers, and at least she has the wherewithal to look a little ashamed. Heat creeps up on her cheeks as Dillon squeezes her close into his side.

But why is she ashamed? Is it because of the kiss we shared or the fact that she never even mentioned him before now? Is it possible that while spending time with me this last week, she actually forgot about her boyfriend? She sure as hell wasn't thinking about him last night when she whimpered into my mouth the second my tongue brushed hers. He wasn't on her mind when her fingers gripped the front of my shirt, pulling me closer.

I should bring up the kiss. The thought makes my eyes focus on her pouting lips, but I decide against bringing it up. I could blow their relationship apart with one single confession, but this man just lost his granddad, and as much as he's trying to be strong, I can tell it hurts him. Plus, I'm no longer the asshole that ruins peoples' lives, using any and all means necessary to kick them while they're down.

Even with the ammunition I have, I'll keep my lips sealed. I know she expects me to act like an asshole. That's why the look on her face is almost comical when I keep my lips sealed.

I don't need to worry about Dillon. All I need to focus on is my girl. I know I won't win her with scathing words and a reminder that it was me she had her mouth on last night, not him. She probably already regrets the kiss. She doesn't seem like the type to cheat, but she also doesn't seem like the kind of person that would keep something like that a secret for long. The guilt would eat her alive, so I know she'll tell him, eventually. I'll leave her to it.

"Have we met before?" I figure bringing up the fact that I've lost all of my memories will knock him off his game. He's already taken back his arm from around her, and she even scooted closer to the window an inch or so. There's a level of victory in that as well. Does he suspect something is going on between the two of us?

There's definitely an air of familiarity surrounding them, and that's a given considering how long they've been friends. Their connection was obvious by the way she jumped into his arms in her driveway, but he didn't press his lips to hers then, and I know it would be the first thing I'd do if I'd been away from her for any length of time. I wanted to do it now, even with her boyfriend at her side.

I wouldn't be able to keep my hands off her for any length of time. Hell, I wouldn't be at the diner eating pie. I'd have her pressed against the wall with my tongue down her throat, needing the warmth of her body against mine, but maybe he isn't controlled by his hormones.

That knowledge pisses me off even more. He's more mature than me, and she teaches kids to read. She doesn't seem to be ruled by her physical needs either. He's better for her than I am, that much is clear, but it doesn't make me want her any less. She's liked him at least since the summer before sixth grade according to her journals, but there's still something off about the way they're behaving.

"We have," Dillon answers, bringing me back to the inside of the diner instead of being stuck in my head, trying to figure out what the hell is actually going on. "I went to school here until halfway through the sixth-grade year."

"I don't remember any of it." Has she told him about my memory loss, or is it only a big deal for me?

"That look." Dillon points at me and smiles before turning toward Piper. "That's the same look he had on his face in kindergarten when you chose to play with me rather than him."

I swallow, hating to be the brunt of his joke, but I keep silent. Piper has suffered as such for years, so sitting here while her boyfriend makes fun of me isn't a big deal. If anything, maybe it'll make her realize I actually have changed. I don't think the old Dalton would sit around while someone was intentionally making fun of him.

Piper smiles, too. "I chose mini marshmallows over fruit because I'm—"

"You're allergic to strawberries," I interrupt. My eyes find hers, and there's a softness to her face when she looks at me. It's reminiscent of the way she looked yesterday when she agreed to stop being rude and promised me, she wouldn't ignore me when I walked into a room. "Is that the day I pushed you down and got your dress dirty?"

Dillon looks from her to me and back, but he doesn't seem annoyed with the realization that she and I have been talking, and that doesn't make sense either. Another thing that confuses me is the fact that I'm still breathing. Surely, she tells her soulmate about the way she's treated at school. Why hasn't this fucker kicked my ass? Why isn't he ramming my head into the cinder block walls of the diner? I honestly deserve nothing less. Instead of doing any of that, he's got a little smile on his face.

Her eyes widen with my question, but she nods. "I think that's the day you started hating me."

Her voice is soft, and for a split second, I can forget that she's sitting beside a man who had his arm on her shoulder earlier and his hands cupping her ass when she ran into his arms. He no longer exists. It's only her and me in this moment.

"That can't be it," I mutter, the whole time locking my eyes with hers. "And if it is, I'm so fucking sorry."

"For bringing strawberries to school?" Dillon huffs a laugh. "How would you even know?"

I don't answer him, and Piper keeps her eyes on mine.

"If I could take it all back." I swallow around the lump forming in my throat. "I wou—"

"Crap," Dillon says as he stands abruptly from the table after looking at his watch. "I'm going to be late."

Piper looks nervous suddenly.

"I don't mind being late," Dillon offers, still holding his hand out for her to take. "I'll make sure you get home."

"I'll take her home," I offer because I'm a nice guy, of course. I have no ulterior motives.

Piper stands, taking Dillon's hand before looking between the two of us.

"It's up to you... baby."

Piper's lip twitches oddly at his delayed sentiment. She nods, and I'm actually surprised that she's agreeing to ride in the car with me considering what happened the last time we rode together. But it's daylight, and we're only a few miles from our neighborhood, so I guess those things factor in her decision as well.

They share the most awkward kiss I've ever witnessed before she wraps her arms around his neck. She says something that's muffled in his ear, and he holds her even tighter. This reaction is real, and I hate that they share that kind of connection with each other.

I watch, standing to the side as Dillon cups her cheek and promises to see her again soon.

Piper nods, blinking away tears as he walks away. She loves him, that's evident, but I have a sneaking feeling that she doesn't love him that way.

Even though we both just watched her boyfriend drive off in his loud car, she doesn't shrug me off when I press my palm to her back and guide her to the passenger side of my mom's car.

Chapter 22

Piper

This was a mistake. This was a mistake. This was a mistake.

The sentence is on repeat in my head, echoing over and over as Dalton makes his way around the front of the car. I've decided to call my mom to come pick me up by the time he climbs inside. There's no way I need to spend another moment alone with this man. I did that last night and look where it got me.

"I don't think this is a good idea," I mutter when he cranks the car.

"Home is only a few miles away," he says as he latches his seat belt across his chest.

If only he'd worn it that night.

But even as I think it, I can't regret what happened. Even as horrible as it is and as much as I want to think differently, I know Dalton has changed. He hasn't shown one hint of being the same guy he was before his car went off the ravine. Knowing this is my main cause for concern because as much as I can admit to tolerating, maybe even liking this new guy, it won't last. The second he finds out I was driving the car or when his memories come back, it's only going to make things worse.

"Did you follow me?"

Why else would he happen to show up during the single hour I had to spend with Dillon before he was due at the funeral home for his granddad's viewing? The coincidence is just too much.

"Oh, shit," he snaps, putting the car back in park before we even rolled back an inch. "Mom's pie. Be right back."

Like a kid hopped up on candy, he throws the door open and runs back into the diner. Instead of texting Mom, who's at the funeral home anyway, I gawk at the door he just disappeared through. Am I so wrapped up in myself that I thought I was the only reason he'd show up here? What a joke.

He emerges a few minutes later with two pie boxes stacked on top of each other. He climbs back inside after placing them in the back seat.

"I can't remember if she said apple and blueberry if they don't have it or the other way around." He grins over at me. "So, I got one of each."

"Is that..." I snap my jaw shut before finishing. I shouldn't ask him things about the accident, but I'm dying to know if he has short-term memory loss as well.

"Is that, what?" he says as he pulls on his seatbelt again.

"I shouldn't ask you things about the accident. It's rude, and I know I hate it when people ask me about it." Mainly, because I don't want to slip up and confess my role in it.

"What's rude," he begins, turning back in my direction with a pointed stare rather than making a move to reverse out of the parking spot, "is kissing me when you have a boyfriend."

"You stole that kiss," I remind him.

"You whimpered like you enjoyed it."

Just the reminder makes my thigh muscles clench. My palms grow sweaty, and my lips tingle with the need for it to happen again.

"I was appalled. You stole my first kiss."

My mouth snaps shut again, and I know I've given too much away. There's no way he'll believe that I'm dating a tattooed-covered hottie like Dillon and never kissed him.

But it's the truth. That kiss last night with Dalton was my very first. My second came moments ago when Dillon pressed his lips to mine in the diner. That one was awkward beyond belief for me, and I'll get back at my friend for putting me on the spot like that, but I have bigger things to worry about right now—namely, the handsome bully sitting in the car with me.

"It was my first kiss, too," he whispers, instead of making fun of me for not having any experience.

"What?" My head snaps in his direction. "Dalton, you've kissed most of the girls in Westover and half the girls in Wise County from what I've heard."

"And yet, all I can remember is your kiss. Your lips. The sound of that little moan that escaped when my tongue touched yours for the first time. It's going to haunt me for the rest of my life."

Are charisma and charm innate gifts? Because this boy is oozing with both.

"We sh-shouldn't talk about that kiss."

I focus on my hands in my lap because I know by the tone of his voice that if I turn in his direction, he's going to press his mouth against mine just like he did last night, and I'd be unable to resist him.

"That kiss is all I want to talk about. Or we could kiss again and talk about that instead."

"No more kissing," I tell him with as much bravado as I can manage.

"Why?" he asks, genuinely sounding confused. "Because I thought it was a great kiss."

I can agree with him on that, but since I have nothing to compare it to, I keep my mouth sealed shut. Plus, continuing to talk about what happened last night will only lead to me wanting to do it more, and that's the worst idea in the history of ideas.

"Is it because you have a boyfriend?"

That would be a great reason if it were true, but I have a feeling Dalton knows that I don't have a boyfriend. The situation in the diner was awkward at best, and the boy sitting next to me is many things, but an idiot isn't one of them.

"Can we please change the subject? No more kissing talk."

"Why didn't you go to the funeral home with Dillion?"

This conversation isn't any better, but I'll take the reprieve from talk of his mouth on mine.

"My grandfather died when I was eleven."

"I'm sorry."

He seems sincere, but he hasn't heard what happened next, so I don't allow myself empathy for him.

"And going there would remind you about your own loss?"

I huff. "No. You convinced me that my grandfather was going to become a zombie and come back from the grave to kill my entire family."

He laughs until he sees the serious look on my face.

"Really?" He frowns, but I can see the corner of his lip twitch like he's still fighting back a laugh. "Zombies aren't real."

"I know that now. I didn't back then. It took months before I could sleep in my own bed again. My parents were so annoyed with me every night when I crawled into their bed with them."

"Probably the reason you're an only child, too." He winks at me, but it only agitates me. He doesn't see how much this affected me.

I can look back now and realize how ridiculous it was, but back then, I was traumatized.

"And that would be another thing you ruined for me," I mutter, turning my attention out the passenger side window, ready to be home and far away from him.

"Fuck," he mutters.

"And if you could not cuss so much around me, I'd appreciate that, too."

"Sorry," he grumbles. "And I'm sorry for the zombie stuff, too. Was I ever decent to you?"

"Only when you were trying to convince me that you weren't as bad as you actually were, and all of those times, you only pretended to be nice, so when you were mean to me, it hurt me more."

"Will there ever come a time when we can do things together or make plans when it doesn't come back to this?"

"Why do you even ask?" I'll never forget the past. Doing so will only lead to more pain, and I've had my fair share of that in my life already.

"Because I'm tired of reliving a past I can't remember, a past I can't change. Eventually, we're going to have to move into the future, Piper. It's not healthy spending every moment we have together discussing things we can't change."

"We shouldn't be spending time together at all," I remind him. "I think it's best that we go back to avoiding each other."

"I haven't been avoiding you. I've given you space, and it's not the same thing." He leans closer but stays far enough away that he isn't touching my skin. "And I'm tired of the distance between us. That kiss last night set me on fire."

"You should see a doctor about that."

He chuckles, and as much as I hate to admit it even to myself, I love the sound of it.

"You're funny, too. I love that about you."

"Just take me home, Dalton."

He grumbles as he puts the car in reverse, but he doesn't say a word on the way home. I thank him for the ride but head straight home when I get out of the car. I don't bother to turn around or respond to him as he calls after me. I've had enough of Dalton Payne this week to last a lifetime.

Thankfully, tomorrow is Sunday, which means I have no tutoring and no Preston duties. The next twenty-four Dalton-free hours will be blissful.

Chapter 23

Dalton

"You're up early," my dad says as he pours coffee into a travel mug. "How was the party?"

"My old friends are ass... jerks," I correct. "They won't be coming back over again."

"What did they do?" Mom asks as she walks into the kitchen, but she doesn't seem genuinely interested.

"They just seem immature. I don't need that around me."

There's no point in telling them the truth. One, it will make them realize how big of an asshole I was, and two, I don't think they really care.

They spent the entire day in the den yesterday preparing for the trial that starts this morning. I don't think there would've been dinner if I hadn't ordered pizza for us. I tried to ask Peyton if they were always like this, but she literally hissed at me when I opened my mouth and then locked herself in her room. I did something, or Piper told her something that makes her hate me, but after the stuff I've been told I did, I'm not surprised. I can't even be mad at either of them for it, but I was being honest when I told Piper yesterday that I'm tired of everyone living in the past. Right now is all I know, and I just want to move on from the shit I pulled before.

After a twenty-minute petty argument about a lack of exculpatory evidence on their case, my parents leave for the courthouse with parting information that they may be late getting home this evening.

And now I just wait.

Right on time, Piper arrives, but instead of just walking in like she has been all week, she knocks on the door.

She doesn't look a bit impressed when it opens, and she sees me standing there.

"Where's Peyton?" she asks from the front stoop, making no move to come inside.

"Shower." At least I could hear her shower going when I came down earlier.

"And Preston?"

"Either asleep or already playing video games."

"I'll wait for your sister in the kitchen," she says as she steps past me.

"We can't have a relationship based on lies," I tell her back as she walks away.

Piper freezes in her tracks, a long-suffered sigh escaping her lips.

"You're delusional."

"I'm delusional?" I ask as I walk around, so she has to look at me. "I'm not the one with the fake boyfriend."

"I love him."

"I don't doubt that for a second," I tell her, and it's the truth. Their connection would be evident to a blind man. "But I think he loves something you can't give him."

She swallows, the apples of her cheeks turning the bright red that I love so much.

"Like what?" she asks weakly.

"Dick," I answer simply, pulling my phone from my pocket.

I turn it around when I open the pictures I screenshotted after hours of research yesterday. After going through old yearbooks, something I kicked myself for not thinking of sooner, I found his real last name. After entering that into the social media platforms, I was rewarded with a plethora of evidence that Piper lied to me yesterday.

"So?" she says, barely glancing at the picture of the two guys snuggling. "He's affectionate with his friends."

I swipe the image, bringing up the one I found of him in a heated lip-lock with another guy.

"Crap," Piper mutters. "You're stalking Dillon now, too? His family knows he's out, so you can't use him as ammunition against me."

"What?" My brows crease. "I wasn't planning on blackmailing you to keep his secret."

She doesn't look like she believes me.

"I'm not that guy, Piper."

Frustrated, I shove my phone back in my pocket and pinch the bridge of my nose.

"I keep telling you that, but you seem to have a hearing problem."

"I hear you just fine," she argues.

"Let me prove to you I'm not that guy."

We had this same conversation two days ago before we got in the pool, and I ruined everything by putting my lips on hers. Now I regret doing that. I mean, I don't regret the kiss, but the timing was shitty. If I had waited until I had more control of the situation, she wouldn't be pulling away from me right now.

"So, just friends?"

My eyes snap to hers. I was prepared to beg and barter to get her to agree to what we'd already settled on, so I'm a little surprised right now.

"No labels," I clarify.

Her head immediately shakes, and she takes a step back even though I've maintained a couple feet of distance between us already.

"I can't. We can be cordial, but I won't ever trust you." Tears well on her lower lashes, but she takes another step back when I reach up to swipe them away. "When you get your memories back, it'll only make things ten times worse."

"I don't want my memories back. I don't want to be that guy. I can't be the guy who avoids his family, keeps crappy friends, and is mean to pretty girls. My memories won't matter because I'll never forget how I feel when I'm close to you."

"You don't know what you're talking about," she mutters before turning back toward the door.

"Where are you going?"

She doesn't stop her stride. "Home."

"You have to keep an eye on Preston."

"You're more than capable of watching after your brother and making him a sandwich," she says as she pulls open the front door. "Tell Peyton I'll call her and let your parents know I couldn't make it today."

"You want me to lie to them?" I'm grasping at straws. I already spent all day yesterday without seeing her or hearing her voice, two days in a row is bullshit.

She spins around. "You can tell them the truth."

"Which is?"

"That you keep pushing yourself on me when I repeatedly turn you down."

"That's not exactly the full truth, though, is it?"

She gives me a wicked smile I've never seen cross her lips before, and just the sight of it makes my heartrate ramp up. She's going to be mean back to me, and for some reason that turns me on more than it should. I deserve it more than anyone else, and I've been waiting for her wrath, knowing she couldn't keep it bottled up forever.

"I think I'll make a list for you, detailing all the hateful things you've done, all the mean things you've said over the years. I have them all written in my journals, as you know, so I'd never risk forgetting what you're really like. You can read them off to your parents. If you want to rat me out for going home today rather than suffering through another round of *please forgive me,* I'd like them to be fully informed of why I made that decision."

Drawn to her when she's like this, I take several steps in her direction.

"Wh-what are you doing?" she stammers when I invade her space.

"You're sexy when you're mad."

"You haven't heard a word I've said," she mutters. "Typical."

"Oh, baby, I'm listening, but your body is saying something your mouth isn't."

"Oh, yeah? And what's that?" She props her hand on her hip in agitation.

"How much you want me, too."

I don't give her the time to deny it before my lips are once again on hers. Instead of shoving me away like I expect, her fingers scrape across my scalp as she scrambles for purchase in my hair. This kiss is nothing like the one we shared the other night. That one was slow and filled with promise. This one is fierce and brimming with hate and anger. Only the animosity rushing through her veins isn't about me taking something she doesn't want to give. No, the way her tongue battles with mine, it's clear she's upset with herself for wanting it as much as I do.

"Dalton," she pants against my mouth when we come up for air, but I don't let her push me away this time.

"Shh," I urge against her mouth before pressing even closer.

I ignore the dart of pain in my wrist when I lift her from the floor. In the next second, I have her legs around me, and her back pressed to the front door. My cock is at full-mast, but I don't grind it against her like my brain is urging me to do. She admitted that our kiss was her first, so it's obvious she's a virgin. I'm already crossing a line that will give me trouble at a later date. I won't push things that far right now.

So as much of a gentleman as I can be in this situation, I keep my mouth on hers and my hands a respectable distance from her ass.

"Dalton," she moans again, and this time it's accompanied with her fingers ripping at my hair.

"Jesus, baby," I moan against her neck, licking at the raging pulse point under her ear.

"Dalton!" she yells this time. "Stop!"

I pull my head back immediately. "What's wrong?"

"Let me down."

I swallow the ball of emotion in my throat. "Piper, please don't do this again. Don't shove me away and pretend we don't have chemistry."

Her eyes flutter closed, and her chest heaves with sharp breaths. "Please let me go."

"You enjoyed kissing me," I remind her as I let her feet lower to the ground.

"I did," she admits. "Too much."

She clears her throat before bending to grab the strap of her backpack that must've slid off her shoulder at some point.

"We can take things slow," I tell her. So long as she isn't walking away because she regrets it, that's something I can work with.

"I have to go."

She walks out and leaves, but she doesn't reject my offer completely, and that's the single thing I hold onto.

Chapter 24

Piper

I feel like the biggest jerk in the world as I walk to my house.

I've left Peyton in a lurch. She has so little time before her test but staying in that house with him isn't possible.

She can come over here and work on math if she wants. I need to get myself out of the danger zone.

As expected, my house is as silent as a tomb when I enter. My parents have already left for work, and I'll have the entire day to stew over what I just let happen, again, with Dalton Payne.

Take things slow, my foot. There was nothing slow about the way he lifted me and propped me against his front door. We were both traveling at the speed of light when he pressed his mouth against mine.

I'm angry at myself for enjoying the warmth of his lips on mine, and I hate that I admitted that out loud to him. He shouldn't know these things. It'll only get me in trouble.

My palms itch, remembering the texture of his hair, and my body aches for the promises he never even said.

Dang it!

Why does he get to me? Do I react this way to him because my aching heart needs some form of positive to hold onto?

Needing a voice of reason, I drop my backpack by the door and fly up the stairs. If there's a person on this earth that can talk me down from the ledge I'm teetering on, it's Frankie.

"Hey," comes her sleepy voice when I call.

"Did I wake you up?"

"Yeah," she grumbles.

"You're usually up with the dawn," I remind her when she sounds agitated about her sleep being interrupted.

"Back home, I actually have things to get out of bed for. It sucks here, Piper. I figured summer would go by faster if I sleep more."

"I don't think that's healthy," I hedge.

"I'm not depressed." She yawns. "No, that's not true. I'm utterly depressed. I want to come home."

"I want that, too," I whisper. "Maybe you can call your parents, and they'll let you stay here while they're out of town?"

"I wish." Sheets rustle on her end of the line, and I wait for her to situate herself. "I already asked last week. They refuse to change the plane ticket and keep giving me this crap about family being important. They act like Granny is helpless. That woman is stronger and healthier than any other eighty-year-old I've met."

"I'm sorry you hate it there. I'd come to you if I could."

I don't mention that it would only be to get away from Dalton and his plush lips, but she doesn't have to know that.

"Shouldn't you be tutoring Peyton right now?"

"I left," I confess. "I couldn't be there today."

Silence fills the hundreds of miles between us.

"Frankie?"

"What has he done?"

I smile at her defensive tone. She may think the guy is smoking hot, but she's never excused his behavior. Her protectiveness makes me grin.

God, I want to tell her everything, but I'm not sure how she'll take it.

"He had a pool party," I begin, planning to tell her exactly what I told Dillon.

"And?"

"All of the regular deviants from school showed up."

"Piper, if you tell me he teamed up against you, I'm going to hitchhike back to Westover and set his house on fire."

Another smile spreads across my face. Fierce loyalty and the willingness to maim and kill is hard to find these days. Frankie gives it in spades, and I'm one lucky girl to have her on my side.

"He didn't," I assure her. "He caught them being mean to me, and he made them all leave. I told him about what we saw Bronwyn, Vaughn, and Kyle doing that night."

"Really?" Her voice is a squeak, still filled with sleep and not ready for this conversation.

"Really," I tell her. "He didn't seem too bothered by that. He was more concerned about the way they were treating me."

"Did he beat the crap out of Kyle? Someone needs to take that jerk down a peg or two."

"I left the room, but I don't think there were any fists thrown."

"And what happened next?"

"Are you living vicariously through my drama because you're bored being stuck on the farm?"

"Of course," she says. "Now get on with the story. What happened next?"

"We got in the pool."

"We?"

"You know." I twist my hair around my fingers nervously. I just want to spit it all out, and even I'm growing agitated by retelling the story a couple of words at a time. "Peyton, Preston, and me."

"And Dalton?"

"He kissed me, okay!"

"Whoa. What?"

"We kissed. Well, he kissed me twice."

"Is he a good kisser?"

"That is not what you're supposed to say. You're supposed to yell at me for letting it happen. You're supposed to warn me against all evil things Dalton Payne. Remind me of the horrible things he's done since the day we met. As my best friend, you're not supposed to ask me if he's a good kisser!"

"So, he isn't?"

I sigh in agitation, and Frankie laughs.

"He's a great kisser."

"I knew he would be. You can't have lips like his and suck at sucking face, you know?"

"Jesus, Frankie." I rub my forehead, but it seems the irritation is there to stay.

"What do you want me to say?" I can hear the smile in her voice. "So, you kissed Dalton. It doesn't have to be a big deal unless you make it one."

"I hate him," I remind her. "We hate him. I can't go around kissing people I hate."

"Hate kisses may be the best kisses ever," she counters. "There are no hard and fast kissing rules. That's not even a thing."

"What do you know about hate kissing?"

She mutters something unintelligible.

"What? Frankie! Have you been kissing on someone in Utah?"

"No!" she screams, but even on the phone, I can tell my best friend is lying. She's as bad at it as I am.

"Who have you been kissing, Frankie?"

"He's a jerk. I don't want to talk about it."

I allow silence to fill the space between us, knowing that she'll cave, eventually. She wants to talk about her guy as much as I want to talk about Dalton.

"He's no one," she says quietly. "Just some fool that works here on the ranch."

"So now you're going around kissing fools?" I tease.

Frankie is always purposeful in how she behaves. She isn't going to convince me she accidentally kissed some guy.

"He's the biggest jerk I've ever met," she snaps. "I hate him."

"I think Dalton has the market cornered on the biggest jerk," I remind her.

"Zeke is worse," she mutters.

"Twelve years of torture worse?"

"I don't want to talk about Zeke," she hisses. "Tell me more about kissing Dalton."

"I don't want to talk about Dalton."

"Yes, you do, or you wouldn't have called me so dang early."

"I gave him some of my journals," I confess, and I swear I could hear a pin drop.

There isn't a hint of noise, not a whisper of sound between us for what seems like an eternity.

"Has he done or said anything mean to you since the accident?" she asks, completely ignoring the questions she really wants to ask. Knowing Frankie, we'll come full circle, eventually.

"He's been nice."

"Am I going to have to pull this information from you? Quit wasting both of our time and tell me what is going on."

"He wants to be friends." She huffs. "He wants to be more than friends. He *likes* me, or so he claims."

"Has he done anything to make you doubt that?"

"Besides years and years of torment?"

"All of that is in the past."

"Now you sound like him," I mumble.

"Let the past go."

"Did he tell you to say that?"

She chuckles, and I know it was a stupid question to ask. Frankie would tell me the second our call connected if Dalton was brazened enough to call her. It reminds me that I told him I was dating Dillon, and I also told him Frankie was my boyfriend when I was on the phone with her the first time I saw him at the diner. He hasn't called me out on that yet, but I have no doubt it'll come. The fake boyfriend trick with Dillon has already been blown out of the water.

"What if he really does like you?" Frankie whispers. "What do you do then?"

"I don't have a clue. I want to run as far as I can get, but at the same time, I want to see where it takes me. That makes me crazy, doesn't it?"

"I think you should—"

A knock on Frankie's end interrupts what she was about to say.

"Cause me to hear thy lovingkindness in the morning," a husky voice says.

"Who is that?" I hiss.

"I have to go."

The line goes dead before I can find out who the man was speaking to her, but more importantly, she didn't finish telling me what she thought I should do.

"Crap," I hiss, readying my arm to throw my phone across the room when it rings.

Peyton's pretty face flashes across my screen with a request to video chat.

"I'm sorry." I apologize the second the video connects. "I just couldn't be over there today."

"I understand," she says. "Maybe I can come to your house in a little bit?"

"Of course. How was the funeral?"

"Sad," she says with a frown. "Everyone loved Mr. Clark."

"Yeah."

"Dillon is the hottest guy I've ever seen before in my life."

"He's pretty good-looking," I agree.

"Why does he have to be so much older than me?" she whines.

"He's also gay," I inform her.

"All the gorgeous ones are."

We both smile.

"So, see you in about an hour?"

"Sounds good."

"I think I need to focus on—"

Peyton stops talking, looking up from her phone.

"Knock much?"

"I didn't know you were here," Dalton says, his voice low and hard to hear across the room.

"Do you normally creep into my room when you think I'm away?"

"You know why I'm here," he mutters.

"Of course, the window." Peyton looks down at the phone, smiling when she sees how wide my eyes are. She winks before looking back up at her brother. "No matter how hard you stare at her curtains, she's not going to pull them back while standing naked in her room."

Oh, Jesus. What is this girl doing?

Chapter 25

Dalton

"I don't want to see her naked," I mutter.

Peyton raises an eyebrow at me. Just mentioning it makes me think of her in the bathing suit and shorts. Even with the naked nerdy girls I found in my phone, I haven't seen a sexier sight than Piper Schofield in a one-piece. I'm a guy, of course I want to see her naked.

"Okay. I don't *only* want to see her naked."

My sister huffs.

I swear I have more than a one-track mind, but I can't help where it ends up where Piper is concerned. I want her naked. I want her clothed. I want her in pajamas and in a white dress as I wait at the other end of the church for her. I want it all. And yes, I want her naked.

Naked and wet, sweaty and reaching for me.

Peyton clears her throat in irritation, and I force those thoughts and dreams down so I can focus on what needs to be said and done right now. Yes, I came into Peyton's room for a reason, but I also need to talk with her.

"I need your help."

She's been a brat to me since the night Piper stayed over, but that has to end. She's my only connection to the girl, and I'm losing my mind already. They're both shutting me out, and it's killing me.

"I'm not going to help you."

I knew she was going to say that. She can't even stand to look at me recently.

"Will you at least tell me why you're mad at me? What the hell did I do to you?"

One day we were fine, and then the next she hates me, looking at me with pity the same way Piper does when she doesn't know I can see her.

Only paying me half attention, Peyton looks back down at her phone before meeting my eyes. She re-situates her body until she's facing me, and I'm grateful she may be giving this conversation a chance rather than telling me to fuck off and get out of her room. After pressing a few buttons on her phone, she looks at me again.

"I don't like the way you treated Piper."

Well, that's a given. I hate the way I treated her, too.

"I haven't mistreated Piper."

"Not since the accident, but before the wreck."

I roll my eyes. Will it always come back to that?

"You sound just like her." I drop to the floor in front of the window, crossing my legs. There isn't so much as a draft from the air conditioner in Piper's room. Her curtains are unmoving, just another barrier between the two of us. "I wish you both would forgive me."

"This is hard for her," Peyton says. "You can't expect her to forget what's happened overnight."

"Hard for her?" I huff. "What about me?"

"Really? You're going to make this about you?"

"It's impossible knowing that I love her, knowing that she's meant for me, and I ruined everything in a past I can't even remember." I drop my head, focusing on my hands because I can't look at my sister, risking the sight of her judgmental eyes on me. I didn't plan this method of attack, but honesty seems like the best thing, so I go for it. "The reprehensible things I've done to her can't be redeemed. I can't go back twelve years and take it all back, but if I could, I'd do it in a heartbeat. Not being able to imagine a world where she isn't mine..."

I shake my head, unable to put into words what I'm feeling in my soul.

"Love? Really, Dalton?" The tone of my sister's voice makes the hair on my arms stand on end in frustration. "It's been less than two weeks."

"What else could it be, if not love?" I snap my head up to look at her.

"Infatuation? Opportunity? A challenge? Any number of things," Peyton counters. "You've never had a girl turn you down before. Maybe it's a reaction to your fragile ego."

"I don't remember anyone else!" I roar. "Her first kiss was my first kiss, too!"

"What?" Peyton's eyes grow wild, and she looks from me to her phone twice. "She kissed you?"

"Well," I begin, embarrassment flushing my cheeks, "I kissed her, but she kissed me back."

"Unbelievable," Peyton mutters, and for some reason, her shoulders relax a bit. "This changes things doesn't it?"

"All of her firsts could be my firsts, too," I blurt, unable to control the words coming out of my mouth.

I've dreamed of experiencing everything with Piper. Those fantasies are all I have to draw from. I doubt I'm a virgin, technically. Bronwyn said as much when she was crawling all over me the other day, but does it even count if I can't remember it?

"Ew." Peyton's nose scrunches up. "Little sister, remember?"

She looks down at her phone once again, and then I see her wink. Is she taking selfies while I'm spilling my guts?

"You never know." Her eyes leave her phone and look up at me. "She may come around."

"And what exactly should I do to convince her?" I don't think my sister has much relationship experience, but since I'm working with nothing of my own, it doesn't hurt to get help and advice wherever I can.

"Just go talk to her," Peyton responds.

"Jesus!" I hiss, throwing myself on my back on her carpet. "I've tried talking with her. She's stubborn and won't listen to me."

"Maybe she will this time."

"Yeah, okay." I swing myself up from the floor.

I didn't get anywhere with my confessions. My sister just wants to give me canned advice, knowing that Piper has pushed me away at every turn. Is she getting back at me for something?

"See you later," I mutter as I walk toward the hallway.

"Are you going to go talk to her?"

"No clue," I tell her as I leave.

"Go talk to her!" Peyton screams after me, but instead of heading to Piper's house, I go to my room.

Pacing hasn't helped before, and yet it's what I find myself doing right now. Tying her up and forcing her to listen to me seems like a twisted option, and I honestly don't think it would breed trust between the two of us.

Peyton was my last chance at figuring out what to do, and that failed epically. Just talking to Piper sounds easy enough, and I'd think it was a great idea if I hadn't already attempted to do it a million times already.

She'll kiss me back when I kiss her, but then she gets lost in her head, remembering all the shitty things I did to her, and she pushes me away.

I'm out of luck and hope, so I grab a quick shower and head over to do exactly what my sister suggested. I'll try to talk to her one more time.

Hell, what am I thinking? I'll try it a million times until she finally understands that the guy she hates no longer exists, and he's never coming back. Even if my memories make a miraculous appearance, there's no changing the way I feel about her.

With determination in my stride, I leave the house, crossing my yard and into hers. I don't even want to knock. I want to shove the door open and tell her how it's going to be, force her to listen and understand, but that doesn't seem like it would work either.

I'm thinking of how I'm going to reword the things I've said over and over as I lift my finger to ring the doorbell.

Chapter 26

Piper

Peyton's bedroom door snaps shut, and all I can do is stare at my friend's smiling face on my phone.

"What just happened?"

"Why are you crying?"

I didn't realize my face was wet with tears until she asked.

I dash them away with the back of my hand.

"Are you going to let him talk to you?"

"Did he know you were on the phone with me?"

Is she playing me to help her brother? Did they just set all of this up? A familiar sense of betrayal begins to seep inside of me.

"He just barged in my room. He didn't have a clue," she assures me. "He comes in here to stare at your bedroom window."

I ignore that little piece of information because it has the ability to either creep me out or make me smile with knowing he thinks of me when I'm not there.

"He said you were mad at him. What did he do to piss you off?"

"I know you don't want to talk about the scars on your legs, Piper, but I can't get them out of my head. I hate him for pushing you to that point."

Shame washes over me, but I can't focus on that right now either.

"What am I going to do?" I whisper.

"I suggest washing your face and brushing your hair. He's on his way over there."

I squeak with anticipation, hanging up the phone without even saying goodbye before hauling tail to the bathroom.

I do as she said, washing my face and brushing my hair. After the kiss we shared less than an hour ago, I also brush my teeth, knowing he may try to do that again.

When the doorbell rings, I'm staring at my face in the mirror. My eyes are still swollen from crying from hearing the desperation in his voice when he explained to his sister how he felt about me. I never expected him to feel that way, and more importantly, I never expected to feel how I am right now with his confession.

He loves me?

There was doubt in Peyton's voice when she questioned his ability to feel that way in such a short period of time, but I heard the truth in his voice. It was laced through his words like restricting ivy, and he seemed to be drowning in it.

That's why the tears were on my face. That's why I feel like I've been punched in the gut as I descend the stairs. But it's the memories I can't seem to let go of that stop me inches from the door.

"Please, Piper," Dalton mutters on the other side of the door. "Please let me in."

The desperation in his voice makes me feel like a fool for only thinking about the past and not considering what the future could hold.

The doorbell rings again, but I'm frozen in place, stuck, knowing that if I open the door, I'm doing more than letting Dalton Payne in my house. I'd be letting him into my heart, and that stupid muscle is frantic with the need to be loved and nurtured.

Let go of the past. That was Frankie's suggestion. Dillon told me to make him fall in love with me, then break his heart, and if I go by the confession to his sister, he's already there. The breaking of the heart is the difficult thing, though. I just don't have it in me. I'm not composed of the things required to do that.

It's what makes it so difficult to put myself in his path.

And yet, I open the door when the bell rings for the fifth time.

"Hey," I say as soon as his head darts up to look at me.

Surprise is clear on his face, and I grin, knowing he didn't expect me to open the door. I love being able to shock him.

"Hey," he says back.

We stand and stare at each other, and after hearing what he said to Peyton, it's like I'm looking at a new person. I'm finally allowing myself to see the person he claims he is rather than the monster that's haunted me for years.

"I just came over to..." He grips the back of his neck. "I wanted to see if you wanted to go grab a snow cone."

My brows shoot up. Not exactly what I was expecting him to say.

"A snow cone?"

"Yeah. You know, shaved ice covered in like flavored syrup?"

Two months ago, I would see his explanation as a way to call me an idiot, but the cute smile on his face reads of playful sarcasm. He isn't insulting me but trying to make me smile.

I reward him with exactly what he's aiming for.

"That's pretty." His hand raises a few inches but then drops back down at his side.

I did that to him. I made him unsure of his permission to touch me.

"I love your smile."

I clamp my lips closed, refusing to snap out that he would've seen it more often if he wasn't so mean, because we're turning over a new leaf. If he's changed, then I have to do the same. If I'm going to give him even half a chance, I can't keep throwing our past in his face at every turn.

"I think a snow cone sounds amazing."

His face displays his shock when I agree rather than reject his offer.

"Really?"

"So long as you're paying." I wink at him and suddenly feel like an idiot. Who winks at people anymore?

"Of course," he agrees. "Can you drive? I don't have a car."

Guilt slams into me once again.

"Yeah, I can drive."

He waits in the doorway while I grab my purse and keys before guiding me to the driveway. He doesn't reach out to touch me, but he's close enough that I can smell his cologne, and I can admit that I want his hand on me, even if it is at the small of my back while we walk together. The thought no longer makes my skin crawl or bile rise up in my throat, but at the same time it also makes me wonder if I've lost my mind.

I'm willingly getting back into a car with Dalton. The last time this happened, I nearly killed us both.

"You can go the speed limit," he teases ten minutes later as we slowly make our way to the snow cone stand.

"I don't want to wreck," I mutter, maintaining my slow speed and refusing to give in to his playful peer pressure.

"Will you tell me about that night?"

The car jerks abruptly as we pull up to a red light.

He doesn't laugh like I expect him to, and when I look over at him, I wonder if he's getting his memories back. It's my number one worry these days.

I don't want to keep lying to him but confessing the truth will ruin everything. He just told his sister that he loves me, and as much as that shocked me, it also made my heart smile.

"You were mean to me that night," I admit. "We'd just found out about your friends."

"They're no longer my friends," he says. "I don't need them. I need you."

A lump forms in my throat as I try to figure out how to give him what he wants without admitting my role in the entire thing, but that's impossible.

I glide the car into a gas station, parking off to the side so I don't interrupt the flow of traffic for those that are actually here to use the facilities.

"What's wrong?" he asks as I turn to him.

"I'm so sorry," I manage before the sobs wrack my body.

He reaches for me, managing to wrap his arms around my back. My seat belt doesn't allow him to pull me against him, but the sentiment is there.

"Don't apologize," I tell him. "I can't handle it."

"I shouldn't have been drinking that night," he continues. "I'll never do it again. Drinking and driving were incredibly stupid. I can't believe I put you in danger."

My head shakes back and forth, and the guilt in his own voice kills me.

"You didn't," I tell him past the lump in my throat.

"The doctor's said my blood alcohol level was more than double the legal limit. I should be in jail."

"I was driving," I blurt. I can't look at him, so I focus on his chest as the rest of it just flies out of my mouth. "You were so hateful that night, blaming me for what happened at the party. You insulted me the entire drive home. I wasn't paying attention. The car drifted on the shoulder, and I was correcting it when you grabbed the wheel. We overcorrected. There was another car coming, and the wheel was jerked, and we went off into the ravine."

Silence fills the car with my confession, and Dalton grows stiff beside me.

I rush to tell him the rest because he may never talk to me again after this.

"The car toppled over and over, and I wasn't even mad as we rolled down the hill. I didn't care that I wrecked your perfect car. I didn't get upset until I looked over and you were no longer there. One minute you were berating me, and the next you were gone." I finally find the courage to look up at him. "I looked for you. I yelled until I couldn't speak, but you were nowhere. You were just—gone."

"Hey." He cups my face, and for a split second I wonder if he's going to wrap his fingers around my throat. "It was just a car."

My eyes search his as shock and confusion war with each other in my head.

"You loved that car. It meant everything to you."

His thumb swipes at the tears that continue to roll down my cheeks.

"I was a materialistic ass. It was just a car." His eyes search mine before settling on my lips. "I'm just glad you're okay."

"But, you're not."

"I'm perfect," he argues, but not in a narcissistic sort of way.

"Your memories are gone. That's my fault."

"I'm glad my memories are gone." His hand trembles as he cups my face. "I wish I could wipe yours as well. I wish I could go back in time and undo every terrible thing I did to you, take back every hateful word, and do things differently."

"I didn't mean to lie, but your mom visited me in the hospital, and when I found out she presumed you were driving, I didn't correct her."

Since I'm confessing, I might as well put it all out there.

"Everyone thinks you were driving because you never let anyone drive that car, and I just let them. Everyone is going to hate me when they find out. Not like that changes much for the people at school, but my parents may never forgive me."

"It was an accident." He forces my chin up when I try to look away. "I'm not mad, not about any of it. You could've kept it all a secret, but you're an amazing person."

"D-do you hate me?"

His face softens even more. "Baby, I could never hate you, and you don't have to worry about anyone else finding out. I'm going to let them keep thinking I was driving."

"Wh-what? Why would you do that?" I don't even want that if I'm being honest with myself. The guilt is too much to keep dealing with every day.

"The truth doesn't change anything, so there's no point." He shrugs as if the pain and disgrace I've suffered with for the last month were for nothing.

"I'm not asking that of you."

"I know." He gives me a weak smile. "Are you still up for that snow cone?"

I can't help but chuckle. My confession has been eating me alive, and he's acting like I just told him I broke a plate in his kitchen, rather than drove his car off a ravine and totaled it.

"I need a minute," I confess. "My face must be a mess."

A sharp breath escapes his lips when I lean closer and reach for the napkins in the glovebox.

"Your face is as beautiful as always."

I smile at his generous lie, but otherwise, keep my lips shut. My luck has to run out soon. Not long ago he confessed he loved me, and he doesn't seem to care that I ruined his life. The other shoe will drop soon, and I don't know that I'll be ready for it. He's already broken down the walls around my heart.

His next blow will be deadly.

I'm sure of it.

Chapter 27

Dalton

I watch Piper as she dabs the tissue under her eyes. She's absolutely gorgeous, and I'd scream it from the rooftops if I could.

Am I shocked at hearing her confess that she was driving my car that night? I guess I am, but it doesn't change anything.

"Are you sure you don't hate me?" she asks, keeping her eyes on her hands.

"Positive."

She sighs and leans back against the driver's seat. She's no longer sobbing, but the tears haven't stopped flowing down her pink cheeks.

"I saw you in the hospital," I whisper. "You walked past my room, but all I got was a cursory glance. My mom had to tell me who you were, and I hated myself. I hated that I couldn't remember you. How in the hell does someone forget an angel?"

She snorts, unladylike and loud.

I'm grinning when she turns her head to look at me.

"Really?"

"It sounds corny, but it's true. While I was out, my entire world was black and gray. Then you walked by with long blonde hair and the brightest blue eyes I'd ever seen."

"Did they do a personality transplant during your surgery, too?"

She smiles at me, and I want to take a snapshot of this moment and hold it in my heart forever. God, I'd be the luckiest man in the world if this girl actually gave me a chance, if she actually let me love her.

"I love how you don't give me an inch when I'm being corny," I say instead of laying the confessions I said to Peyton at her feet. "It's only going to make this so much sweeter when you're mine."

"Don't get ahead of yourself." Those are her words, but they no longer hold the bite of anger or unease that they had each time we've talked.

"Let's go get that snow cone," I tell her, because all I want to do is unhook her seat belt and pull her across to sit on my lap. I want to bury my nose in her hair while my arms are holding her close.

And maybe something more than losing my memories did happen because of the accident, because all of that, although one hundred percent true, sounds ridiculously cheesy, even in my head.

She agrees by putting the car back in gear and merging into traffic.

"Crap," she mutters as we draw closer.

Lined up on the picnic tables beside the snow cone stand are all the people I could go a lifetime without seeing again. Bronwyn is sitting on Kyle's lap while everyone else is either sitting or standing nearby. They're all laughing and having a good time, and I don't begrudge anyone of that, but it's the unsure look on Piper's face that makes me wish they'd all disappear.

"Maybe this wasn't such a good idea," Piper mutters as she pulls into the crowded parking lot. "I won't mind just getting ice cream down the street. I'll understand."

"Understand? Look at me, Piper." Her eyes are slow to meet mine. "What are you talking about?"

"We can go somewhere else if you don't want to go here."

"This is exactly where I want to be." I lean in closer to her. "I'm not hiding you away, baby. I'd be a fool to keep the prettiest girl in the world in the dark."

"If we go out there together, there's no going back for you. Even if you get your memories back and decide against whatever it is you think you feel about me, you'll be a pariah."

"Whatever it is, I *think* I feel about you, huh?" I huff a humorless laugh as I sling open my car door.

Either this woman isn't listening, or she's so broken from the pain I've caused in the past she just can't believe what she's hearing. That changes here and now.

"Get out," I tell her after yanking open her car door. "Now, Piper."

With the quickness of honey in the winter, she unbuckles and slides out of the car.

"Everyone is staring at us," she whispers as she stands in front of me.

I ease her door closed and press her against it.

"Are you nervous?" I ask as I inch toward her.

Her hands are trembling at her sides, but instead of letting her eyes dart toward the group of people who are exceptionally quiet, considering how animated they were when we pulled in, she keeps her focus on her feet.

"I'm a little nervous. Are you nervous?"

"I am," I admit. "I want to hold your hand, but I'm terrified you're going to hit me in front of everyone."

"That would be embarrassing," she says quietly, and I'm going to be in serious trouble if she doesn't stop watching my mouth.

"Incredibly so," I agree, my face mere inches from hers.

"They're still staring at us," she repeats.

"They don't exist, baby. It's only you and me here."

"What are you doing?" Fear laces her tone when I lean my face closer.

"Making sure everyone here knows you're mine."

"Dalton—"

I swallow her worries.

I lick away her fears.

I press my body against hers and give her all the strength she'll ever need to stand at my side.

Her fingers tangle in the sides of my t-shirt, and even though she's shoved me away twice when we've done this before, right now, she's pulling me closer. There's no longer hesitancy in the way she opens her mouth and lets me in. She doesn't draw her tongue back to get away from mine. She gives as good as she gets, and I'm grateful we're in public because I don't think I could be a gentleman if we were alone.

My blood is on fire, my breath short and ragged when I pull my mouth from hers. Her eyes glisten, but the tears from earlier are gone, replaced with a sheen of adoration and happiness.

"Get a room whore!" I tense at the insulting words as they're thrown our way. I'm not all that familiar with Bronwyn's voice, but I know she's the one who just said it.

"Don't," Piper says, her fingers in my shirt holding me tighter when I begin to pull away.

"I won't let her treat you this way," I seethe.

"They don't exist."

My jaw clenches, tightening to the point of pain, but I can't look away from her.

"Do you want to go set them straight, or do you want to kiss me again?"

All I can do is lean in and press my lips to hers again. From the outside, the kiss is rated PG, but with the way my blood is pumping to every area of my body but my actual brain, it feels erotic and intoxicating. I feel ashamed for having my mouth on her like this in public. Not because I'm embarrassed about standing here with her like this, but because others have opinions about things that shouldn't concern them.

"You're hard," Piper whispers against my lips, and it makes me realize I'm crushing my hips against hers.

The pressure is phenomenal, but clearly, she's uncomfortable.

"I'm sorry." I try to take a step back, but she's still tangled in my shirt. Fire and need for her are burning through my veins.

"Don't apologize. I think it's sweet."

"Sweet?" I choke on a laugh. "I would've guessed you'd be disgusted."

Her brows draw in as she looks up at me. "Why would I be disgusted? It just means that you are attracted to me, so much that you can't control your body's reactions. It's sweet."

"I don't want to embarrass you," I confess, "but if we walk to the snow cone stand to order right now, the entire world is going to know exactly how you make me feel."

She bites the corner of her lip, and it's easy to tell she's actually working through the possible scenarios of this.

"You've got that devious look in your eyes, baby, and believe me, I love it. I'll do it if you want me to."

"Are you implying that I want you to strut around the snow cone stand with a boner just to make your ex-girlfriend aware of what I do to you?"

Man, how in the hell did I resist this girl for so long?

I pull away from her, adjusting my dick, so it's more pronounced and turn to walk toward the ordering window.

She squeals and pulls me back.

"Please don't," she pants against my lips. "Put that thing away."

She kisses *me* this time. This time it's her tongue demanding entrance to my mouth, and right here in the parking lot of *Mr. Cones*, Piper Schofield steals my entire heart.

I cup her neck, running my thumb along her cheek as she takes everything I'm offering her, and when she pulls back, we're both breathless and smiling like idiots.

"Better?"

"Baby," I swipe her swollen lower lip with the very tip of my thumb, "if you think that's what makes an erection go away, you have a lot to learn about a man's body."

"All of that is true," she whispers against my lips. "I don't know anything. Think you can teach me a thing or two?"

Where did this little vixen come from?

"I'll tutor you day and night until you've learned it all," I promise, but I pull my hips away from hers. "But this isn't the place for your first lesson. I'll need you alone and away from prying eyes for that."

She grins, and the fear and trepidation twisting her face up when we arrived are no longer visible.

"Tell me what happens after we get our snow cones."

I grip her hip with my hand but do my best to keep my body from touching hers. I wasn't joking about being turned on when she's within eyesight.

"We're going to go sit on that picnic table under the tree and enjoy them," I tell her.

She frowns. "I figured we were going to get them and leave. My parents aren't at home. We could start my first lesson today."

"Jesus, Piper." I rest my forehead against hers, totally in love with the suggestion, but knowing it can't happen.

Jumping into bed with her isn't the way to her heart. I don't doubt that a couple of minutes of kissing her would make it easy enough to slide between her trim thighs, but sex isn't all I want from her. That comes as a reward after she gives me her heart, and I won't take the bonus until I have the main prize.

Chapter 28

Piper

"Don't give me that look," I tell Dalton as we settle on the picnic table under the tree just like he suggested. "It's good!"

"Pickle juice?" His nose scrunches even more. "It's disgusting. I figured you'd go for something like blue coconut or banana."

I scoop another heaping spoonful of my snow cone in my mouth and smile. "I can't risk a flavor that may have strawberries in it."

He looks down at his cherry-flavored snow cone. "Well, crap. I didn't even think of that."

He places it to the side, making it obvious he doesn't plan on eating any more of it, then he jumps down from the tabletop and starts to walk away.

"Where are you going?"

"To buy a bottle of water."

"You can eat the snow cone, Dalton."

He places his hands on my knees and moves in closer. "But can I kiss you if it has strawberry in it?"

Despite the pickle-flavored juice melting on my tongue, my mouth runs dry. Everything is different from how it was this morning. After hearing his confession while on the phone with Peyton, after him not hating me when I confessed about driving his car, how could it not be?

I've finally given in to what my gut has been telling me for a while. Dalton Payne is not the same man he was weeks ago, and that realization has opened my eyes to what we could be together.

"Y-You better go grab that water," I suggest.

His lips on me are about all that I want right now, and I'm grateful he's doing something to remedy the possible allergic reaction I could have to his snow cone choice because honestly, I'd probably risk the anaphylaxis to kiss him again.

He licks his lips suggestively but pulls away at the last second. My breaths don't come easier until he's standing behind a mom with two little boys waiting to place their order.

How is it that I miss him when he's only a dozen feet away from me? Am I so starved for attention from the opposite sex that I go crazy with a couple of kisses? I think I need to have my head checked because I can't help but feel like this is just another prank. My heart is telling me that Dalton really means what he says, that his confession to his sister came from a good place, but the tortured and tormented girl in me is still cautious.

"Hey." I snap my head up at the feminine voice, my hands already beginning to shake with what's coming.

Violet, a girl from school that I don't really know, is standing in front of me with a bright smile. She was never one to be mean to me at school, but she also never did anything to stop the bullying either. In my opinion, those people who just stand on the outskirts of the group and watch while others are humiliated are just as guilty as the ones actively abusing others.

"Hi," I say with caution.

"Can I join you?"

My eyes instinctively dart toward the snow cone stand, searching for Dalton. I'm not looking so he can rescue me but trying to find his eyes and reaction to determine if he's involved with this setup.

Dalton isn't even looking this way. He's smiling at the woman behind the counter with his money in hand, ready to pay for his bottle of water.

"Why?" I ask, giving Violet my full attention. "Did your friends send you over here?"

"They're not my friends." She doesn't snap the words at me, but disgust drips from her tone.

"You're hanging out with them," I remind her. "Doesn't that make them your friends?"

"No," she answers, sitting beside my feet on the picnic table.

I'm sitting on the tabletop, and the distance between us, even though she's close makes me feel a little better.

"I only hang around them because I'm bored," she says, but it's not the full truth.

I simply stare at her, wondering why she's here to begin with.

"It's super shitty, and I know I've never said anything when they've picked on you, but I didn't want to be included in their tormenting." She heaves a harsh sigh from her lips. "I never laughed like the others. I don't know if you know that or not."

"I know you were at Dalton's little pool party the other day. If you're not friends with them, why would you go?"

Does this girl really think that I'm so hard up for friends that she can slide right over here, and I'll welcome her with open arms? I have twelve years of built-up cynicism that wouldn't allow for that even if I wanted to be friends with her, which I don't.

"Boredom?" She shrugs her shoulders, looking past me toward the crowd of rowdy teenagers on the other side of the lot. "I just wanted to say sorry for not speaking up. They didn't send me here, and I don't want to associate with them at all. I figured if Dalton was starting a new group, one that didn't treat people poorly, then I could—"

"You thought you could what?" I snap. This girl has lost her mind, thinking she can hop from one side to the other. I've decided people like her are worse than the ones participating in being mean.

"I just want friends," she mutters, and just like that, she makes me feel sorry for her.

"They're going to be mean to you if you stick around much longer," I warn her.

"I know." Her back straightens, but she never pulls her eyes from mine.

"Hi. I'm Dalton." Saved by the handsome boy. He holds his hand out to her. "You were the one at the pool party that was happy I put those jerks in their place."

This is news to me.

"Violet," she says with a hint of awe in her voice as she shakes his hand. "It's been a long time coming."

Dalton has to pull his hand away from hers when she holds it a little too long, and I can't really fault her for the hearts practically dancing in her eyes. He's incredibly good-looking, but the thought of her crushing on him bothers me more than her keeping her lips closed when she had witnessed me getting bullied at school.

Dalton takes his place by my side, making a point to swish his mouth several times with the water he just purchased before speaking again.

My cheeks flush with his actions, knowing that he's thinking of kissing me just like I have been doing since he pulled his lips away from mine a few minutes ago.

"Are you going to be a senior, too?" Dalton asks Violet, and I bristle at the fact that he's interacting with her at all.

Then I do my best to step back and look at his point of view. He doesn't know anyone, and he's able to approach each person as if they're brand new. He isn't worried about what happened in the past. He's only concerned with how they act now. Maybe I should do the same.

"Junior," Violet answers.

"Hey, Vi."

We all turn our heads to the person that just walked up. Drake is another one of those that sort of floated around the mean people, and like Violet, he never participated in the daily doses of torture.

Dalton introduces himself to Drake, and before long, we have a group of about ten people at our table. I remain silent, watching these people gravitate to Dalton like shelter in the storm. Is it possible that there's an entire populous at Westover Prep that has just been waiting for things to change?

Dalton, even with no memories, doesn't miss a beat becoming the center focus once again to the group. He smiles and chats, asking questions about school and sports, but he keeps my hand clasped in his the entire time, even taking breaks while others are talking to grin at me and press his lips to the back of my hand. Everyone that's joined us takes it in stride. They don't bat an eyelash at the affection he's showing me, and it makes my nerves calm a little.

He glances my way, concern marking his brow when I wince from brain freeze after taking too big of a bite of my snow cone.

"You okay?"

"I think the pickle juice is eating a hole in my head," I mutter through the pain.

He rubs my temples, not missing a beat in the conversation with those that have gathered around us.

Kyle and Bronwyn's group has dwindled. Many of their inner circle watched us for a while, but then left the snow cone shop altogether. Thankfully, they didn't bother to come over and fake being friends. I don't know that I could've handled that if they had. I'm not a mean person, even after being bullied for a long time. I've never wanted to outwardly criticize or gloat, but watching Bronwyn huff and puff as our group got more attention as time passed, I can't help the little smile pulling at my lips.

I will never be friends with the trio of hatefulness and spite, but maybe they will quit being vile now that Dalton is different.

When we get up to leave, my snow cone long forgotten and melted, several of the people ask about meeting up again later in the week. Dalton smiles at them but doesn't confirm any plans.

"See?" he says as we climb back into my car. "That wasn't so bad."

"I feel like I'm in the middle of a teen drama series," I mutter as we drive back to my house. My head still aches, but it's not bad enough to really worry about right now.

He laughs, a husky sound that fills the inside of the car.

"You didn't have a good time?"

I don't answer him, but only because I don't know how. Yes, it was nice being around people that weren't being hateful, but the entire time I was waiting for someone to slip up and call me Mary, or for someone to walk up and say something harsh. I've been on pins and needles the entire time, and two hours of stress has left me exhausted.

"It was fine," I finally answer when I feel his eyes burning a hole in the side of my head.

"Just fine?" He takes my hand when I park in my driveway. "We can do better than fine."

A weak smile pulls up one corner of my mouth, but it's the best I can give. I can't even explain the way I feel. Today was what I've hoped for years but having it didn't bring the elation I dreamed of many times.

"Did you hear me?"

I turn my head toward him. "I'm sorry. What?"

"I asked if you wanted to go for a walk. I could push you on the swing."

My eyes narrow at the suggestion. "The swing? What are we nine?"

He shrugs. "It could be fun."

I don't respond, and I don't make a move to get out of the car either. I'm struggling between asking him for some time alone and suggesting we go inside my house.

Feeling drawn to him is really messing with my head, and yet I don't want to spend a second away from him. I don't know if I'm worried that with distance he'll change his mind, maybe realize he doesn't love me and that one of the girls back at the snow cone stand would be a better fit. My lip curls in irritation at the thought of Violet dating him.

"What's that look for?" His finger presses against my lip, and I hang my head in shame for doubting him.

"I just..." I shake my head because it's filled with warring thoughts that are bound to drive me crazy. "I don't know. Maybe you should go home."

"Nope." He doesn't hesitate when he speaks. "We aren't doing this again. I'll say it a million times if I need to. I'll apologize every day for the rest of my life until you believe me, but I'm not letting you get lost in your head while you think of ways to push me out of your life. Don't do this, Piper. Please."

"Dalton." I shake my head again. "I can't help it. I have a lot of stuff to work through."

"We can work through it together. Tell me what you need, and I'll give it to you." I sigh. "Not space. I'll give you anything but space."

"Are you a mind reader now?"

He frowns at me even though I'm trying to be playful.

"It's easy for you to move past what's happened because you can't remember it, but it's going to take longer for me."

"What can I do to help?"

"Nothing," I answer honestly. "I feel like a fool for even sitting here with you. Like I'm crazy for even considering dating you."

"You're mine," he whispers.

"The alpha routine doesn't help," I tell him, but it kind of does in a way.

Not having to make that decision, knowing that he's going to be there regardless of how I treat him, is a powerful thing. And even though I'm not a vindictive person at heart, it makes me want to test his loyalty, to push him and see what I can get away with as retribution for how he's treated me.

Then I remember the shine in Violet's eyes when he introduced himself earlier. He's got options whether he wants to use them right now or not.

"Piper?" His finger hooks under my chin as he urges me to look at him. "Tell me what I can do, and I'll do it. I know it's going to take time, but please promise me that you'll at least try. Give me a chance, baby, and I'll prove to you that I'm worth it."

Chapter 29

Dalton

"This isn't what I had in mind," I mutter.

"You said, and I quote, 'Tell me what to do, and I'll do it.' Did you not tell me that earlier this week?" She raises an eyebrow, a tiny smile playing on her pink lips, and I'm a goner for this girl.

"I did, but I didn't think you'd have me dressed as 'Clifford the Big Red Dog' on the hottest day of the year."

"It's barely eighty-five," she tells me.

"But it's like a million degrees in this costume." I don't mention that my balls are sticking to my damn legs because I don't think she can appreciate the torture that entails.

"We'll only be out here for a few more minutes. It's almost time to go inside and read."

She asked me to help with her volunteer hours at the library, and I readily agreed, knowing that I'd do just about anything to spend a little more time with her. I'd still be here right now, even if I knew what I was getting into.

"It's so hot," I grumble again as she greets families of small children with a wide smile like she's living her best life right now.

"I'll make it up to you," she purrs in my ear as a family of five walks away.

"How so?" I ask, my blood already growing warmer with the thoughts of how the repayment could go.

She's different than she was in the car on Monday, but every once in a while, I catch a look in her eyes that makes me want to wrap my arms around her and assure her that I'm the man she needs me to be. It's when she's alone that I worry the doubt will take over, and I wait, holding my breath every morning until she shows up at the house to tutor Peyton. Three out of the last four days, she's walked right into my arms, pressing her lips to mine before going to find my sister, but Thursday was a rough day for her, and she just gave me a sad smile and a peck on the lips before disappearing into the kitchen. That day I gave her space, not knowing if she needed that or for me to make myself more visible. The space seemed to work because when she was done, she found Preston and me in the pool splashing around, and she finally had the smile I love so much on her pretty face.

Today is a good day, too.

Today, she came to my front door and pressed her lips to mine before she even spoke a word. Today, she didn't pull her hand from mine when my dad saw us standing on the front porch together. Today, she grinned the entire time on the way to the library, and now I know why.

She's rejoicing in my misery.

"How so?" I repeat when she winks at me as another family makes their way into the library.

Her teeth dig into her bottom lip before she speaks, "How do you *want* me to repay you?"

I don't know if she means for her voice to be sultry or if she's just curious, but my cock jerks in the costume because of the way she's looking at me.

"I'm sweating bullets," I remind her. "Maybe you could help me in the shower later?"

I'm pressing my luck right now. Other than a few hands above the shoulders make-out sessions, we haven't even gotten as close as we did earlier this week at the snow cone stand. I'm proud to say I've had herculean restraint where she's concerned.

"You want me to pick out a change of clothes?" She inches closer, and my eyes do their best to stay focused on hers rather than her mouth or the tiny amount of cleavage swelling at the top of her tank top. "Maybe get you a fresh towel?"

"I was thinking more along the lines of washing my back." I clear my throat when the words come out husky and barely intelligible. "Maybe making sure my legs are clean?"

"My clothes would get wet."

"You could take them off," I suggest as she steps even closer to me. "Maybe shower with me."

Her throat works on a swallow, and then she nearly kills me by licking her lips. "I don't hate the idea."

"That's a start." My mouth is dry, and I'm moments away from grabbing her hand and insisting we go back to my house.

"Why do you turn me on so much?" she whispers. "I probably shouldn't even admit it out loud, but I find you almost irresistible."

Words that should make me smile in victory are like buckets of ice-cold water being poured on my head. It's clear she still feels like she can't be completely honest with me, and it's a barrier I've been fighting against. I know I need to give her time, and I'm doing my best, but the one step forward two steps back is frustrating. I'm not upset with her, but at myself, for the monster I used to be, that's made her so apprehensive in the first place.

I palm her face, looking directly into her eyes. "I'm not filing things away to use against you later, Piper. We're working at your pace here. There's no pressure on my end. Please tell me that you know that?"

"I do," she responds immediately.

"Look, Momma! It's Clifford!" Before I can pull away from Piper, a little girl, no older than three runs toward us with a huge smile on her face.

"Hi, there!" I tell her, using a fake voice for some reason.

Many kids have been leery of getting close to me in this costume, but this girl isn't afraid at all.

"Are you ready for storytime?" I ask her.

She nods enthusiastically before sprinting ahead of her mom to go inside.

"Ready to read to them?" Piper asks with a brilliant smile.

I nod, just as the little girl did, but I don't think I'm giving off the same effect. The big red head just slips back and forth, and I probably look like I'm headbanging to silent music from Piper's point of view.

***

"That wasn't so bad," I admit as I strip out of the stifling costume in the library's employee breakroom.

"I knew you'd have a great time." Piper beams.

"I didn't say I had a great time," I confess, sticking with my vow to never lie to her again. "I said it wasn't bad."

"So, you don't want to help next weekend?"

My eyes narrow at her because she already knows the answer. "Does it include another costume that's going to have to be dry-cleaned before someone else wears it?"

"Next week is *Harold and the Purple Crayon*. We're going to draw pictures. No costumes involved."

"That I can do," I tell her, wanting to pull her into my arms just like I've wanted since we arrived, but I wasn't lying about the temp inside that suit.

"What are your plans for the rest of the day?" she asks as she gathers the suit up.

I wipe sweat off my face with the bottom of my t-shirt, loving the way her eyes are glued to my abs.

"I can think of a few things. What are you thinking right now?"

Her guilty eyes snap up to mine, and I grin at her.

"We haven't been alone all week," she says, derailing my thoughts of grabbing ice cream or heading to the mall in the next town.

"That's been purposeful on my part," I admit.

"You don't want to be alone with me?"

"I want nothing more."

"But you've purposely kept that from happening?"

Her head tilts in confusion, but the saucy look in her eyes makes me wonder if she's merely playing coy.

"I don't want to take things any further than what you're comfortable with."

"And you think if I'm alone with you, I won't be able to resist you?" She bites her damn lip again, and the sight of that flesh between her teeth makes my body come alive with need.

"I think you may want things in the moment, but I couldn't live with myself if you regretted something you did with me. I know you still struggle with trusting me."

She sobers with my words, the playful look on her face melting away until she's frowning in my direction.

"I'm trying," she whispers.

"I know. That's why I've wanted to keep things light with no pressure. Your pace, remember?"

"We can do things other than having sex."

Oh, God. This woman is going to kill me.

"We could go to the mall," I offer, "or grab some ice cream?"

Lord knows I need something to cool me down. I'm pretty sure I've had sex before, but since I can't remember it, I'm a ball of horny energy. My mind is always on sex. Always. And even though in my head I want to take things slowly, I know my body will be able to change my mind if I'm in the position to make it happen.

"Or," her tone changes back from cautious Piper to the vixen I love more and more each day, "we could go make out at the park."

"The park?" That seems like a semi-private, yet very public place. We could be mostly safe from my overactive libido there.

"You want to go for a walk?"

She smiles, the wicked thoughts in her head displayed blatantly on her pretty face. "I don't want to walk."

I swallow thickly, both hating and loving that a simple conversation has set my body on fire. If I thought she was ready, and it was her suggestion, I'd take her right here in this breakroom; consequences be damned.

But we're not there yet.

"You want to make out," I clarify, "in the park."

"Yes," she answers. "And if you're a good boy, I may even let you get to second base."

My eyes dart to her chest, watching it rise and fall rapidly with her elevated breathing.

"You like that idea," she says with a chuckle.

"I love any idea that involves touching you or spending time with you. I'd be almost as happy just hanging out with you watching a movie."

It's mostly the truth, but the laughter that emits from Piper tells me that she knows it's not one-hundred-percent honesty.

"Let's drop this," she holds the Clifford costume up, "at the dry cleaners, and we'll go from there."

Chapter 30

Piper

"Why are you whispering the alphabet?" I laugh at the sight of Dalton with his eyes squeezed closed. His lips have been repeating letters rather than kissing mine like I want them to be doing.

"Your hand," he mutters between M and N.

"This one?" I flex my fingers on his thigh.

"Y-yeah. Every time you do that, it makes my jeans tighter. Well, my—" He clears his throat. "Let's go for that walk."

"I think that bulge is the problem, not your jeans."

His lips work faster, already back to XYZ for the second time since he last spoke.

"Dalton?" I remove my hand from his leg and cup his face. "Are you freaking out?"

His head shakes back and forth. "I'm trying not to nut in my jeans."

A bark of laughter escapes my lips. "Seriously?"

"Are you making fun of me? That's really mean, Piper."

I can't tell if he's joking or if he's serious.

"I'm not making fun of you." I sit back in my seat since I was practically on top of him and pout. "I just didn't think I affected you that much."

He shakes his head, eyes still closed, but at least he's no longer repeating the dang alphabet. "You just don't understand."

"Is this the part where you make fun of me for being a virgin and not knowing anything about guys?"

His eyes snap to mine. "I love that you don't have any experience, but what you're not understanding is that I don't remember anything from my past. I might as well be a virgin, too."

He huffs, and I don't know if he's irritated with himself or me.

"So, you're keyed up?" I hedge. He nods, tongue sneaking out to lick his lips. The action shoots straight between my thighs, and it's my turn to swallow the lump forming in my throat. "Well, I am, too."

His eyelids lower, heat filling his gaze as he watches my mouth. "And I'm ecstatic about that, but you can hide your reaction to me. I can't do that."

He motions to the erection straining in his jeans.

"You want me to describe in detail how wet my panties are?"

He groans again, head rolling on the headrest before he focuses outside of the car.

He suggested the park, but I'm driving, so we ended up in the most secluded place I could find. The lone woman walking her dog is so far away, I can't even tell what breed is on the other end of her leash.

"I'd love to find out how wet you are," he says after a long moment.

I bite my lips, on the verge of offering him just that, but he seems tortured and turned on by the suggestion. I don't want to pressure him into anything, not that I think he'd turn me down. But it's the sting of possibly being rejected that makes me take pause.

"We can just make out," I offer instead. "Kissing and above the waist stuff."

He rolls his head back in my direction. "And that may still be enough to make a mess in my jeans."

"Okaaay," I draw out. "Then, I'm up for suggestions."

He shakes his head as if he's battling inside of it. "Come here."

He holds his arms open wide, and I lean in closer.

"No," he says when I pucker my lips playfully for him to kiss. "Straddle me."

"What?"

That doesn't seem very conducive to preventing what he doesn't want to happen. My core throbs at the suggestion, but I don't move.

"Come here," he repeats. "Just kissing, promise."

"And what about your problem?" I point to the thickness in his lap.

"That's not going to go away until I take care of it."

"Then take care of it."

His eyes widen as his frantic eyes dart back and forth between mine. "You want me to jack off in your car?"

"Eww!" I swat his chest. "No. That's gross."

"That's the only way to make it go away," he grumbles.

"Go into the bathroom over there." I motion my head to the concrete building at the beginning of the trailhead.

"That would be pointless because I'm always hard around you. Plus, I'm not going to rub one out in a public bathroom."

"Then what—"

"Hush." He presses his fingers to my lips. "Come here. Let me worry about it later. Climb on my lap."

I realize I should exercise more, or at least stretch more often because climbing into his lap in my car is clunky and not as easy as I've seen it done in the movies. I nearly knee Dalton in the face, but he has quick reflexes and somehow prevents my leg from making contact with his nose.

"Sexy, right?" I mutter when I finally settle on top of him.

The door is digging into my left knee, and the other one is crammed in beside the gear shift, but the warmth of his body is a lovely reward.

"Everything about you is sexy."

"I'm already in your lap. Don't get corny now."

"Lower," he urges with his hands on my lower back.

I drop down, coming to rest exactly where he wants me. His thickness is to the left and under my leg, and it doesn't seem like it would be comfortable for him, but he doesn't complain.

"Mouth," he whispers, and I move without a second thought.

His lips are warm, teasing, and slow against mine. There isn't a hint of the frenzy filling my own veins, and I let him lead, willing to follow him anywhere at this point.

I whimper a moan, my hips moving of their own accord.

"Stay still," he whispers. "Just let me kiss you."

Need as I've never felt before thrums through my body, and even though I want to rub myself all over him like a cat desperate for attention, I stay as still as possible.

His hands flex on my back, kneading my muscles in all the right places as his tongue explores my mouth with sensual licks that begin to drive me crazy.

"Touch me," I beg, and I'm not sure where I want him to start because I need him everywhere.

I want his hands and mouth on my breasts, but my core is also craving attention.

"Where?" he asks, his lips trailing hot kisses down my neck.

I don't answer him, afraid of sounding too reckless at this moment, but he must be a mind reader because his lips leave my neck as he begins to lick and kiss the swell of my breasts.

"Is this okay?" he asks on a pant as his tongue teases the seam of my tank top.

"Yes," I moan.

My nose scrunches up as I cringe with the need evident in my voice, but I don't spend long worrying if I sound like a fool because Dalton hooks a finger into the top of my tank, pulling it down to give his mouth more room to explore. The top of my lacy bra is exposed to him, and I can see what he's talking about when I look down to watch him. My chest is flushed with my arousal, and from this angle, my boobs look spectacular. Now I know why so many women take selfies from a higher angle. It's very flattering.

"You're perfect," he praises against my heaving chest. "So perfect."

Emboldened by his praise, I reach up and pull down the cup of my bra. Dalton just stares. He doesn't open his mouth to speak or swipe his tongue at my nipple that's beading to the point of pain at his perusal.

He. Just. Stares.

Heat fills my cheeks, making my embarrassment clear to anyone who might see me, but when I apologize and move to pull my clothes back up, he grips my hand preventing me from doing it.

"Don't," he whispers, and the tone is reverent and grateful. "Let me look at you."

My mouth turns into a desert as my breaths rush out in uneven puffs.

"Show them both to me."

My hands tremble as I pull down the other side of my bra, and we both watch as the second nipple furls to match the first.

"This is the most magnificent thing I've ever seen." His voice is a whisper, but it seeps into me like warmth on a cold winter's day. He looks up at me, his eyes sparkling with some unknown emotion. "C-can I touch them."

"Please," I beg.

And when he does, when he reaches both hands up and palms each of my breasts, I'm certain I've never felt anything more powerful in my life.

"Jesus," he grunts, rubbing his thumbs over the peaks before pinching them lightly between two fingers. "You're amazing. These... God... I'm a lucky bastard."

His eyes find mine once more, and they're filled with an unspoken pleading, and all I can do is nod my agreement. I don't know what he's asking, but I'm willing to let him do just about anything at this point.

My dreams are fulfilled when he lowers his head, licking at one nipple and then the other.

And I was wrong about his touch being the most powerful thing because his mouth on my sensitive flesh outranks it by leaps and bounds.

"Dalton," I moan when he sucks my nipple into his mouth, his cheeks hollowing out with the action.

"Feel good?" he asks as he turns his head to lavish the same attention on my other breast.

"So good. Don't stop."

He doesn't. He keeps his mouth on me until my hips are working against his of their own volition. He keeps kneading, sucking, and nipping at my breasts, grunting his own pleasure when I press my core against him, looking for relief.

Something akin to a howl spews from my throat when the combination of everything takes me over the edge. His mouth slows as my orgasm ebbs, and even though I'm satiated with all of it, I still bury my face in his throat, embarrassed by what just happened. The orgasm was so powerful my head throbs with each pulse, making my eyes scrunch from the radiating pain.

"Don't hide from me," he says as he urges my head back.

His lips are red and puffy, and it makes his mouth that much more delectable. I kiss him because I just have to, and he kisses me back with the same needy fervor. The headache fades away as my heart rate evens out, and I'm grateful for it.

"You came," he mumbles against my mouth as his lips turn up in a smile.

"Sorry."

His smile grows even wider. "Don't ever apologize for something like that. It thrills me that I was able to help."

"Yeah?"

He nods. "But you need to get back over there."

He motions to the driver's seat, but I'm not interested in that suggestion. He's still thick and hard under me, and that's an issue I want to resolve. He brought me pleasure, now it's his turn.

"That doesn't interest me at all," I tell him as I reach for the button on his jeans.

"Piper." He swallows, and I can tell he's pained by what he's going to say next. "Two cars pulled up while we were umm... while you were... there are more people at the park now."

"What?" I hiss rubbing my hand over the fogged-up window. Sure enough, there are not two cars like he thought, but a handful lined up in the parking lot beside us. "Do you think they saw?"

I scramble into the driver's seat, managing it much faster than the crawl into his lap.

He chuckles, and I watch as he adjusts his erection in his jeans. "I think the windows were fogged up enough, but anyone could guess what was going on."

My hands tremble as I push my hair out of my face.

"Calm down," he says, grabbing my hands and pulling them to his lips. "They didn't see anything."

"But it could be people who recognize this car. What if they tell my dad?"

"I don't think anyone would bat an eye at knowing a high school senior is making out with her boyfriend at the park."

There are so many angles I could approach that statement, but it's the word boyfriend that stops me in my tracks.

"Boyfriend?"

He grins. "I better be your boyfriend. If not, I'd feel used. I don't just go around making random girls c—"

I squeal, cupping my hands over his lips.

"Let's never talk about that again."

"Really?" His eyebrows rise as he mumbles behind my hands. "The sounds you made. The way you arched into my mouth—"

"Enough!" My smile is wide, and I feel his lips turn up under my hands.

"Thank you for sharing that with me," he says as he draws my hands away from his face with his own. "Now, we better get home before your dad sends out a search team."

The sun is beginning to set, which means we've been at the park for hours, and yet it seems like our time is over in the blink of an eye.

"What about your..." I indicate his still straining erection.

"I'll deal with that later."

He gives me the side-eye when I open my mouth to make a few suggestions.

The drive home is happy, but I can feel how tense he is. I've heard stories of how guys peer pressure their girlfriends into doing stuff. Most guys wouldn't be worried about my parents, only able to focus on their own needs, but Dalton is different. It's just one more thing to add to the plus column.

"Why don't you video call me in thirty minutes," I whisper against his lips when he kisses me in my driveway a few minutes later.

"Yeah?"

I nod. "Wait to deal with your problem until then."

His eyes spark. "What do you have in mind?"

"Just wait, and you'll find out."

He nips at my bottom lip. "Thirty minutes, got it."

He presses one last kiss to my lips before standing in my driveway until I make it safely inside.

My dad is waiting near the door with his arms crossed over his chest and a scowl on his face.

"Was that Dalton Payne you were kissing in the driveway?"

My heart races, pounding in my chest. I've had the sex talk with my parents, albeit very formal and anatomically correct seeing as they're both in the medical field, but I've never had a boy talk with either of them.

"Yeah," I answer awkwardly, hoping this conversation doesn't last past the thirty minutes I told Dalton to wait.

"I don't think you should hang around that boy," he says evenly. This is Dad, though, even when he's angry or frustrated, he's calm and collected.

"Dad," I groan. "He's a nice guy."

"He's the reason you got in that wreck." I open my mouth to tell him the truth, but he snaps his hand up. "You're almost eighteen, Piper, and I know I can't control your life, but I think you should think about the consequences of spending time with him. Give it some thought, and I know you'll come to the right decision."

He walks away without another word, leaving me standing there torn between the guy I'm most likely falling for and the disappointment my parents will feel if I date him.

The decision is easy.

Too bad my dad thinks I'll be on his side after the coin toss, he just sent my way.

I rush up the stairs, anxious for that video chat with Dalton.

Chapter 31

Dalton

I don't know where everyone is that lives here, but I don't see a single person on my rush up the stairs. I lock my bedroom door before rushing to my bathroom. My mind is racing with ideas of what Piper has in mind, but I'm still gross from being in that stupid costume, so I rush through a shower, doing everything in my power to ignore the persistent boner hanging between my thighs.

Like I'm preparing for a first date with the prettiest girl in class, I can't decide what to wear after I get out of the shower. I don't want to be presumptuous about her intent, but I leave my shirt off to tempt her, tugging basketball shorts up my legs before falling on the bed.

I test the camera angle, making sure I look okay before video dialing Piper.

Her cheeks are flushed, hair still wet from her own shower when she answers.

"Hey," she says before her perfect teeth dig into the lip, I had the privilege of nibbling on earlier.

"Hey, yourself," I respond.

A few moments of silence pass as we just stare at each other.

"So umm…" She grins wide. "That was fun in the car earlier."

"I enjoyed myself." If I concentrate hard enough, I bet I can still feel the soft texture of her nipples against my tongue.

And that's all it takes for me to go from half-mast to fully erect.

I shift my hips, holding the phone with one hand while resting the other on my dick in a bid to make it calm down.

"It felt really good," she confesses, but she must be embarrassed to be talking about it because she isn't looking directly into the camera anymore. "I want you to feel good, too."

"Yeah?" My heart is racing. "How do we make that happen?"

"I thought…" She swallows so hard, I can see her throat working on camera. "Maybe you can touch yourself."

"And you watch me?" My cock jerks, loving the idea already.

"And I could maybe touch myself."

If she keeps talking like this, I won't even have to have skin on skin contact with my dick. I'm already leaking from the tip at the sight of her fresh face and the bare skin visible from her tank top.

"Is that a dumb idea?" she asks when I take too long to answer her.

"No," I snap. "That's an amazing idea."

"Can I umm, can I see you while you do it?"

I know what she's asking, but I act like I don't. "You can see me now, right?"

I grin just for her.

"I mean your... umm... never mind. This is fine."

"Oh, do you mean this?" I angle the camera down, letting the video pick up the trail of my abs down my happy trail until it skates over my basketball shorts. My erection is evident on my end, but I don't know if it's decipherable on video.

She gasps, and that answers that question.

"What about you?" I ask, turning the camera back to my face. "Do I get to see you, too?"

"If you want."

"Oh, baby. I want that so much." I look around my bed, wanting both hands for this, before spotting an extra pillow. I prop the phone against it, adjusting it slightly so she can get a full view of my face, torso, and the straining member below the waist.

"Wow," she whispers. "Great camera angle. Hold on."

The camera on her end goes wonky, but before long, she's done the same, propping it up, so I have an incredible angle of her body.

"Stop," I tell her when she lifts her hips to pull her shorts off. "Just dip your fingers into your shorts. The first time I see you completely naked, I want it to be in person."

"Okay," she pants. "Do we start now?"

"You're running this show, Piper. You tell me what to do."

"Is this awkward for you?" Her brow furrows. "I don't know that I can tell you what to do. How about you tell me?"

Jesus, this girl is going to be the death of me.

"Slip your left hand under your waistband," I begin. "Pull your tank top up and play with your nipple with your other hand."

"Will you touch yourself, too?" she asks as her hands move to obey my commands.

"Do you want me to?"

"Yes," she moans, and it sends a rush of cold chills over my entire body. "I want to see it."

Without preamble, I lift my hips and shove my shorts down to my knees. My cock springs free, celebrating the cool air with the anticipation of being touched.

"Fast or slow?" she asks, breathlessly.

"Do whatever feels good." I choose slow for myself because there's no way I can make this last, and I want to prolong it as much as possible.

"It all feels good," she whispers, "but my hand doesn't feel as good as your mouth did."

The mention of what happened in her car while I'm touching myself sends a bolt of electricity up my spine.

"I can't wait to taste you again. To put my mouth exactly where those fingers are exploring right now."

She shudders with my dirty words, but I'm being completely honest. I want to taste every inch of her body. I want to spend hours, days, months even finding out exactly what she likes and then giving it to her at every possible opportunity.

"I w-want that, too, Dalton."

"I want to spread you open with my fingers and find every secret you've been hiding under your clothes. I want to spend a lifetime worshipping your body and making you mine."

"Dalton," she moans.

"Fuck, I'm gonna come," I grunt. "Jesus, Piper."

She whimpers, and the tiny sound coming from her own pleasure sends me over the edge. Rope after rope of cum spurts onto my heaving chest, and I look back at the camera just in time to see her stomach contract with the convulsions of her own orgasm.

She moans with pleasure before hissing with pain.

"What's wrong?" I ask when her brow scrunches up.

Her right hand moves from her breast to push against her temple.

"Headache," she answers after a long moment. "I don't think I drank enough water today. I'll be fine."

"Are you sure? I can come over and—"

"I'll be fine," she reassures me, but it takes her a long moment before she realizes her breasts are still on display. Not that I'm complaining, but I recall how quickly she clammed up in the car, so I know her head must be hurting pretty bad if she hasn't pulled her tank down yet.

"I'll see you tomorrow, Dalton." She gives me a weak smile. "I had a lot of fun today."

"I did, too. You should come over a little early tomorrow so I can kiss you before you start helping Peyton."

"Maybe, I will." She winks at me before ending the call.

***

Piper came over early this morning just like I'd hoped she would. We made out like two people who hadn't seen each other in years, even though it was less than twelve hours.

I couldn't convince her to not tutor today, however. I begged and promised all sorts of delicious rewards if she cut the tutoring short, but since Peyton's test is on Friday, Piper refused, saying that she needed these last couple of days to get ready.

I waited all damn day to get her alone, and I think she knew I was waiting not so patiently because they studied an hour longer than normal, only leaving us two hours to hang out before my parents were due home.

But, I'm an optimistic guy because a ton can get accomplished in two hours.

"Where are you going?" I ask Piper when I walk into the kitchen to find her loading her backpack up. "Were you just going to leave?"

Her cheeks redden.

"What's this about?" I press my finger to her heated face.

"What we did last night was crazy," she whispers, her head hung low.

"Do you regret it?"

"No, but—"

I halt her words by stepping in closer to her.

"You were fine this morning when you got here. Where's this coming from now?"

She holds up her phone, and I have to bite the inside of my cheek to keep from smiling. Frustrated with spending the day alone while Piper tutored my sister, I got revenge by sending her a line of texts describing in nauseating detail what I wanted to do to her after she was done.

She never responded back, but clearly, she read them.

"We don't have to do any of that stuff if you don't want to," I assure her.

Most of the things I sent were way over the top and an attempt to get her up to my room even if it was to tell me to stop, but she never showed up.

She doesn't answer me, and it makes me curious. "Unless there's something on the list that interests you?"

Her face is flaming by now, but I take a step back, giving her some space because she isn't smiling.

"Piper?"

Once her notebooks and pens are shoved in her backpack, she looks up at me.

"Is this just sex and messing around? If it is, let me know. I'm not saying I'll be completely turned off by the idea, but I need to know where it's heading. I don't want to get hurt."

The words come out in a rush with barely a breath in the middle.

"No," I answer honestly. "We can slow things way down. I don't want you to think that's all I'm after because it isn't."

"Your lips are on mine before I can even speak, recently. The car in the park. Last night on video." She shakes her. "I feel like that's all there is to us. You said I was your girlfriend, but—"

I press my fingers to her lips, hating that she's always going to second guess my motives. I don't remind her that she instigated the call last night, knowing that it wouldn't be beneficial to either of us.

"Then we take sex off the table. Let's just hang out. Watch a movie or something."

"And that won't make you mad?"

My head snaps back. "No, of course not. Why would I be mad that I get to spend time with the prettiest girl I've ever met?"

She grins now and allows me to lead her into the living room. She holds my hand on the couch, and we make it halfway through the first Harry Potter movie before my parents get home.

Chapter 32

Piper

I woke up this morning with a migraine that even maximum-strength headache medicine couldn't get rid of.

I called Peyton and told her that even opening my eyes hurt, but I'd be over later if I got to feeling better. She was actually happy I wasn't able to make it, complaining that her brain is fried, and it needed a break.

I turned my phone to silent and went right back to sleep, the pain in my temples subsiding just enough to let me drift off.

What seems like mere seconds later, my bed dips, and Dalton's familiar scent fills my nose.

"Hey," I mumble as my covers lift.

"Peyton said you weren't feeling well," he says after pressing a soft kiss to the back of my head. "Is there anything I can do?"

"How did you get into my house?" I know the front door was locked. My parents left this morning through the garage like usual, and I'm the only one who really uses the front door, and I know I locked it when I got home from his house yesterday evening.

"The key under the rock," he explains. "You didn't answer my question. Is there anything I can do to help?"

"Just hold me," I whisper. "I can take more medicine in an hour."

Without another word, Dalton wraps himself around my body, and I doze off again.

Time is meaningless in my dreams, but the pain in my head manages to manifest itself until it's so unbearable that it wakes me.

"Medicine?" Dalton whispers, and it takes all that I can manage to nod my head.

He climbs off the bed, and I'm grateful that he doesn't turn on the lights as he reaches for the bottle on my bedside, offering two pills to me and a glass of water.

I swallow the pills with a groan and fall back onto my pillows. Sleep eludes me this time around, but I find comfort in Dalton's arms. When the meds kick in, I turn in his arms, resting my face against his chest.

"Do you get headaches often?" he says, keeping his voice low.

"Not really. Last year when I had the flu, I had horrible headaches. Well, everything hurt, actually."

"I wish I was here then to help you."

"Oh, you helped," I snort. "My mom asked yours if you could get my assignments. I was so worried about missing school."

"Did I?" he asks.

"You brought assignments alright, but they weren't the ones we'd been given in class."

He groans, the sound a low rumble in his chest, and it makes me smile against his skin.

"But the teachers took sympathy on me since I never get into trouble or cause problems. They counted the grades, but it was still hell trying to get caught up since I worked on a bunch of stuff that wasn't required."

"I'm sorry."

"It's in the past," I tell him. It's the best I can manage because I'll never say, 'It's okay.' That's a form of forgiveness, and even though I love that I'm resting against him right now, I still don't know that I'll ever be able to forgive him for what he's done.

"I wish there was a way to make it up to you. I feel like we missed so much time that could've been spent just like this because I was an asshole. Sorry, I mean a jerk."

"Then let's not waste any more time," I offer.

"What do you mean?"

"Let's get to know one another. Where do you want to go to college?"

"I haven't really thought about it. Where do you want to go?"

"Harvard," I tell him without missing a beat.

"Really?"

"I mean, I don't think I can afford it, so I'll probably end up at State."

"Maybe you'll get a scholarship," he muses. "I think I'd like to go to State, too, but I don't even know what my grades are like."

"You haven't checked into that yet?"

He shrugs, and I feel the movement against my own body. "I've been a little preoccupied."

I know he's talking about me, and I won't even let myself feel bad about that. I don't know his exact GPA, but Dalton Payne isn't some dumb jock. I wouldn't be surprised if he was a straight-A student like me.

"I think we should make plans to go to the same school," he whispers.

"Seriously?" I don't lift my head, but I also don't manage to disguise my surprise.

College is over a year away, and as often as I think about getting out of this town, it still seems like a lifetime until it happens. Is he thinking about us being together in a year? I inwardly kick myself for wondering if our shelf life would extend past the end of the summer.

"Maybe even think of living off-campus so we can share an apartment or something?"

I want to argue with him, tell him that the idea of living together thrills me and terrifies me at the same time, but thinking about that step right now is a little premature. I don't do that, though. I keep my mouth closed and let myself wonder what that would look like.

Would we both have jobs? Take some of the same classes? Time together would be hard to find with a heavy class load, and living together would make it easier, but we don't really have the same desires.

I'd find a library or youth center to volunteer at in my spare time, and he'd probably rush the biggest fraternity on campus, attending parties every weekend. It just wouldn't work.

"You hate the idea, don't you?" He wraps his arm tighter around my back, pulling me impossibly closer. "I still have a year to convince you otherwise."

"We still have to make it through senior year," I mutter. "I don't even know what our first day back to school is going to look like much less the last day."

"Close your eyes," he urges. "Let me describe it to you."

I've spent most of the last ten years living out my own fantasies in my head, imagining a day when I can walk into a classroom with my head held high rather than with darting eyes wondering which idiot was going to make fun of me or trip me, so I figure I can humor him for a moment.

My eyes flutter closed, and for a long moment, I concentrate on the sound of his breathing and the upward rise of his chest as he inhales.

"The first day of our senior year, I'm going to offer you my letterman jacket so you can be reminded of me in the classes we don't have together. You'll refuse it, telling me that I don't own you, but there will be a smile on your pretty lips because we both know that I do." I grin against him. "We'll ride together. You'll probably be driving, seeing as I still don't have a car."

I cringe with the reminder.

"Get out of your head, Piper, and back in my fantasy. We'll make out in the parking lot until the first bell rings, but because I'm so addicted to your lips, we'll kiss for a few minutes longer. You'll be nervous to get out of the car, so you'll offer to drive us to a secluded area so I can have my way with your body."

I huff a laugh but wonder if it's something I would do to avoid walking into school while people are still milling around with the possibility of pulling a prank or shooting scathing words in my direction.

"As much as I'll want to take you up on that offer, I'll manage to refuse, with the promise of exploring your phenomenal body after classes are over. You'll pout, once again, tempting me with the need to bite your lip, but I drag you out of the car, take your hand, and we walk into the front of the school like the king and queen we are."

"Hmm. It sounds like you have it all figured out. What does the last day of school look like then, Predictor of My Future?"

"That's an easy one. We skip the last day of school because we can't be bothered to get out of bed long enough to get dressed."

I chuckle at the surety in his voice.

"We may not even like each other by that point. A year is a long time."

"Not when I'm betting on forever," he whispers, pressing his warm lips to my forehead.

"And if you get your memories back? You may realize that you can't stand me."

I don't know why I'm pressing him so hard, but it's one way to keep some sort of guard up around him. He's done nothing to make me doubt his changes, but the lingering wariness that he'll hate me once he remembers me is always there.

"I don't think I hated you," he says.

"Well, if it wasn't hatred, I don't want to see you angry at me. I know I sound like a broken record, but you were vile to me."

"I know." He presses his lips to my skin once again. "But I had these..."

"What?" I prod when he stops speaking. "Tell me."

"It's a little embarrassing."

"You can survive a little embarrassment," I tell him. "Believe me. I should know."

He sighs, his weight shifting under mine like he's suddenly uncomfortable.

"You can't judge me if I tell you."

"I make no promises," I tease. "Just tell me. You're probably making it into a bigger deal than it actually is."

"After the accident, I went through my phone."

I stiffen, unsure of where this is going.

"There were..." he pauses. "There were naked pictures."

I gasp, my fingers clinging to his shirt when all I want to do is run into the bathroom and hide.

"Of m-me?"

Was he planning to use them against me?

"Fuck, I wish," he rushes out. "I mean, I'd love to have those kinds of... dammit, I sound like a pervert. They weren't *of* you."

"Why do you say it like that?" I'm honest with myself enough to admit that I wouldn't mind having a few racy, candid shots of him.

"They were nerdy girls, but they all resembled you. They had long blonde hair and bright blue eyes, just like you have, like they were my type. Like you were my type, even though I was a complete jerk to you for years."

I raise my head from his chest to look him in the eye. "Are you telling me you created a spank bank with nerdy girls that looked like me?"

Un-freaking-real.

He nods. "Does that make you mad?"

I drop my head back down to his chest, a small smile playing on my lips. I reach my hand up. "Show them to me. I want to see them."

"Wh-what? I don't have them anymore. I cleared my phone."

"What do you jack off to now, then?"

He doesn't respond, but his breathing changes.

"Tell me," I urge. "What is it? Is it super kinky? I won't make fun of you, promise. Unless it's like a foot fetish or something, then I'll make fun of you."

"I don't—" I pinch his side until he yelps. "I think of you. I jack off to you."

"Like Saturday night?"

"Nothing was more amazing than Saturday night. I've relived that a dozen times since then."

"You've been a busy boy." My grin is so wide, it's making my headache come back. "Will you stay here until close to the time for my parents to get home?"

"Headache coming back?" he predicts.

"Yeah."

"Sleep, baby. I'll stay."

I fall back asleep with his lips pressed to my forehead and thoughts of our future together drifting around in my achy head.

Chapter 33

Dalton

"That's it!" Piper praises when Peyton works out a complicated problem from start to finish on her own. "I think you're ready."

"Ugh." Peyton shoves the notebook away from her. "I don't think I'll ever be ready."

"You're working on sophomore-level problems, Peyton. You're going to rock that test Friday."

"Maybe," my sister grumbles, but I can tell it's hard for her to keep doubting herself when Piper has so much faith in her. "Does that mean we're done? No more math this summer?"

Piper looks to me briefly before turning her attention back to my sister. "We should probably brush up before the school year starts but—"

Peyton grumbles her displeasure like only a thirteen-year-old can.

"Fine," Piper concedes. "No more math, but I can help you during the school year if you get stuck. Just don't let yourself get behind like you did last year. High school math gets harder every year and falling behind makes it nearly impossible to get caught back up."

"Believe me," Peyton says as she stands from the kitchen and stretches her back, "I won't fall behind. I never want to spend another half of summer doing math homework."

My little sister walks toward the fridge, leaving my girl and me alone at the table.

"Are you really done?" She grins at me as she begins to gather her things. "Does this mean I have you to myself for the rest of the summer?"

I rub my hands together like a supervillain with diabolical plans, and all I get from her is a weak smile.

She's more pale than usual, and it's clear that the headache from yesterday hasn't completely gone away.

"Are you feeling alright?" I hook a finger under her chin and make her look up at me. "Does your head still hurt?"

"It's like a dull ache. It'll be fine."

"Have you talked to your dad about it?"

"It's just a headache, Dalton. I'll be fine."

When she stands, I pull her against my chest. "Does this mean you're going back home? I can come with you and hold you while you sleep."

Doing that yesterday was the most intimate thing I've ever experienced. Listening to her soft breathing and holding her against my chest on her bed was amazing, and I can see myself scheduling cuddle time with her on a daily basis.

"I'm so sick of staring at my bedroom walls. Can we lay down in your bed instead?"

I know her head hurts, but that doesn't stop my dick from thinking of better things to do with her in my bed besides sleeping.

She chuckles, well aware of what's going on south of the border when I pull my hips back from her a few inches. She doesn't give me shit for it, though, and that's a warning sign that she feels worse than she's letting on.

"How about we turn the TV down low and watch a movie in the living room?"

"That's a great idea," Peyton interrupts. "I'm going to go see if I can pull Preston away from his video games. Wanna watch Harry Potter?"

I shrug, leaving it up to Piper to decide on the movie, and she nods her head, but I imagine she doesn't really plan on watching anything, so she doesn't really care what's playing.

Before we leave the kitchen, I guide Piper to the fridge, grabbing each of us a bottle of water. I remember her saying on Saturday that she hadn't drunk enough water, and her headache was probably because she was a little dehydrated. I doubt that's still the case because I practically poured water down her throat the entire time she was awake yesterday, but a little more water won't hurt.

"Are you hungry?" I ask before we leave the kitchen.

When she shakes her head, I guide her to the couch, plopping down and letting her lay across me with her head in my lap. I'll let my siblings decide what to watch when they get back in here. Right now, I'm quite content to just massage Piper's scalp while her eyes drift closed.

I have to shush Preston the second he comes racing into the room like his ass is on fire, but when he sees Piper resting on my lap, he snaps his lips closed. I think the little guy has a crush on my girl, but it works to everyone's benefit right now because he grabs a blanket off the back of the couch and covers her with it before settling into the recliner on the opposite side of the room. Peyton comes in and pops in the DVD for the second Harry Potter movie, and for the first hour, my little brother doesn't make a peep.

The music at the end of the movie rouses Piper, but even though she's awake, she doesn't lift her head from my lap. She seems content to stay there as the third movie is put in.

When Peyton gets up to make something to eat, she's gracious enough to make everyone a sandwich, and I manage to convince Piper to sit up and eat hers.

"Want some ice cream instead?" I offer when she only manages a few bites.

She shakes her head, and the look she has on her face reminds of the way she did when she got the brain freeze from the snow cone.

"Maybe something warm?"

"Hot chocolate!" Preston yells, suddenly wincing when Piper moves to cover her ears. "Sorry."

She gives him a weak smile. "Hot chocolate would be wonderful."

I don't think she really wants it and is only asking because she knows it would make my little brother happy, but I take our plates to the kitchen and pull out a pan and milk to heat on the stove.

"It's summertime," my sister comes in, stating the obvious.

"And?" I rummage through the crowded pantry until I find the familiar blue box.

"How did you remember he likes hot chocolate with milk instead of water?"

I look from the box in my hand to the pan of milk.

"I didn't." But somehow, I knew.

"I read that sometimes that's how the memories come back. They're not like a flash, but just muscle memory more than anything."

"Cool," I tell her because it seems like everyone but me is concerned about my memories. I don't know what Peyton is worried about, but from her own confession, I know Piper is terrified I will hate her if they come back.

I don't ever see that happening. She was worried about my reaction when she told me about driving the car the night of the accident, but I didn't blink an eye. Apparently, I loved that car, but what she doesn't know is that I love her more.

"Are you and Piper like official or something now?"

I keep my back to her while grabbing mugs from the cabinet.

"Yes," I answer her.

"Does she know that?"

I chuckle at the surprise in my sister's voice. "I've told her."

"Told her? Does she not get a say? Is this just some other way you're manipulating her?"

Carefully, I set the mugs on the counter. I could get angry and tell my brat of a sister to stay out of my business, and honestly, I'm tempted to. I don't want anything coming in between Piper and me, but hostility isn't going to convince this girl that I've changed. If anything, it would only set us back a few steps.

"I like her a lot. You already know that. I'm not manipulating her. She should probably stay a million miles away from me because of all of the shit I've pulled over the years, but for some reason, she's giving me a chance." Peyton shifts her weight on her feet. "She's giving *me* a chance, and I'm not going to do anything to mess that up. You don't have to worry about her, Peyton. She's safe with me. I promise."

"You talk a good talk," she huffs, and I know she's not one hundred percent convinced even though just last week she was the one urging me to go talk to Piper after I confessed my feelings to her.

"Then step back and watch me walk the walk, too." I wink at her and decide when she laughs a little that she doesn't completely hate me after all.

I mix the cocoa powder in the pan and stir it until all the lumps are gone before pouring it into the mugs. I'm on my way to the fridge, hand under the ice dispenser when Peyton pipes up.

"You'll need two cubes of—"

The machine whirs, dropping two cubes of ice into my hand before she can finish her thought.

"Preston will complain it's too hot if I don't put two cubes in his," I say with my eyebrows raised.

"How did you know that?"

"I don't know."

"But seriously. You were never around before. How would you know something like that?"

"I don't know," I repeat, but I don't have time to stand in the kitchen and ponder all the weird shit that's going on. My girl is in the other room, waiting for a steaming cup of hot chocolate.

Just like I predicted, Piper doesn't drink the hot chocolate, offering her mug to Preston when he finishes his own, but she does lean back into me and let me wrap my arm around her shoulder so we can watch the third Harry Potter movie, so I call it a win.

My parents get home, both pissed off and snapping at each other because their client was found guilty with only two hours of deliberation from the jury. Piper excused herself shortly after, no doubt unable to handle the shrill sound of Mom's voice when she tore into Dad for his lack of rebuttal on some comment from the state's attorney.

I kiss her on the lips with the promise to call her later before heading up to my own room for the night. This is the first time I can remember them actually raising their voices at each other, but from the way Peyton rolled her eyes when they got home, it's more than a regular occurrence.

I plug headphones into my ears, letting my music blare until enough time has passed to call Piper.

I call three times over the course of two hours.

She never answers.

Chapter 34

Piper

"What happened last night?"

These are the words Dalton greets me with when I knock on his door shortly after his parents drive off for the day.

"Happened?" I tilt my head in confusion.

"You didn't answer your phone. I called like a million times."

I roll my eyes, stepping past him into his house. "You called me three times."

He's glaring at me when I turn back in his direction.

"I went home, took some nighttime headache medicine and passed out."

His eyes soften with my admission, and I know he's been worried about me.

"And I woke up this morning feeling like a million bucks."

"I thought something bad happened. I was worried."

"I'm fine." I raise on the tips of my toes and press my lips to his.

"Are you here to tutor? I thought Peyton was done."

"I'm here to see you."

"It's early."

My smile falters, now realizing that his hair is a mess, and he's only wearing a pair of low-riding basketball shorts. My mouth waters at the sight of the muscles laced together down his torso.

"Did I wake you?"

"The doorbell did," he grumbles.

"Then come on." I grab his hand and tug. "Let's go back to bed."

I squeal like a lunatic when he scoops me up in his arms and runs up the stairs with me. Thankfully, neither Peyton nor Preston's door swings open. We'd have to end this really quick if his little brother comes out wondering what we're doing.

"Mmm," I moan when he tosses me on the bed that's still warm from his body.

His sheets are a mix of his cologne and body wash, and the combination makes my skin tingle.

"Don't make sex noises in my bed, Piper." Dalton shuts the door, making a point to flip the lock before turning back to me.

"Where else would I make sex noises then, Dalton?"

His eyes narrow as my hands roam over the top of his blankets.

"You're frisky this morning," he says with a smile as he stalks toward the bed.

"I had an amazing night of sleep," I remind him.

"But we came back up here to go back to bed."

"You can go back to bed if you want." I sit up on his bed and snap my tank top over my head, tossing it to the floor with a grin when his jaw hangs open.

"Where's your bra?" he asks after swallowing twice.

His feet are planted halfway across the room, but I'm no longer worried about whether he wants me or not. The erection forming in his shorts answers that question.

I'm also no longer concerned whether he's really into me or if he's playing some long, drawn-out prank. I married him in my dreams last night, and when I woke up this morning to the sun shining and the birds singing outside, I didn't roll my eyes at the ridiculous thought. I dressed quickly and ran over here, finally ready to begin working on our happily ever after.

Thoughts of joining him at the same school, living in the same apartment while in college no longer worries me. I felt sincerity in his words the other day. He believes every word that came out of his mouth. It wasn't a ploy to get into my pants or a practiced speech just because he thinks I wanted to hear it. He said those things because he meant them.

And Lord, help me, I want everything he offered. I want it all. I want it today, tomorrow, and every other day thereafter.

"It's at home," I tell him with a wicked grin. "Probably tossed on my closet floor. Do you want me to go get it?"

I twirl a lock of my hair, and I know he's watching it go around my finger, brushing against the side of my breast with every rotation.

"Am I being too presumptuous?" I bite my lip, knowing he loves when I do that. "Do you want me to get dressed and leave?"

"N-no. It's just..." His hand skates over the top of his head, and I can tell he's trying to get his breathing under control. "I didn't think this was going to happen. What *is* actually happening right now?"

His eyes lock on mine, and I should give him credit where it's due. I know it must be extremely hard for him to look away from my tight-tipped breasts to focus on my face, but somehow, he manages it. It only makes this decision that much easier for me because I know it's the right one.

"I want you to make love to me." He swallows again. "Do you want that, too?"

"Yes," he responds immediately. "I want that."

"Yet, you're glued to that spot." I point to his feet for impact. "If you want to wait, we can. I'm not trying to pressure you."

"I n-need to brush my teeth." He's scrambling across the room and snapping the bathroom door closed behind him in the next second.

Rolling my teeth between my lips to keep from laughing, I strip out of my shorts and toss those to the side with my tank before crawling between his sheets.

The water in the sink turns on, but a grunt and groan, having nothing to do with brushing teeth, comes from the bathroom. I'm still staring at the door five minutes later when he reemerges.

"What just happened in there?" I ask the question, but I already know the answer.

The erection that was tenting his shorts before he left the room is smaller. He isn't soft by any means, but he's not a raging bull any longer either.

"Did you just jack off in the bathroom?"

His cheeks pink. "Please don't be mad. I would've nutted in like ten seconds, and I don't want to ruin our first time."

"How do you know?" I ask as I toss back the blankets so he can join me on the bed.

His eyes widen to a comical size when he sees me under them with nothing but a pair of lace panties on.

"H-how did I know what?" he stammers, once again frozen to the floor rather than climbing under the blankets to join me.

I think I may have fried this poor boy's brains.

"How did you know you would come in ten seconds?"

"Please don't say come," he begs. "Jesus, look at you, Piper. I've never seen a more beautiful girl before in my life."

"Does that mean you want to join me, or do you just want to stand there and stare?"

"Both," he answers without missing a beat. "I want to watch you. I want to devour you. I want to make you come on my fingers, my tongue, and my cock."

"You can't do any of that from over there," I tease. "Come here, and we can start with a kiss."

"Hell yeah," he snaps, springing into action and climbing onto the bed. "No blankets. I want to see you."

My bravado falters with him this close. I needed the blankets as a shield. I want him. That part isn't a lie, but I have secrets that I want to stay hidden. I know it won't last. He'll see them eventually, but I wanted our first time to be magical, not tainted by the pain of my past.

"So perfect," he praises as he crooks a finger and runs the back over my nipple. It tightens to the extreme, and I whimper with the need to be touched. I want his mouth on me like it was in my car, days ago. With the headache that wouldn't go away, that seems like a lifetime ago, and I'm desperate for him right now.

"Kiss me," I plead, and for once, he doesn't freeze. He lowers his mouth to mine, his hand still toying with the tips of my breasts.

He urges me back, covering my nearly naked body with his, and the warmth of his skin against me is nothing short of divine. His lips tangle with mine as he lifts my leg, hiking it over his hips as he presses into me. Even blocked by my panties and his shorts, the ridge of his penis settles on me exactly where I need him, and I can't help but moan into his mouth when he pushes against me, the perfect roll of his hips igniting a fire that's been simmering for weeks.

"Wait," he pants against my lips before he pulls back.

I miss the heat of his body immediately, but the fire in his eyes lights me up once again as he peers down at me.

"Are you sure?"

"Only if you keep your promise." I lick my lips, smiling when he looks confused. "Fingers. Tongue. Cock."

I see the second realization hits him, and he's like a man possessed.

"Promise," he vows, crouching down between my legs before I can stop him.

"Dalton, don't."

I wasn't even thinking when I toyed with him just a second ago.

"Piper." Tears burn my eyes when his fingers trace the numerous scars on my inner thighs. "What is this? Is this from the accident?"

I don't answer him, but it doesn't take long for him to put two and two together.

"My God," he gasps, his voice filled with pain and regret. "I did this. This is because of me, because of what I did to you."

I manage the courage to look down at him, and I shatter even further at the sight of tears pooling in his eyes.

"That's in the past," I assure him, but he pulls out of my grasp when I reach for him. "Dalton, look at me."

I let my own tears fall at the sight of his losing the battle to hold back. My eyes follow his tears as they trace down the curves of his handsome face.

"Please," I beg. Vulnerable to his eyes as they refocus on my thighs, I begin to tremble.

He's no longer looking at me with lust and unfiltered desire. He's broken and dealing with something I boxed away and put up on a shelf weeks ago. The desire to cut was like a switch he flipped off when he kissed me the first time in his backyard, and it had been a while since I'd done it even before then.

"Look at me!" I roar.

He jolts with the yell, but his eyes are slow to look up at me. When they find mine, I can already tell it's going to be a long road to get back to where we were only moments ago.

My throat clogs with emotion as that tiny hint of a headache begins to renew, a low throbbing pulse at the base of my neck. I know it only gets worse from here.

I want to tell him I forgive him. I want to shout the words for everyone to hear, the very words I refused to even entertain until I woke up this morning. I knew they were coming, but they don't hold the power at this moment as they deserve, so I keep my mouth shut.

The headache intensifies.

My pulse pounds in my ears, and my skin grows oddly cold.

"I sh-should go." I try to stand from the bed, but my legs don't want to work.

I'm too upset to function right now. Lost in his own mind and remorse, Dalton stairs at a spot on the bed that only he can see.

"I'm going to—" I tip over, and my world goes black.

Chapter 35

Dalton

"Piper!" Her eyes roll back as she collapses.

By some miracle, I'm able to catch her before her head slams against my bedside table.

"Please, baby. Please wake up." Holding her in my lap, I press my palms to her flushed cheeks.

Her breathing is ragged, but it's like she isn't even there. Her full weight is in my lap, and an eerie sense of foreboding washes over me.

"Peyton!" I scream, the sound echoing around my room. "Peyton!"

I don't have a clue what to do. Did she pass out? Does this have something to do with the headaches she's been having since the snow cone stand? I feel helpless, impotent with my inability to do anything. I can't reach my phone and releasing her to go get help doesn't even occur to me.

"Dalton!" Peyton screams from the other side of the door. "What the hell is going on?"

The sound of the door rattling snaps me back into a reality I'm not sure I can face, but it motivates me to cautiously lay her on my floor and unlock my bedroom door.

"What the hell did you do?" Peyton screeches when she sees Piper laid out in nothing but her panties.

"Sh-she just passed out. I can't wake her up." I rush back to Piper's side, but there's no change. "Grab something to cover her up with. We need to get her to the hospital."

Peyton disappears, returning an eternity later with a robe, and I don't even bother to put her arms in the sleeves. I wrap it around her and scoop her up into my arms.

"We need to call an ambulance," Peyton says.

"It'll take too long," I argue as I carry her out of my room.

"You don't have a car!" Peyton yells at my back. "Call for help."

"Her keys," I snap. "Get her keys from my room."

There's no way I can sit idle and wait for medical help. I can get her to the hospital before help even leaves the station.

"Please, Piper. Please be okay," I whisper as I carry her out the front door to the car in her own driveway.

Peyton tosses the keys in the front seat while I situate Piper as best I can in the back seat.

"I'm going with you," my sister says, but my head is already shaking with rejection.

"Someone has to stay with Preston."

"I'll call her parents and have them meet you there. What is going on with her?"

"I don't know."

I honestly don't. She was fine before. She was playful and ready for us to take things to the next level. Although she was sad at my discovery, she was trying to comfort me.

I shake my head, ridding it of the things I made this beautiful girl do to her own body because of the way I treated her.

"I have to go," I mumble to myself.

Peyton is standing in the yard, arms crossed over her stomach as I drive away. The hospital is only a couple of miles away, but the drive seems like an eternity. I manage to hit every red light, and my foot bounces with uncontrolled anger as I wait. The last light is already yellow when I pull up, but I rush through it with a prayer that we don't get sideswiped.

The wreck.

This has to have something to do with the accident.

My fingers are drumming on the steering wheel as I pull into the parking lot of the hospital, and I lay on the horn when some idiot with three kids, they can't seem to control, take their sweet ass time crossing the crosswalk.

"Get out of my fucking way!" I yell when the mom gives me a snide look, making no effort to move faster.

Finally, with the speed of a sloth, they move, and I'm able to pull up right outside of the ER doors. I don't bother turning off the car. I just swing my door open and pull Piper back into my arms. Her breathing is different, but I can't tell if it's more even or slowed because she's dying.

Tears streak down my face as I carry her inside.

"Help! Someone, please help!"

It's nothing like the movies. A swarm of people doesn't rush to my aid, pulling a gurney.

One nurse stares in shock on the other side of a glass wall for a long moment before she actually moves into action.

I'm near collapsing on the floor with Piper in my arms when the heavy wooden doors swing open, and two people in scrubs rush toward me.

"Carry her inside," the taller woman advises. I follow her past the doors to a small bay with a curtain pulled back. "On this table, hurry."

"What happened?" the other medical person asks.

"She passed out."

"How long ago?" I don't even see the person who asks, but they pull the robe back, revealing her naked flesh to the entire room, and I seethe with anger. She deserves more modesty and respect than what they're giving her.

"Twenty minutes, maybe?" I answer when the question is asked again.

The medical staff is rushing around, taking her pulse, blood pressure, and listening to her chest with a stethoscope. One is starting an IV.

"Do you know if she's taken any drugs?"

I see red. "She doesn't fucking do drugs!"

"You need to calm down," someone tells me. "We just need all the information so we can make informed medical decisions."

"She's been having bad headaches. We were in a car crash five weeks ago. She had a concussion and a sprained—"

"Piper!"

I swivel on my feet so fast at the approaching voice that I nearly fall over.

Dr. Schofield, Piper's dad, is rushing in our direction. Mrs. Schofield is right behind him with red splotchy eyes and tears streaming down her face.

"What happened?" he asks. He's not looking at me but down at his unconscious daughter. "Why is she naked?"

"She passed out," I somehow manage. "We were—"

Before I can give him the dirty details, I'm certain no father wants to hear, Piper begins to shake on the table. Her body manages to jolt and stiffen at the same time.

"Push four of Ativan," the guy who seems to be in the lead says.

My whole world narrows to the tip of the needle being inserted into Piper's IV. Mrs. Schofield is sobbing beside me, and Dr. Schofield is standing stock still and looking as helpless as I feel.

Piper stops shaking, but there's still a flurry of activity around her body.

"Possible subdural hematoma," the doctor says as he steps back to let someone on the team lift the bedrails. "Let's get her to CT."

They unlock the wheels on the bed and push her away. I'm frozen, watching all of them, including her parents, disappear through another set of double doors that reads MEDICAL PERSONNEL ONLY with the love of my life.

I'm not allowed to stay in the patient part of the emergency room. Before long, a sweet old lady ushers me back out to the waiting room, and she only frowns when I ask her if I'll get updates.

"If you're not family, dear, you're not privileged to that information."

It's midday, the sun blazing through the windows when Mrs. Schofield comes back out into the waiting room. I rush to stand as she approaches. Her movements are slow, like it's taking everything in her power just to cross the room. Her face is unreadable, but her red-rimmed eyes make my chest heave. My knees weaken, threatening to make me crash to the floor.

"Is sh-she okay?" My words come out on a sob.

Mrs. Schofield reaches for me, placing a calming hand on my arm, but it feels like a brick, as if she's transferring the weight of the world from her shoulders to mine.

"She's going to be fine."

She gives me a weak, reassuring smile, but the relief weighs as much as the horrible news I thought she was delivering. Knees first, I crash to the floor at her feet. With my head lowered into my hands, I sob like a child. Elation fills every cell in my body. I'm so happy she's okay, but it's the burden of the vow I made myself while sitting here for hours that's going to kill me.

"Can I see her?"

She nods, turning without a word and walks toward the elevator bank.

"Devin doesn't want you here, but he went back to the office for a little bit. You'll need to be gone before he returns."

I nod in understanding. If I were Dr. Schofield, I wouldn't want my amazing daughter near a man like me either.

"What was wrong with her?" I ask.

"She had a subdural hematoma," she says, but that just makes me stare at her harder in confusion. "She had a small brain bleed."

"From the accident?" Her lip twitches, and I can tell she's mad at me, too.

"Yes. They got it under control with medicine."

"I won't be long," I promise when she points me toward a door. "I only need to say goodbye."

My throat burns with tears, with hatred for myself, with pity I shouldn't be allowed to feel when I step inside and see her small body in the hospital bed.

My feet feel like stones, my legs infused with lead as I walk closer. I've lost my memories, a blessing and a tragedy all rolled into one, but it's what I have to do now that is going to destroy me.

This is the coward's way out. Asking for forgiveness doesn't even enter into my head because I don't deserve it. I never did.

Insisting such from her was just another thing I need to atone for.

I clasp her hand between mine, the warmth of her skin assuring me that she's going to be okay. I whisper that I love her, and it's because of this love that I have to walk away.

Chapter 36

Piper

"I said I'm fine." I swipe at my mother's hands as she once again straightens my covers.

"You're in the hospital for the second time this summer," she huffs as she drops her hands to her sides. "I don't think there's anything *fine* about that."

"I don't even have a headache," I mumble. "When do I get to go home?"

I do my best to ignore my silent phone, but even though it's not ringing or sounding out alerts for texts, it has had all my focus since I woke up a couple of hours ago.

This hospital visit is different from the last one. I'm not covered with aches and pains. I'm not worried that I killed someone. I'm only concerned with why Dalton hasn't answered when I called and hasn't once responded to one of my texts.

"You want to go home to see that boy," my dad snaps from the other side of the room. "And that's not going to happen."

I narrow my eyes at my father. Days ago, he left the ball in my court, left the decision to date Dalton on me, but he's changed his tune. He's putting his foot down, which is ridiculous. The man is a pediatrician for Christ's sake. He should know better than to forbid a teenager anything.

"He's—" I begin, but he interrupts.

"He brought you to the emergency room naked," Dad seethes.

My skin heats with embarrassment, but if I'm going to be doing adult things with my boyfriend, then I need to approach this situation like an adult.

I'm not ashamed of what Dalton and I have done so far but speaking about it with my parents isn't something I want to do.

"We didn't have sex," I tell him honestly.

"Only because you passed out before it got that far."

What did Dalton tell them? Surely, he wouldn't go into explicit detail about the twenty minutes in his room before I was unconscious.

"I'm seventeen," I remind him. "Eighteen in a couple of weeks. I'm mature enough to make my own decisions about sex."

"Yet, you're not intelligent enough to stay out of a car when the driver has been drinking?" He raises a challenging eyebrow at me. "You're back here again because of him."

"This isn't his fault," I begin, but snap my lips closed.

Dalton didn't want me to tell anyone that I was driving. I'm not saying that I won't confess eventually, but I also don't want to break my promise to him without talking to him about it first.

"The hell it isn't," Dad seethes.

Mom places a hand on his back, and it seems to comfort him some, but I know it's not enough to make him forget about the entire situation.

I'm opening to argue further when the nurse walks into the room.

"How are we feeling?" Her bright smile is a stark contrast to the atmosphere filling the room.

"I'm fine."

Mom frowns at my snappy reply, but I ignore her.

The nurse's smile doesn't falter as she checks something on the IV machine.

"Who are you?"

I roll my eyes but answer, "Piper Schofield."

"Where are you?"

"Westover Regional Hospital."

"What happened to you earlier today?"

"I had a delayed brain bleed due to a car accident a few weeks ago. I got a headache at my *boyfriend's* house right before we were going to have sex." I look at my dad and emphasize my connection to Dalton. He doesn't seem impressed. "I passed out and ended up here."

"And what—"

I answer her next question, stating the time after looking down at my phone and the date.

This is the third time they've been in my room to conduct neuro checks. They said I could go home after the fourth one, and I'm just biding my time. It's late, the sun already giving up for the day and falling below the horizon, but after sleeping some, I feel rejuvenated and ready to go home.

"Very good, Piper," the nurse praises. "You'll be out of here in no time."

"See?" I glare at my dad when the nurse excuses herself. "I'm fine."

"You haven't been fine for a long time," Mom says.

My skin begins to tingle, and the healed cuts on the inside of my thighs burn as if they're reopening and coming back to life.

"Wh-what?"

"When I went back to the house to get your phone and some clothes for you..." Dad swallows, looking away from my eyes.

"What did you do?"

"We have every right as parents to go through your things."

My pulse pounds in my ears, but the headache I expect stays away this time. It's only a simple relief because if he's saying what I think he's saying, there's no hope for Dalton and me.

"What did you do?"

Tears fill my eyes, and I don't bother trying to wipe them away as they cascade down my cheeks in a torrent. I don't care that my itchy hospital gown is getting soaked around my neck. It's the pain on my parents' faces that nearly gut me.

I never wanted them to find any of this out, especially after Dalton has changed.

They won't care. They won't bother to take the time to see him as anything other than the monster they've clearly read about.

"He's done horrible things to you," Dad whispers.

"I care about him," I argue. "He's not the same man as the one you read about."

"You didn't tell us any of it," Mom adds. "You've been suffering this whole time..."

She drops her head into her hands and sobs. Dad wraps his arm around her shoulder and pulls her in close to his chest. Sad eyes look up at me over her head.

"You've scarred your body because of him."

"Not just him." I say the words before I realize they don't really help my case. Everything everyone did to me was because of Dalton, and depending on how much they read, they'd know that, too.

"Exactly," Dad says.

I want to remind them of the times I came to them to tell them that Dalton was mean to me, and they just made excuses for the way little boys act around pretty girls, but this isn't their fault any more than it is mine. All of this is on Dalton, and I just have to figure out a way to make them understand that forgiving him is my responsibility, not theirs.

"This is the second time I've been in the hospital. Why didn't you mention the scars on my legs before? Surely the doctors noticed them after the accident."

I cross my arms over my chest, needing to deflect as much of this spotlight off of Dalton and me and point it somewhere else.

"The doctor mentioned them," Dad admits. "But they were secondary to the head injury. You seemed happier shortly after you got home, so I didn't mention them."

"I was happier because of Dalton." Everything is completely different than it was the day Dalton sprayed me with the water hose the night of the party.

"He's tortured you for years," Dad says like I need the reminder. "You cut yourself because of him."

I don't have an argument for this because it's true. The pain I've endured for as long as I can remember hasn't faded. I don't have on rose-colored glasses where Dalton is concerned, and I wouldn't be arguing with my parents if I truly didn't believe he's changed.

"I should've come to you about the way I was being treated at school, but I was handling it."

"By cutting?" Mom pulls her face from Dad's shirt to look at me. "Oh, sweetheart, that isn't the way to handle things like this. You should've come to us."

I bite my tongue until I taste blood. Even if I had come to my parents about what was going on, there's a good chance they couldn't have stopped it. Dalton and his band of idiots were relentless, and I've seen what happens when kids speak up. Things get worse for them, and worse for me would've been an early grave because I was always teetering on that edge anyway.

"I care about him," I repeat.

"It's Stockholm Syndrome," my dad mutters. "I never should've allowed you to tutor Peyton. It put you in his evil path."

I scoff. "It's not Stockholm Syndrome."

"I'm a doctor," he reminds me.

"And I'm the person going through all of this. Things were fine after the accident. The Paynes came over and had dinner with us. Why the sudden change? Why now? Even if I wasn't dating Dalton, I probably would've ended up here. This isn't his fault. We both made mistakes that night."

"You could've died," Mom sobs, her emotions taking over again.

"I could die walking to the mailbox!" I yell. "I could die from a million things that have nothing to do with the accident. I'm not going to stop seeing him."

My father grinds his back teeth, but he doesn't open his mouth to insist I never speak to Dalton again, and for that I'm grateful.

When they head to the cafeteria for more coffee and something to eat, I drop Peyton a text to find out what's going on with Dalton and why he won't respond to me.

It's late, and she has the test tomorrow. That's what I tell myself when she doesn't text me back either.

Chapter 37

Dalton

They tell me I used to love the color black.

There are many things from my past that I hate.

Myself and the dark color surrounding me are the two things leading the pack right now.

People whimper and cry beside me, and I'm just numb, so broken that my pieces can't combine enough to form wetness in my own eyes.

I deserve this.

I deserve watching the love of my life with her ashen face and hands crossed on her stomach in constant repose as the preacher talks about her devotion to life and helping others.

I deserve the looks from her mother and father that speak of the million ungodly things they wish would happen to me.

I deserve the blame my own parents planted at my feet for my involvement in the steps that led up to today.

I deserve it all.

The torture.

The wreck.

The getting my heart ripped from my chest because of an undiagnosed brain bleed that snuffed out the life of the most beautiful girl in the world.

She was fine when I left the hospital that day. Even her mother assured me she would be okay.

She didn't deserve this, though.

She didn't deserve the monster that tormented her daily.

She didn't deserve to suffer at the hands of an idiotic boy and the army of bastards willing to hurt her at his command.

She deserved the world, and yet she gets a wooden box and six feet of dirt, all the while I'm left on earth without her.

I can't do that.

That can't happen.

Our story doesn't end this way.

It should be me in that casket. Me leaving this world behind so she can shine in the bright light of the sun and live her life to all its glory.

It should be me.

It should be me.

It should be me.

My hand trembles as I reach into the inside pocket of my sports coat.

I'm not scared or afraid of what comes next.

It's the anticipation, the thrill of joining her that makes my blood sing, the unused energy making my fingers twitch.

July sun glints off the barrel as I hold my salvation to my head and pull the trigger.

I wake with a start, heart pounding in my ears like drums. Cold sweat covers my skin in a sheen so thick my clothes stick to every inch of my body. My hands are trembling so hard they thump against my forehead when I try to push my hair out of my face.

I check my phone once again. Seeing that she had texted me twenty minutes ago, the pain from my dream ebbs a little.

I made promises.

I vowed to myself that I'd stay away.

I knew it wasn't going to be easy, but I didn't expect it to be pure torture either.

She's called.

She's texted.

She left a voicemail filled with sobs and tears, explaining that her dad read her journals and knows all of the horrific things I did to her.

She begged me to come see her, but I can't face the pain on her face.

I can't face the girl I love because of what I saw.

Every time I close my eyes, the wounds on her thighs are front and center. Some were older, thinned and fading to a light silvery color, but there were others that were still pink and angry, proof of the pain I caused her. I hurt her so much that she hurt herself.

What kind of monster does that make me?

What kind of person pushes someone else so far that they take a razor and cut into their own skin?

And yet I want her.

I need her like I need air, and it's killing me to keep my distance.

Going to her would be selfish. It would calm my pain, but it does nothing to ease hers.

There's nothing I can say, nothing I can do to make things better. I can't erase the past, not like mine has been erased from my mind.

I don't deserve the reprieve. I shouldn't be able to sit on my bed with her journals spread all around and merely read about the things I've done to her. I need to be wrapped in her torment, cocooned in her pain until I'm suffocated in retribution.

A soft knock on my door doesn't even make me lift my eyes.

"Hey." Peyton has stopped in to chat more than once since I took Piper to the emergency room three days ago, so I know exactly how this conversation is going to go. "Did you finally text her back?"

She knows the answer, so I don't bother to speak it out loud.

"You need to go see her." Peyton sighs when I continue to ignore her. "She's been blowing up my phone checking on you."

Now I raise my eyes to hers. "What did you tell her?"

"I told her that you have exiled yourself to this room, and you're heartbroken and that she needs to get better so she can come over here and slap you until you snap out of it."

"Pey—"

She holds her hand up. "I didn't tell her anything. You aren't responding to her calls and texts, so I haven't either."

"What?" My brow furrows. "You shouldn't ignore her."

She shrugs. "You shouldn't either. When you respond, I'll respond."

"She needs someone right now," I remind her. "Frankie is still in Utah. She doesn't have anyone else to talk to."

I hurt even more knowing that my sister has been ignoring her as well.

"She needs *you*," Peyton specifies. "So, you need to call her. I'm dying to tell her how easy the test was the other day."

"I'm the last thing Piper needs," I mutter, my eyes drifting back to the open journal on my bed. "Did you know that I told the entire school that I caught her making out with a pillow?"

Peyton smiles. "Big deal. I've made out with my pillow before."

My nose scrunches. "I didn't need to know that, but what if everyone at school found out?"

Her eyes widen. "I'd kill you."

"See? It's not that it happened, which I don't think it even did because she doesn't mention that in her journal, just the aftermath of me telling people that it did. It was in seventh grade, and that's the first night she—"

I snap my jaw shut. I'm ashamed of what I caused Piper to do, but that secret is hers to tell or keep, not mine.

"The first time she cut herself?" Peyton whispers.

I swallow to try to dislodge the lump in my throat, but I don't think a semi-truck could move it at this point.

"Yeah. You knew about that?"

"I saw them after we swam in the pool. She didn't want to talk about it."

"Now you understand why I haven't answered."

Without warning, Peyton raises her hand and slaps me in the back of the head. "You're so fucking stupid! She has forgiven you, and if she hasn't, she was getting really close to it."

"She should hate me."

"And she did for a long time, but she doesn't now. A girl that hates you wouldn't have been up here naked in your room." She narrows her eyes at me. "Unless you stripped her against her will."

I roll my eyes at her, still rubbing the back of my head where she smacked me. "Don't be ridiculous."

"Then you need to call her. You're torturing yourself over what you've done, but it's only hurting her more for you to ignore her."

"It's what's best."

"Did you explain that to her?"

"Sort of," I mutter.

"What the hell does *sort of* even mean? You either had the conversation with her, or you didn't."

"She was still out when I did it."

Like an asshole, she rears back and hits me again.

"She probably thinks you're playing some sort of prank on her or that the last couple of weeks you've spent going after her was just part of some big joke."

I shake my head. "It hasn't been. I lo—"

"You love her. Yes, I know that, but does she?"

"I can't tell her now!" I roar as I stand up from the bed and point an accusing finger down at the journals. "Look at what I've done to her! My love is tainted. The way I acted has ruined any chance for us."

"Yet she was here, in your room with you, by choice. What does that tell you?"

My hands fist my hair, but I ignore the pain in my scalp when I pull. It pales in comparison to the agony in my chest.

"I'm no good for her." A sob escapes my throat.

"Yet, you're exactly who she wants." Peyton crosses the room but stops short of touching me. I'm sure she can tell just how crazed I am right now. "The least you have to do is explain to her why you can't be with her. Say it to her face instead of whispering it like a coward while she's knocked out. Not doing so is only hurting her more, and by the way you're acting right now, you have enough guilt from the pain you caused her."

She walks out of the room, closing the door behind her, and once again I'm left alone with only my remorse and regret to keep me company.

Chapter 38

Piper

"So, you're brain-damaged?"

I huff a laugh at Frankie. "Something like that."

"When did they cut you loose?"

"I got home late yesterday evening."

It's now ten in the morning, and I once again woke my sleeping best friend.

"How are things there?"

"Nope," she snaps. "We're not talking about me. I want to talk about you."

There's a hint of a secret in there somewhere, but I called because I wanted to tell her what was going on and get her advice.

"I really like him," I confess.

"Dalton Payne?"

I chuckle at the confused tone in her voice. "Yes, Dalton Payne."

"He's very good-looking," she muses, and if she were here, I bet she'd have a wide smile on her face. "But he tormented you for forever. Are you really going to just forget about all of that?"

"I won't ever forget." There's isn't a chance of that, but I don't think holding it against him for the rest of our lives is the right thing to do either. "He's different."

"So you've said, but you've not given me much proof that it's true. How is he different? He's not treating you poorly, but that's common decency. Have you fallen in love with the boy because he hasn't made people laugh at you recently? Please, Piper, don't be that girl."

"I'm not that girl," I mutter. "He looks at me like I'm the beginning and end of his day. Just the way he caresses my face—"

"Caresses your face? What have I missed?" Frankie interrupts.

"We're together," I whisper.

I don't know why I lower my voice. My parents have left for work, my dad warning me against going to see Dalton.

"I'm sorry. I didn't catch that. It sounds like you said you and Dalton Payne were together."

"I did," I tell her with a stronger voice. "At least I thought we were."

"You're confused about it? If you were together, you'd know. Oh, Piper." I'm getting really sick of hearing my name said that way. "If you're not sure it's because he's messing with you. Please, don't fall for this. It feels like Vaughn all over again."

"You're the one who pushed me to talk to Vaughn," I remind her. "This isn't like that. He's probably embarrassed because he had to carry me into the ER with nothing but panties and a robe on."

I slide that information in there, hoping she'll ignore it and we can—

"In nothing but panties and a robe!" she shrieks. "You need to start at the beginning and tell me everything. Only giving me half of the info isn't okay. If you want me to help you with this—and I know you called for that very reason—I need to know everything, so spill."

I do just that. I start with the kiss in his backyard, and I tell her about the snow cone stand, and all of the making out. I even confess to what happened in the car at the park, and we spend way too much valuable time discussing that at length before she lets me continue, all the way up until I woke up in the hospital for the second time, and he wasn't there.

I cry when I tell her how many times I've called and texted, only to be ignored. I even explain that Peyton isn't answering her phone, and even though I can tell it agitates her, Frankie doesn't say anything about being temporarily replaced by the younger Payne.

"How did he react when he saw the cuts?"

"He was zoned out, like I was the ugliest thing on the planet. He was disgusted by the sight of them."

And then it hits me like an explosive strapped to my heart.

"That's why he isn't calling or answering texts, Frankie. He finds me disgusting."

Silence fills the line between us for a long minute.

"Crap," she mutters. "I can't believe I'm about to say this."

"Just say it," I demand with a sigh. "It's not like things could get any worse."

Tears have been falling down my cheeks for the last half hour, and I've stopped brushing them away.

"He doesn't hate you." She makes a rude noise when I try to interrupt. "You've just spent the last half hour telling me what's going on. It's my turn to talk."

"Fine," I grumble.

"He doesn't hate you," she repeats. "From the sound of it, he hates himself right now. He hates what he caused you to do. Now I'm not saying I trust the man fully, but if I take a step back and only use the information you just gave me, not taking into account the crap I know he's pulled in the past, I'd say he's been genuine this summer. His reaction to your scars is about him, and when we get through all of this, we're going to sit down and talk about that. I can't believe you kept something like that from me."

"I'm sorry," I mutter.

"I'm sorry you were hurting more than I ever knew. I would've killed him long ago had I known you were doing that crap."

"I hid it from everyone, and he wasn't even supposed to see that day. I didn't think he'd pull the covers back that far."

"Well, from what I know about teenage boys, they want to see the entire package."

"What?" I chuckle. "What do you know about teenage boys?"

She makes a weird noise in the back of her throat but doesn't answer my question. "And we'll go back to that once this issue is settled as well."

She remains silent, and all it does is double my suspicions about what my dear friend has been doing while on her grandmother's farm this summer.

"What should I do?"

"Go talk to him," she answers without pause.

"It's not that simple."

"It *is* that simple, Piper. Go talk to the boy that went from monster to lover."

"He's ignoring me."

"And that is easy to do on the phone, but not when you're right in his face."

"And what if he tells me to leave and that he hates me?"

"I don't think that's going to happen, but if it does, then you'll finally know, and we can work on ruining his life senior year."

I grin, knowing she's full of it. We're not mean people, and we're already at the bottom of the social hierarchy at Westover Prep, and since this isn't some stupid romantic drama that would never work out in our favor.

"And say what?"

"Tell him that you love him."

"I don—"

"Un-uh," she huffs. "Don't start lying now. Be honest with yourself and be honest with him."

"I'm shaking," I confess.

"What are you afraid of?" Softness fills her tone while I take a second to actually ask myself that very question.

"Everything," I tell her. "I'm scared he'll ask me to leave. Afraid he's going to tell me none of it was real. Terrified that I've given him my heart and he's just going to walk all over it like he's done to me for as long as I can remember."

"And you may go over there, and he'll wrap his arms around you and tell you what you overheard when he was talking to his sister. You won't know until you speak with him. Not knowing is going to tear you up more than anything else. You know that as much as I do."

"You're right."

She laughs. "Piper, we've been friends for how long? You know I'm always right. Now go over and talk to your boy toy. Keep in mind that a warm bath will help your bits if you get too sore."

"Too sore?" My eyes widen when I realize what she's talking about. "Oh, God!"

She laughs, and for the first time since I woke up in the hospital, I feel a little of the weight lift off my chest.

"Just go talk to him."

"Simple," Frankie assures me.

"When do you get home? I miss you like crazy."

"Still another two weeks," she says with a sigh. "I'm ready to be there now."

"Okay, then tell me about Zeke." She doesn't say anything, and I have to pull the phone from my ear to make sure the call didn't drop.

"I'm not talking about him. The boy drives me crazy. He wants to pretend like he's a man, but then when he's..." she draws in a long breath.

"Go talk to Dalton, Piper. Call me later this evening and let me know how it went."

"Maybe sooner than that," I mutter.

If he tells me to kick bricks, I may be sobbing on another phone call with her here shortly.

"It's all going to work out," she assures me. "Trust me. I have a gut feeling about this. He didn't shun you in front of the people at the snow cone stand, and he's probably over there wallowing in his misery and kicking himself for all of the horrific things he's done. And let me just say that you need to make that boy work for you, more than you have already."

"Kind of hard to make that happen when I'm going over there to beg him to not break up with me."

"Stop," she snaps. "That's not what's going to happen. You're going to go over there and remind him why you were worth fighting for to begin with. So, go brush your teeth and hair and make up with your boyfriend."

Chapter 39

Dalton

I know Piper got home yesterday. By dinner time, both of her parents' cars were in the drive. When she was in the hospital one or both of them were gone at all times.

My skin has been prickly and itching just knowing she's so close, but I've managed to maintain my resolve.

The conversation with Peyton yesterday plays over and over in my head, but I know it's just my selfishness trying to convince me that I can have her. Keeping a girl like Piper Schofield is impossible, especially for me, no matter how much my brain tries to convince me otherwise.

I want her. I don't think I'll ever stop wanting the girl next door, but after the things I've done to her, the extremes I pushed her to, there's no turning back from that.

She hasn't forgiven me. How could she? I've done nothing but turn her life upside down for years. I'm a fool to think that a month of being different is enough to change me. Although I pray I never get my memories back, I'm just as terrified as she is that if they do come back, I'll be the same unrepentant asshole that I was before. I don't know how that would be possible with how much I love her, but it's one of my biggest concerns.

"Are you going to just sit there all day?"

I don't bother to turn my head to look at my sister. Peyton hasn't complained too much that I've taken up residence in her room, looking out her window with the hopes of seeing Piper. It's another way I've been torturing myself. I'm strong enough to stay away from her, but not seeing her at all is killing me. It's another form of punishment and torture I've been doling out to myself in tiny doses.

"She's home, you know."

I still don't respond.

"I bet she'd love to see you. She's still been texting and calling my phone. I wish you'd get your crap together because I miss my friend."

"And I told you to stop ignoring her."

"Maybe you're right." Peyton's tone makes me pull my eyes from the coral-colored curtains twenty feet away and look at her. "Maybe I should invite her over so we can catch up."

"You'd really do that to me?"

She frowns. "I miss her. Are you asking me to stop being friends with her because you're playing the martyr and punishing both of you?"

"No." Even as I say the word, I know it's mostly a lie.

I don't want Piper here because it would be impossible to stay away from her. My resolve only goes so far and keeping distance between the two of us is the only way I can keep my hands off her.

"You love her." Her tone softens as sadness fills her eyes. "I don't understand any of this at all."

"It's not meant for you to understand," I mutter, my eyes drifting back to Piper's house.

"You're not going to catch a glimpse of her over there."

I begin to ignore her. I've found that if I don't engage with her, she'll walk away and leave me to my own racing thoughts and wishes for things to be different.

"You won't see her," she says again, "because she's waiting for you in your room."

My heart gallops, pounding against my ribcage as adrenaline fills my blood. My eyes are focused on her house, but I don't see a single thing. My blood heats, demanding my legs to move, to go seek her out, but I'm frozen, stuck in this position while my head wars over what to do next.

"Did you hear me?" Peyton snaps. "Go talk to her. If you can't be with her for whatever stupid reasons you've conjured in your head, then she deserves for you to say those things to her face. Ghosting her is being a jerk, and you've said over and over that you're no longer a jerk."

"What do I say?"

Peyton huffs, her arms taking up residence across her chest. She's annoyed with me. That much is clear, but I need help. I need guidance. I need someone who can support my decision to let Piper go. I know I'm not going to get those things from my sister.

"You tell her the truth. All of it. Not just the stuff to push her away. You lay it all out, and then you listen to her, and you take her truths and then decide if they change what you said. It can't be one-sided."

"Talk to her." I say the words out loud, testing them for merit.

"See? Simple?"

There's nothing simple about walking into my room and seeing Piper. But then again, there's nothing simple about the way I feel for her. Not seeing her for the last couple of days has left a hole inside of me, an aching void of despair that longs for her constantly.

"Go." Peyton literally shoos her arms to get me to leave her room.

My bedroom door is closed, and thoughts of how I'll find her fill my mind. Unable to just stride in there, I lean my head against the cold hardwood, and pray for strength.

Piper is standing at my window when I finally manage the courage to turn the knob and open the door. She doesn't look in my direction immediately, but her shoulders tense.

"I always know when you enter a room," she says without looking back at me. "It's like the air around you is charged. My heart starts to beat faster, and my fingers tingle."

Her hands open and close like she's feeling that very thing now.

"It's the same with you," I confess.

Slowly, she turns around, and although I expected her to be ashen, the way she was the last time we were in my room, her cheeks are full of color, and her eyes sparkle with vibrancy.

I hate the fact that she was sick for so long, and I was so wrapped up in winning her over that I didn't even recognize the signs of her pending illness. This beautiful girl could've died while I was so focused on making her mine that I didn't even see it. Add that to the ever-growing list of shit I did wrong where she's concerned.

"Why have you been ignoring me?"

Straight to the point. It's pure Piper, and I shouldn't have expected anything less.

"You were in that hospital because of me."

"I was in the hospital because the doctors missed something before I got home, or the bleed was delayed. Neither reason is because of you."

"The accident was my fault," I tell her.

"I was driving. That means the accident was my fault."

Knowing she's going to argue every single point I make, I cross the room to my desk. From the window, it creates the greatest distance between us that the room allows, and it's already hard enough not going to her and wrapping her in my arms. This is worse than I imagined it would be. Sharing the same space with her, knowing what we were going to do the last time we were in here is killing me. My brain and body are getting on the same page, and that can only mean trouble for my resolve.

"We can't be together," I tell her, my back straightening as I say the words.

"Care to elaborate?" She watches my face as if she's a life-sized lie detector. "And don't give me any of that bull about the things that happened in the past."

Repeatedly swallowing doesn't remove the lump that's threatening to cut off my air supply in my throat, but she's patient, waiting for me to speak again.

"I saw your thighs, Piper." My words come out on a whisper, reminding me just how upset I was the other day.

I wanted to make her feel good, to run my mouth all over her like I'd brazenly promised, only to find the pain she's always hidden so well under her clothes. The shorts at the pool a few weeks ago make complete sense now.

"So, they disgusted you?"

"Yes," I admit, and she sucks in a breath.

I can tell she thinks I'm confessing to being disgusted at the sight of her, and for a moment in time, I almost go with it. I almost tell her that I can't be with a girl who's marked up like that, but I swore to her I'd always be honest.

"I hate myself for what I made you do. I hate that your gorgeous body will always carry the burden and proof of the pain I've caused you."

"Is that all?" Her question is dry and emotionless.

"I've done nothing but destroy you. I've done a million things to you for no reason other than because I could."

"Do you love me?" Only now does her voice crack with her pent-up emotions.

My mouth snaps shut, refusing to admit that right now. It'll only give her more reason to try to wear me down, and I'm already only hanging on by a thread.

"Because I love you." My head snaps up. "And I refuse. Are you listening to me? I refuse to get my heart broken this way. How dare you make me fall in love with you, only for you to turn around and decide you're just not into me! Do you know how ignorant you sound right now?"

The lump in my throat dislodges, but when I open my mouth to speak, it's clear she isn't going to give me the opportunity to do so.

"Either you really do feel like I deserve better, and honestly, Dalton, I *know* I do. I deserve better than a boy who's only hurt me until that accident. I deserve someone who worships me, someone who isn't afraid to hold me and tell me how they feel. I deserve so much better than that, but you know what? I didn't get to choose. I didn't want to fall in love with you. Hell, I didn't even want to like you as a person. You made me do this." Tears fill her eyes, and I stand as she tries to blink them away. "Either you think that, or you don't care for me at all."

An incredulous laugh escapes her throat.

"That's it, isn't it? This between us is what it's always been. It's a joke, or a prank or some kind of fun for you at my expense." She turns to leave, and I want to stop her, but my feet are planted to the floor. "I should've known better. I should've left well enough alone. Making the sad girl with no friends fall in love with the bully. Just freaking perfect. Have a nice life, Dalton."

"I do love you!" I spit as she reaches for the doorknob. No matter what I feel or think, there's no way I can let her walk away from me right now, not thinking and feeling the way she does. She freezes, but she doesn't turn around. The sight of her shoulders shaking with her sobs is killing me. "I love you more than I ever thought possible, but I'm no good for you."

"No!" she yells, spinning around to face me. "You don't get to do that either! My love for you is unconditional. It doesn't make sense. Even I can admit that, but it doesn't make it any less real. If you want me to walk away, just tell me, and I will. But shoving me away because of things we can't change? I forgive you for all of it. You told me to stop living in the past, and I've done that, but now you want to push me away for the very same reason."

Tears burn my eyes, and the lump in my throat returns.

"You forgive me?" Her head nods immediately. She doesn't even have to think of her answer. "For everything."

"All of it. Everything you've ever done to me, I forgive, but if you walk away from what we have, I'll never forgive you for that. My scars may never heal, but they've made me stronger. They've made it possible for me to open myself up to see who you are now."

"And if I get my memories back?"

"Will it make you stop loving me?"

"No. I don't think there's anything that could make my love for you fade."

"Then what's the problem?"

"I want to save you from me, Piper, from the things I've done, but if I remember, I can't help but feel like we're going to be right back here— right back to me hating myself and feeling like I don't deserve you."

"Then I'll have to remind you of all the good you've done since the accident. I'll remind you every day that you love me."

"I won't need a reminder," I tell her.

"So, where does this leave us?" She hasn't closed the distance between us, and it's killing me.

I give her a small smile. "I guess this means you're mine."

Chapter 40

Piper

His.

God how I want that. It's why I came over here this morning. It's all I've felt for a while now. Thinking I lost him has been ten times more painful than anything he's done in the past.

"Yours?"

"Yes."

"No more pushing me away."

"No more," he agrees.

"I'm serious, Dalton. I don't want to lose you, but I refuse to go through this again. I can't handle the back and forth."

"I promise," he vows. "No more."

"You made me another promise, and you haven't followed through yet," I remind him.

His eyebrows rise in confusion.

"You promised me..." slowly, I walk toward him, my heart hammering inside my chest at being the one to instigate this, "fingers, mouth, cock."

His mouth parts, allowing his breaths to rush out past his lips.

"That's not a good idea."

I pause. "Because of my scars?"

"Because you just got out of the hospital. I nearly killed you last time."

"Death by orgasm?" I tease. "What a way to go."

"I'm serious, Piper. We should wait."

"I'm fine."

He takes a step back, but I can see his hands clenching at his sides with the need to touch me.

"And your doctor cleared you to have sex?"

A laugh erupts from my throat. "I didn't ask the doctor about sex."

"Then we wait."

"I'm not going to call one of my father's colleagues and ask him if I can have sex. I feel great. Better than I have in a long time, and I'm telling you I'm fine."

"I can wait, Piper. We don't have to do this now."

"I can't," I tell him as I tug my t-shirt over my head. "Is this pressuring you into doing something you don't want to do?"

I reach behind me and unsnap my bra, letting it coast down my arms and fall to the floor.

He shakes his head. "I want to. God, do I want to."

He steps closer like he doesn't have any control of his body.

"You'll tell me if you get a headache or if you start feeling bad?"

"Of course," I vow. And I will. I don't want to go another four days without seeing him. "Will you be gentle with me?"

"I can try," he whispers. "You'll tell me if I'm going to fast?"

I laugh because we're moving at a snail's pace right now. "Yes. Will you touch me now?"

His eyes are aimed at my exposed breasts, and he nods, but his legs don't move him any closer to me.

"Touch me here," I tell him as my hand reaches up to caress my own breast.

"Jesus," he pants. "God, I don't deserve you."

"But you still have me," I remind him. "I'm yours."

"Are we really doing this?" Finally, he closes the distance, his hand reaching up for a tentative touch to my flesh.

My chest heats with a mixture of anticipation and shyness. We've been this far before, but it's still so new, I don't know if I'll ever get used to the feel of his eyes on me. Although I'm exposed and vulnerable to him, it's the look of pure reverence in his eyes that lets me know I'm safe with him.

"Only if you want to," he answers, but as the words leave his lips, his mouth lowers to the tip of my right breast.

Warm heat surrounds my nipple, and it's sensation overload, enough that it makes my knees nearly buckle.

I urge him toward his bed, but he seems content to just stand in the middle of the room and lave at my flesh with his wicked tongue.

"Tell me if this doesn't turn you on."

"Dalton," I cup his cheeks in my hands, forcing him to look up at me, "everything you do turns me on. Undress me."

He nods, his head shifting in my hands before I release him. His lips find mine as he works to open the button on my shorts and shoves them over my hips. They fall to the floor, and I kick off my shoes so I can clear my body of my clothes. Now, I'm standing in his room in nothing but my panties, but it's his mouth on mine that I focus on. I've missed everything about him, but his mouth on me is what I've longed for the most. The way his lips move against mine removes all doubt about how he feels for me.

His kiss is powerful, worshipping, and when he groans as our tongues touch, I know that I'll never get enough of him.

As much as I love his lips against mine, my body burns with the need for more. I want it all, all of him, all of this, all of it for eternity.

"Dalton," I whisper against his lips, "we need to get on the bed."

Without pulling his lips from mine, he grabs me behind my thighs and lifts me until my legs are wrapped around his body.

"You're still dressed," I complain as he lowers us to his bed.

"And I'm going to stay that way for now." I pout as his hands skate down my body, my stomach trembling under his fingers. "If I pull my cock out now, I'm going to want inside of you."

"That's the goal," I remind him.

"And I still have a promise to keep."

He pushes his body back, settling between my thighs, resting on his haunches. His eyes rove over me from my kiss-swollen lips and down my stomach until they rest between my thighs. The shaking in my body is renewed with his perusal, but I stiffen when his fingers begin to trace over the scars on my inner thighs.

"I will tell you every day how sorry I am for this." His touch is gentle, the tips of his fingers barely making contact, but his eyes don't well with tears this time, and for that I'm grateful.

When he lowers his head, my core clenches with anticipation, but his lips spend time kissing each and every one of the scars. It's as if I heal from the inside out, and even though the flaws will remain, they no longer matter. If anything, they'll merely serve as a reminder of how we got here today.

"Dalton," I plead when his mouth ghosts over my most sensitive flesh so he can kiss the scars on the other side. "Please."

He smiles, tilting his gorgeous face up so I can see his eyes. "Patience, Piper."

He keeps his eyes focused on mine as his fingers trace the lines of my panties from my hip to my center without touching me where I need him the most.

"Touch me."

"I am," he teases. "And I'm going to have to combine a couple of things together today, because as much as I want you to have patience, mine is quickly running out."

"C-combine?" I pant when his thumb brushes over my clit.

"We're going to have to do fingers and mouth together today, baby. That okay?"

I nod enthusiastically, and he laughs at my eagerness. "I didn't think you'd have a problem with that."

I lift my hips when it's clear he wants my last piece of clothing gone, but when he tosses them away and looks down, his mouth hangs open.

"Jesus... I... fuck, baby. You're pretty here, too." When his thumbs spread me open, my face burns with embarrassment. "So pink and perfect. Makes my mouth water for a taste."

Is he just staring at me? God, it makes me want to crawl in a hole and hide.

"Can I taste you, Piper?"

As much as I want to tell him no and beg him to stop staring at my most delicate flesh, my body has other demands.

"Y-yes," I answer, trying to ignore the urge to clamp my thighs together.

"Fingers and mouth first, okay?"

I nod before squeezing my eyes closed as I feel his warm breath there.

"And we may have to end up with an IOU on the third one because—dammit, Piper, so tight."

I moan with delight when the tip of one finger presses into my entrance.

"I won't last once I'm inside of you." His finger continues to work, and I refuse to look down at him, knowing he's cataloging my responses. "It's going to hurt, and I won't have time to get you there."

"Dalton!" I screech when his thumb gets in on the action and begins to circle my clit at a torturously slow pace.

"Feel good, baby?"

"So good. So, so, so good."

"How about this?"

My eyes snap open at the first luxurious lick of his hot tongue. With his finger still inside of me, curling and pulsing in some magical way, his tongue takes over for his thumb, and it's life-changing.

No longer worried about embarrassment, I flex my neck and prop myself up on my elbows so I can watch what he's doing to me.

He grins, the corners of his mouth curling up as his tongue works me into a frenzy. Like a maniac, I nod my head over and over as something amazing builds inside of me. It only spurs him on, one finger becoming two, his tongue focusing on that one tiny spot that throbs for him.

Without warning, my body convulses, and the pressure that was building inside of me ruptures into a series of moans and pulses, radiating from where he is to each of my extremities. It's so powerful, I have to dash tears from my eyes. So that's what a good orgasm feels like? Give me a million more because it was phenomenal.

His mouth still works me, his fingers edging deeper, but the overload of sensations makes me shove his head away forcefully. He smiles again, undeterred by the aggressiveness I just displayed.

"Feel good?" He licks at his lips as he waits for my answer.

My breathing is ragged as if I had just run a marathon rather than having laid here merely as a semi-active participant in what he just did.

"Can we do it again?" I beg.

Taking me seriously, Dalton begins to lower himself back down.

"Get up here." I pull him to me, pressing my mouth to his before even realizing what I'm doing. A tanginess fills my mouth, and it's almost weird enough to make me back out of the kiss, but then he moans in my mouth, sweeping his tongue over mine, and I'm once again lost to him.

He doesn't pull away from me as he reaches down and shoves his basketball shorts off his hips, and he only pulls his lips away an inch to get his shirt off, and here we are, both completely naked. His warm flesh covers mine, and the thickness between his legs rests perfectly at my core, hot and needy.

"Are you sure?" he asks, his lips trailing down my jaw.

"I'm sure," I tell him. "Condom?"

"Fuck. Yeah. I almost forgot." It's only a matter of seconds before he reaches into his bedside table, opens a new box of condoms, pulls one from the pack, sheaths himself, and settles back between my thighs.

"Be gentle," I remind him.

"Of course. Are you ready?"

I nod, unable to actually say the words, and he lifts up on one side, touching me there again before notching himself against me.

"Jesus, just the anticipation is going to make this end too fast."

My eyes screw shut when he pushes in a few inches. A stinging pain hits next, and I whimper. He's too big, too much all at one time, and I shift my hips to try to ease the burn.

"Please look at me," he begs. "I need to know we're in this together. This is my first time, too, remember?"

"Oh, God," I whisper when I open my eyes and see the vulnerability in his. "Dalton."

"Piper," he moans, pushing deeper into me.

When his legs meet the back of my thighs, I know he's fully inside of me, and even though I expect him to pull back out and slam back inside, he holds his hips still, letting me adjust to him even though I can tell from the strain in his forehead that it's costing him.

"Ready?"

I nod my head because the sharp pain is gone, replaced by a low throbbing that I'm sure won't go away no matter how long he stays still.

"Kiss me," I plead as his hips flex back.

He obliges, lowering his mouth to mine. Lifting my legs, I wrap them around his waist, and it makes him able to push in impossibly deeper. We both moan. Him with pleasure; me with unease.

"Piper, shit." He pushes in again, slow but with unfaltering rhythm. "Fuck, baby. I'm so sorry."

He jerks inside of me, growing thicker as his arms begin to tremble around me.

I don't answer his apology. He has nothing to be sorry for, so I just hold him closer until he pulls out of me to dispose of the condom. He doesn't leave me alone long, using a warm washcloth from the bathroom to clean between my legs, another embarrassing thing that forces my eyes to close until he's done.

When he settles back on the bed, we don't bother to grab clothes, opting to hold each other flesh to flesh.

"Are you okay?" he asks after a long silence that had me believing he was asleep.

"Yes."

"Sore?"

"A little, but I heard it gets better the more you have sex." His penis thumps against my leg, making me chuckle. "But it isn't going to happen again today."

He holds me tighter, resting his chin on the top of my head.

"Thank you," he whispers.

"For the sex?" I chuckle against his chest.

"For loving me. For forgiving me."

I lift my head and look up at him. He's no longer my tormentor. He no longer looks at me with fire in his eyes and a desire to make me fall in shame. His handsome face and gorgeous green eyes are filled with the same kind of love I feel deep in my chest, and it makes me realize that I was right all along.

I killed the tyrant that haunted me day and night. The world is rid of that monster forever because the man in my arms right now is nothing like the evil being I thought would plague me for eternity.

But things are perfect right now.

Right now, we aren't facing the world.

I'm not arguing with my dad about loving a man that hurt me.

He isn't facing his friends that may still want to cause me pain.

No, things are perfect right now, but in a month, we go back to school, and that's when we risk losing each other to the past we're both trying to forget.

Epilogue

Dalton

"I predicted this," I remind Piper as she looks through the windshield of the car toward the front doors of Westover Prep.

"No, you didn't," she mutters, but a smile plays at the corner of her pretty pink lips.

"I did. Six weeks ago, you asked me how I thought today was going to go. I told you I'd offer you my varsity jacket." I point to the clothing in the back seat of my dad's truck. "Told you that you'd refuse it."

"It's too hot for that right now."

"Still predicted it."

"We should leave." She gives me a saucy look, one that never fails to make my cock thicken in my jeans. "Go somewhere secluded."

"Predicted that as well. That's why we left home early and stopped by the park."

My lips still taste like the treasure between her legs. My mouth has been on her dozens of times since that first time in my bedroom when I finally stopped trying to push her away and accepted that we were meant to be together no matter our past.

"The only thing that's off so far is you're supposed to be kissing my lips until the first bell rings."

"That so?" She finally pulls her eyes away from the droves of students walking into the school. "We can remedy that."

I've never been more grateful that my dad is tall and drives a truck. Without hesitation, Piper flips up the console and climbs into my lap. We've done this so many times, she knows the right angle I need her at, and she settles on my lap perfectly.

Her mouth lowers to mine, distracting me from what we're supposed to be doing, but we still have a little time, so I take sips of her lips and grip her delectable ass in both hands. Both of us have been insatiable since our first time. Even though we have to sneak around because her dad has put his foot down about us dating, we find plenty of time to spend together. Now that school is starting, that will be more difficult. It wasn't hard to see each other when both of our parents left for work Monday through Friday, but now we have to contend with the seven-plus hours we'll be at school.

"Let's leave." She grinds her hips down on me, a simple reminder that even though I got her off earlier, the favor hasn't been returned. She likes fast and dirty, and I love to take my time, so we always have to compromise when we're strapped for time.

"We can't," I whisper against her lips before licking into her mouth once again. "And quit grinding on me."

She giggles, keeping her hips rotating, and it's driving me crazy because I know just what this feels like when she's naked, and I'm inside of her. My dick cries to be released.

"I swear it, Piper. I'll fuck you right here in this truck."

"Mmm," she moans, her lips leaving wet kisses along my jaw.

The faint sound of the first bell can be heard on the outside system, and even though it kills me, I grip her waist and gently urge her off my lap.

"Really?" she pouts. "You're gonna leave me all hot and bothered?"

I point to the erection barely contained in my jeans. "I'm no better over here, babe. Let's go."

"Things would be a lot better if you just let me tell my dad what really happened that night." She looks over at me, school forgotten.

This isn't the first time she's tried to convince me to let her spill the truth, but I wouldn't allow it then, and I won't allow it now.

"I think sneaking around will be fun," I lie. I want nothing more than to be welcome in her home, invited to her house for family dinners, and to be accepted by her father, but I have more than just that night to atone for. Telling Dr. Schofield, she was driving is only one small piece of the problems I've caused for Piper.

We don't talk about her scars even though I kiss them each and every time I get the chance. Her parents know about those, and since her dad invaded her privacy, they also know about every mean thing I ever did to this amazing girl. One confession about that night won't change all of that.

"Sneaking around won't be fun. We're both taking advanced placement classes this year. We're both going to be studying a lot, and we should be able to do that together, but it'll be time we have to spend apart."

"We'll make time," I promise.

"It won't be enough."

"Do you love me?" I search her eyes, looking for any sign that she's going to lie to me.

I do it every single time I ask the question or when she offers the words on her own. I still can't believe Piper feels that way about me, and I've had a hard time getting rid of my doubt. But, just like always, sincerity is in her voice and evident in her eyes when she speaks.

"Yes. You know I do."

"Then trust me about this. I'll have a conversation with your father eventually, but right now isn't the time. The sting is still too new. He wouldn't listen to what I have to say, and it'll only make things worse." She gives me a weak smile, and I brush my fingers down her cheek. "Now let's go. We can't be late for the first day of senior year. Are you sure you don't want to wear my varsity jacket?"

She scoffs again, just like she did the first time when I open my door. I'll get her in that damn thing before the week is over. Piper sits in the truck until I climb out and go around to her side.

"Come on," I urge, grabbing her hand and pulling her out and against my chest.

Just like I told her I'd do, I sling my arm over her shoulder and walk into the school with her.

It's not as dramatic as I thought it was going to be when I described today to her all those weeks ago. We've spent many more days at the snow cone stand and even had people over to my house to swim. Piper and I don't have a huge circle, but we do have a few people we feel like we can trust.

"Piper!" Frankie screeches as she runs in our direction.

Frankie got back less than a week ago, and even though I catch her giving me the side-eye every so often, she seems like she's coming around to the idea of me and Piper.

Others aren't, however. Bronwyn literally hisses like a feral cat at Piper when we walk by. Kyle is too busy talking to two girls in cheerleading uniforms to even notice us, but Vaughn is going to be trouble.

Without Bronwyn and Kyle paying attention to him, he watches my girl like he wants to eat her up, and it makes me want to punch him in the nose. I pull Piper closer, tucking her into my chest before brushing my lips against her temple.

"We talked about this," she hisses. "You promised you'd keep the PDAs to a minimum."

"We just nearly got busy in the truck, and you're worried about a little kiss?" I whisper in her ear.

Her cheeks heat, pinking to my favorite new color, but she just rolls her eyes.

"Stop being a caveman, Dalton. We have bigger problems to talk about," Frankie snaps. I still can't get a good read on the girl, but she's Piper's best friend, and I'd never come in between that.

"We talked on the phone for an hour last night," Piper interjects. "What could we possibly talk about now?"

"You remember Zeke?" Frankie asks.

"The farm guy from Utah, you won't give me any information on?"

Frankie scoffs and rolls her eyes. "Yes, that idiot."

"What about him?" Piper asks, and I let the girls talk as I step around Piper to get the books she'll need for her next couple of classes.

"He's here."

I turn back at the tone in Frankie's voice.

"What do you mean *he's here*?" Piper asks, offering me her backpack when I hold up her books.

"He's attending Westover Prep."

"What?"

"And my parents just told me this morning that he's going to be staying with us until his parents can find a place to live in town."

Piper's jaw hangs open, and I don't know a single thing about this Zeke guy. My girl has mentioned before that Frankie has secrets about him that she's trying to get to the bottom of, but other than that, they've never talked about him in front of me.

What I do know is Frankie is twisted up for some reason, and our first day of school has just gotten ten times more interesting.

OTHER BOOKS FROM MARIE JAMES

Standalones
Crowd Pleaser
Macon
We Said Forever
More Than a Memory

Cole Brothers SERIES
Love Me Like That
Teach Me Like That

Hale Series
Coming to Hale
Begging for Hale
Hot as Hale
To Hale and Back
Hale Series Box Set

Cerberus MC

Kincaid: Cerberus MC Book 1
Kid: Cerberus MC Book 2
Shadow: Cerberus MC Book 3
Dominic: Cerberus MC Book 4
Snatch: Cerberus MC Book 5
Lawson: Cerberus MC Book 6
Hound: Cerberus MC Book 7
Griffin: Cerberus MC Book 8
Samson: Cerberus MC Book 9
Tug: Cerberus MC Book 10
Scooter: Cerberus MC Book 11
Cerberus MC Box Set 1
Cerberus MC Box Set 2

Ravens Ruin MC

Desperate Beginnings: Prequel (Book 1)
(Not a romance, but gives all of the back history on the club)
Book 2: Sins of the Father
Book 3: Luck of the Devil
Book 4: Dancing with the Devil

MM Romance

Grinder
Taunting Tony

Printed in Great Britain
by Amazon